CODE WHITE

THE SIERRA VIEW SERIES

MAX WALKER

WALKING PRESS

SYNOPSIS

Dr. Nicholas White was finally pursuing what he wanted. Or rather, who he wanted. After a year of marriage to a woman he was sure was cheating on him, he got a divorce and found himself in bed with the man he couldn't stop thinking about. It was a heated and passionate encounter that left them both wanting more.

So much more.

Shepard Kensworth couldn't believe how strongly he connected with Nick. Shepard was a resident at the hospital and should have had his nose buried in a book, not in Nick's chest. Their moment was brief, but their feelings certainly weren't.

That same day, Nick received news that altered the course of his life forever. A rift cracked between the two men before they could ever solidify anything.

When life pushes them back together, the two men begin to accept just how perfect of a match they are. Not everyone is happy with the reunion, though. When outside forces threaten to tear them apart again, Nick and Shepard must come together stronger than ever before or end up shattered beyond repair.

book Suggestions on next pg ⟶

book suggestions by Mom -

1) Red Queen -Victoria Aveyard

2) Wings -Aprilynne Pike

3) Divergent Series - Vironica Roth

(Groundhog's Day gifts: Max Walker: Code Silver/ Code red:(Sierra View books 1 and 2)

other book suggestions on next pg →

The Experiment:
Rabecca Raine
Kiss me now:
Penny Wylder

ALSO BY MAX WALKER

The Sierra View Series

Code Silver — book 1

Code Red — book 2

Code Blue — book 3

(handwritten annotations: "Will read on Mon.", "will read tonight", "Done")

The Guardian Series:

Cover Me

First Down

Eagle Grip

Fire Flow

Christmas Story:

Daddy Kissing Santa Clause

1 SHEPARD KENSWORTH

(Done)

S hepard was a medical school resident. He should have been at home, studying drug interactions and preparing for his two-week rotation on the surgery floor. He should *not* have been in the on-call room, on all fours, with his ass in the air, an uncomfortable mattress squeaking underneath as one of his attendings slapped his hard dick against Shepard's ass, both of their scrubs discarded in a heap on the floor.

But of course, life isn't always about the "should haves." The "shouldn't haves" are often much more interesting.

Shepard bit down on the flat pillow, preventing a rogue gasp as Dr. Nicholas White pressed the head of his cock against his hole. The doctor's strong hands gripped Shepard's hips and steered his ass for easiest access. Shepard pushed his ass back, asking for more, begging for it. He could feel the doctor's thick cock rub against his crack, already slick with lube. Shepard couldn't help but reach behind and grab Nick's girthy tool, giving a few good tugs, feeling the slick rubber of the condom on his palm mixing with the heat rolling off of Nick in waves. He guided the head of Nick's fat cock to his hole and pushed back. Shepard had been wanting this the minute he laid eyes on the doctor, but he had also believed this would never happen. Nick didn't hold back. He pushed in, drawing a gasp from Shepard and a groan from Nick.

"Did I hurt you?" His tone was immediately caring. It only made Shepard hotter.

"No, no," Shepard reassured, wiggling his ass to take more of the doctor, "just a little fast at first. I'm ok."

Nick went back to gyrating his hips, his cock sinking deeper and deeper as Shepard became more comfortable. It was slow, and passionate and *so fucking hot*. Shepard was seeing stars. He could feel himself accommodating to the size and sensation of being filled as Nick thrust a little deeper, harder, he was going faster. Shepard was biting back the moans. A quick flash of pain morphed into a dose of ecstasy as Nick fucked him deep, burying himself down to his balls before drawing out. Both his hands were holding on tight to Shepard's hips, guiding him as the doctor's thrusts started getting faster. Shepard's ass slapped against Nick's groin. He could hear Nick grunting from behind, low and muffled as he tried to keep it quiet as well. The hospital was still buzzing outside of the locked door with nurses and doctors running past, orders being called over the intercom system, other residents making their rounds. All of them unaware as to what was happening on the other side of the thick wooden door.

Shepard's mind was being blown, that was what was happening.

If someone told him a year ago that he would be having sex with the hottest doctor in all of Sierra View, he would have laughed in their face. Not only was Nicholas White an enigma to most, he had also been married to a bubbly brunette named Anna, leading Shepard to believe that he wasn't Dr. White's type anyway.

"You're so sexy," Nick said in his gravelly growl from behind Shepard. He felt the doctor's hands glide up from his hips and rub over his lower back, giving Shepard a sensation of pure bliss. His lower back was one of his favorite spots to be touched, so that, coupled with the intense pleasure he was getting from having Nick's thick cock fill him, and he was already close to coming. Shepard held himself up on one arm, using the other to reach between his legs and tug on his own leaking cock, his balls already tight against him. He looked and saw a string of precome drip down onto the soft white towel they had placed underneath them. Nick continued to pound him, pushing against Shepard's P-spot and subsequently sending shockwaves with every thrust.

Shepard woke up from plenty of dreams where sex with Nicholas White was the feature presentation, but those were just dreams. They would leave him with a throbbing boner in the morning and that was it. An empty bed and a messy stomach. The dreams had started the moment he met Dr. White months ago, when he had started his residency rotations for the first time. Since then, he had been admiring the doctor from afar, wishing he could have a taste but accepting the fact there was a nearly-impossible chance of that happening.

Nearly being the keyword.

"You're so big," Shepard moaned, keeping his voice low as he spoke into the pillow. This seemed to have spurred the doctor on, because he started driving into Shepard. He could feel the doctor's balls slapping against him, his ass filled with the doctor's entire cock with every thrust. It was enough to have Shepard's arms shaking, his toes curling.

"Come here," Nick said, grabbing Shepard's hips again. He stopped thrusting, but stayed inside Shepard. He pulled Shepard toward him, off of the bed, so that Shepard could stand, all the while his ass was still plugged by Nick's cock. It was incredibly hot. Shepard bit his lower lip as Nick started pounding into him as they stood. He was shorter than the doctor was, so Nick had to bend his knees and drop down a bit. Shepard jerked himself off, starting to get scared his legs would give out soon from the intense pleasure he was feeling. His knees were already shaking.

"Fuck, fuck," Shepard moaned. He bit a knuckle, stopping himself from crying out.

"I'm going to come," Nick growled into Shepard's ear. "Oh, fuck," he said, biting Shepard's ear lobe as his thrusts became erratic. Shepard couldn't hold back, either. He didn't even give a warning. He just grabbed his cock at the base and felt it throb in his grip as he erupted, shooting his seed all over the white towel while Nick unloaded inside him. They were both quivering and huffing and completely overwhelmed with the post orgasmic bliss. Nick kissed Shepard's neck as he pulled out, leaving Shepard feeling empty all of a sudden. He was surprised at how ready he was to go again. His cock was usually the first to tap out, going back to soft status pretty soon after sex. But this time around, Shepard was still hard, ready for more.

Unfortunately, the clock on the wall was saying there wasn't time for more. Shepard had ten minutes before he had to be back outside.

That's enough time for a cuddle, at least.

Shepard was getting ahead of himself. This was a one-time thing and that was it. He highly doubted Dr. White would want to cuddle with him, he had to keep things clear in his head. They were both horny and that was it. Sure,

Shepard had dropped subtle hints during office hours, and sure, he may have given Dr. White the eye a couple of times in the hall, but that was it. Just a sexual attraction where the both of them were looking for a release and both of them got one.

Shepard grabbed the towel from the bed and set it on the floor. "That was... fucking incredible," Nick said, breathless as he fell back onto the bed, condom already wrapped up in a paper towel and thrown away.

Well... if he's going to lie down.

Shepard was equally starved for breath. He felt like a bowl of Jell-O. Completely useless, at the whim of whatever breeze blew their way. He collapsed onto the bed next to Nick. "Honestly?" Shepard said, "That was the best sex I think I've ever had."

Nick nodded. His cheeks were a cherry pink, matching the same flush that had spread across his chest, underneath a sexy dusting of hair. "I'm going to have to second that." He looked up at the ceiling, an arm underneath his head. "Guess that's not too bad considering it was my first time with a man."

"Seriously?" Shepard asked. "Because it felt like you've had a good amount of practice."

Nicholas laughed at that. Shepard enjoyed hearing that sound. It felt good. Especially here, while they were still together on the bed, naked and sweaty. The laugh almost made it feel even more intimate.

Shepard, for a moment, let himself be fooled into thinking this wasn't simply a burst of hormones and nothing else. It was then that Nick surprised him by rolling over and throwing a hand over Shepard's chest. For a second, Shepard froze, not expecting this kind of cuddling. But he quickly warmed up to it. It was exactly what Shepard wanted. He rolled over so that he could scoot back and tuck his butt into the curve of Nick's body. His semi-hard cock pressed against Shepard's butt. Shepard couldn't help but give a wiggle. Nick responded by squeezing his arm a little tighter around Shepard. There was something in the way Nick held him that put Shepard into a trance.

"You know," Nick said in a hushed tone. "The second I laid my eyes on you, I wanted this to happen."

Shepard felt an urge to roll back around so he could look into Nick's eyes. "That's weird. I felt the same thing." Shepard didn't roll over. A kernel of fear kept him looking at the bland yellow wall. He wanted to believe that everything the doctor was saying was certifiably true, he didn't want to witness any evidence of the opposite.

"It was just so complicated."

"With your divorce?"

"Yeah, these past few months have been really rough on me. I couldn't go from a divorce and straight into a relationship, especially since I'd never even been with a man before. I just focused on work and getting through the days without bumping into you. Also, I felt like I was a complicated mess myself, and complicated messes don't make for great relationships. Why risk making things harder for you? Medical school is already hard enough."

Relationship...

Shepard scooted his butt back, rubbing it against Nick. "Tell me about it," he said with a chuckle. "I'm cool with it. Sorry about your ex by the way... well, maybe sorry is the wrong word."

"Yeah, I wouldn't use sorry, either. The divorce was what I needed. If I never ended things with her, I never would have acted on feelings I've had for a long damn time."

"What happened?" Shepard asked. He rolled over for

this one. Nick's amber brown eyes were captivating in their depth. Shepard could stare at him for days and be totally fine.

"We weren't a good fit," Nick said. For a moment, Shepard thought the conversation was going to end there, and that would be fine. Even though Shepard found himself wanting to know more and more about the devilishly handsome doctor, he also felt like that would come in time. The last thing Shepard wanted to think was that this would be their only rendezvous.

No, no.

This felt too good for it to be the last time.

2 NICHOLAS WHITE

"I'm pretty sure she was cheating on me. I just kind of went along with it for a while because I didn't think I had any other choice. I didn't think I'd really be happy again. I felt like I was just kind of floating along." Nick cracked a smile in the dimly lit room. Shepard was still a little flushed, his cheeks slightly pink, his hair messy, a couple of thick dark strands circling down on his forehead. He was the most beautiful thing Nick had ever laid eyes on. Like a work of art created by the most gifted of savants. He wanted to stare at the man for hours. He wanted to memorize every singe freckle on Shepard's face, every small detail, every crinkle next to his eyes. He couldn't believe how attracted he was to this man. "Then you came along." Nick was being way too open, and honestly?

He didn't give a fuck. Not in that moment.

He felt like letting it all out for Shepard. There wasn't a reason in the world he could think of that would prevent him from opening up. It was something in the air. Something in the way Shepard looked at him. With big hazel eyes that expressed captivating depth. "You had such a huge smile, and you're so handsome, and smart. I always see everyone laughing when they're with you. Everyone's always happy when you're around. I was almost jealous. I had to stop myself from being around you because I knew your smile was dangerous, and yet everyone else was around you, enjoying you."

Shepard chewed on his lower lip, a smile on his face. Nick couldn't hold himself back. He went in for a kiss. He thought it would be soft and quick, but that would never happen when Shepard was involved. Their tongues met and danced for what felt like days. Years. Decades. That was how long he felt like he had known Shepard. This was the first actual, deep conversation they had ever shared and yet Nick felt like Shepard had always been a part of his life.

The kiss broke as a pager started going off, vibrating against the floor. "Oh shit," Shepard said, eyes snapping open. He jumped out of bed and hurried to the corner where his scrubs were thrown. He dug through the pocket and silenced the alarm. "I've got to get to work," he said, smiling as he tugged on his underwear, moving to his scrubs next. Nick sat up on the bed, still a little blown away by the fact that he had just made love to a man, and it was beyond his wildest expectations. The pleasure was intense and the sense of intimacy he shared with Shepard was unbeatable. A high he wanted to get hit with again.

"Let's have dinner tomorrow," Nick said as Shepard was working his arms through his shirt.

"Dinner?" Shepard asked again, clearly taken aback. "Sure, yeah, definitely." He smiled at Nick, who was beginning to get dressed as well.

"I'll see you then."

"See you," Nick said, already counting down the minutes left until they met again.

NICK GRABBED two Stellas out of the fridge and popped them open. His best friend, Aaron Diaz, was sitting on a barstool and wasting his time on Tinder, swiping right like it was his job. Nick handed him a beer and walked to the couch, sitting down and taking a sip of the cold beverage, hoping it would be enough to stop his mind from obsessing over Shepard and his naked body.

Fuck.

Just thinking about Shepard made Nick's cock twitch. He squeezed his thighs together and threw his feet up on the glossy white coffee table. Maybe he could redirect blood flow away from his dick. He was definitely going to need more than one beer. Aaron must have matched with someone because he gave a hoot and fist-pumped in the air. "Fuck yeah," he said, hopping off the barstool and making his way over to Nick. He stepped over Nick's legs and sat down on the couch next to him. "Check this one out."

Aaron showed off his phone like he had earned a damn Nobel prize. Nick looked at the screen, seeing a very beautiful girl in a barely-there bright blue bikini, sunning on the deck of a huge boat. She was someone Nick could see Aaron with. His best friend was a lovable douchebag. A frat guy that actually did have a heart and didn't purposefully go out and mess with people. He looked the part, too, in his tan Sperrys, short khaki shorts, and light blue polo with some weird animal logo on the chest.

"Nice, yeah, she's cool."

"Cool?!" Aaron said. He pressed the back of his hand to Nick's forehead. "Dude, are you coming down with something? A weird hospital virus you should be telling me about?"

Nick chuckled. "No, I think I'm already immune to everything out there."

"I dunno, man, I've seen Thirty-Eight Weeks Later."

Nick arched an eyebrow. "You mean Twenty-Eight Weeks Later? The zombie movie? Thirty-eight weeks later sounds like a bad movie about a slightly premature baby."

"Yeah, that one." Aaron laughed before taking a drink of his Stella. His phone vibrated as he matched with someone else on the app. "Oh, oh, ok, look at this girl. She needs way more than a 'cool'."

Aaron flipped his phone, showing Nick a beautiful woman in a bright yellow sundress, her breasts spilling over the top. "Cool."

Aaron dropped the phone on the couch. "Ok, seriously, what's going on?"

"Oh, I don't know, maybe it's the fact that I made my divorce official two months ago?"

And I'm also done with women.

That was something that was going to have to wait to be said. Nick wasn't sure how his best friend was going to take the news. Hell, he wasn't even sure about the news himself. Throughout his entire life, he had always had an inclination for the same sex. That inclination grew as the years passed, evolving into a deep yearning that had been tugging at Nick since he entered medical school. By then, he had met Anna and was perfectly happy dating her, so he never explored the side of him that cried out for a man's touch.

Then, his relationship with Anna began to crack. She became more and more distant, starting fights with Nick over things that previously never even mattered. Things like a pair of socks left by the couch; that would have her close to smashing dishes. She was staying late at work and had surprise meetings on weekends. Things didn't feel right.

Nick also started to suspect something was up when she had left her phone inside the bathroom one night. Nick had stepped in and closed the door, which was almost cracked in half with how fast Anna threw it open, looking for her phone and giving a relieved sigh when she grabbed it from the countertop. A divorce ending their year-long marriage soon followed. In the immediate aftermath, Nick felt lost. He was angry and taking it out on the residents, he could tell. He hated himself for being an asshole, but he was just so damn frustrated. He felt like he had wasted so much time with Anna, in a relationship that was fractured to begin with.

Then he shook Shepard Kensworth's hand, and everything suddenly shifted. The world made a little more sense. It felt like there was a track to get on. Fast forward to the current day, two months later, and Nick had snuck Shepard into the on-call room for the absolute hottest fuck of his entire life. It was more than a spur of the moment thing. Shepard had been making Nick's heart race for weeks, and he knew he wanted to get to know him. Nick wasn't expecting to go all in when he invited Shepard into the room, but both of them instantly discovered that the chemistry between them was stronger than the valium they kept locked up in the cabinets.

Nick couldn't believe how good it had felt. He was getting hard just thinking about it.

"You're right," Aaron said, picking up his phone and beginning to type a message to his potential dates. "Sorry, I'm being stupid. I just thought, maybe getting out there again might get your mind off of her, you know?"

"I think I'll take it easy for now." Nick took another drink of his beer. He couldn't say anything more. He wanted to tell Aaron what had happened, but Nick also knew that religion made up a huge part of Aaron's life and he had never expressed any positive attitudes toward gay people. He never bashed anyone, Nick wouldn't have stood for that, but he also didn't seem thrilled when one of their mutual friends had come out as a lesbian. They had never truly discussed it, but Nick wasn't sure if this was the proper time to bring it up. He wanted to enjoy this feeling. He wanted to ride it as long as possible. Things would get complicated soon enough, but Shepard already proved to be more than worth it. He hadn't been this excited about getting to know someone since... well, since no one. Not even Anna had captured his attention this intensely. Even before their mind-blowing sexual connection, Nick had been captivated by the charming medical school resident with those caring hazel eyes and that sharp wit, all matched with a mastery at the sinful smirk that made Nick's knees weak and his dick swell.

"I dunno, dude," Aaron continued. "Some good pussy is the best kind of medicine. You're the doctor, you should know that."

"Thanks," Nick said. "I must have slept through that lecture in med school."

"Well, you're welcome." Aaron laughed as he took a chug of his beer, finishing it off. He wiped his mouth and placed the empty bottle on the coffee table. Nick offered to grab another one but Aaron mumbled a no, his fingers furiously typing up another message.

"Hey, man," Aaron said, setting his phone aside, "thanks again for letting me crash at your place."

"Of course, Aaron." Nick got up from the couch and went to grab himself another beer. Maybe he'd stop thinking about Shepard when he reached the bottom of this one?

"We've been friends since high school, I'd never turn you away."

"I know, but it's not ideal. I promise, I won't be here longer than another month. I promised a week, and I know it's been a little longer than that, but my fucking philosophy degree is completely useless. I'm getting my real estate license now and should have some property lined up to sell in no time, though. I'll get out of your hair, man, I swear."

Nick stood in his kitchen and waved Aaron off. "I know you'll figure it out soon, Aaron." Nick's home had an open-concept style kitchen with a massive marble island serving as a divider between the kitchen and the living room. It wasn't a huge house, but it was big enough to have Aaron stay over without feeling like he was impeding too much. He mostly kept himself to the guest room on the opposite end of the house, on the first floor. Besides, Aaron was entertaining. It had been a while since they had spent a good amount of time together. Nick had become too busy with his career and Aaron had spent a long time traveling the country on money he had won from a scratcher.

Nick leaned on the kitchen island, drinking the beer and beginning to wonder if the alcohol was actually having the opposite effect of what Nick intended. He wanted his mind cleared of Shepard, but instead, all he found himself wanting to do was grab his phone and call the guy. He didn't even care if they couldn't see each other that night, he just felt a powerful desire to hear his voice.

Wow, Nick thought. *Shepard's dick must be magic.*

That was when his doorbell rang. Aaron had ordered pizza and was getting up from the couch but Nick moved faster, putting his hand out. "I've got it," he said, grabbing his wallet and walking toward the door. He was feeling more than generous. The least he could do was buy his best friend a pizza.

He opened the door and cocked his head in sudden surprise. In the place of a polo shirt-wearing delivery boy holding a box of cheesy goodness was Anna Turron, his ex-wife, and last person he expected to be seeing.

"Anna," Nick said, surprise clear in his voice. She had been crying, Nick could tell by her puffy pink eyes. She was wearing an old red T-shirt from their trip to San Francisco and a pair of baggy white sweats. She held something in her hand. A pen? Why was she holding onto it so tightly? Her fist was balled up at her side, but Nick could see the end of it poking out of her tight fist.

"Nick, we need to talk."

"Come in," Nick said, stepping aside. Anna hurried in, but stopped cold in the entryway when she saw Aaron sitting on the couch.

"Shit," she said. Nick looked from Anna to Aaron, both of them staring at each other like a pair of bank robbers caught in the vault.

"Well... I'm pregnant," Anna said, breaking the thick silence.

Nick took a sharp intake of breath.

"And I'm not sure if it's yours or Aaron's."

Nick momentarily forgot how to breath.

3 | SHEPARD KENSWORTH

ONE YEAR LATER

D r. White was being such a fucking dick.

He was doing this on purpose. He had to be. But why? What had Shepard ever done to the man? Besides give him an incredible fucking orgasm, of course. Both of their bodies had reached heights that neither of them had thought possible. Shepard had felt a surprising and profound connection with Nick that day in the on-call room. He would never be able to explain it, but he damn well knew he had felt it.

That was a year ago, and a lot can change in a year's time.

The exam room was deathly silent as everyone had their eyes turned to Shepard. Even the patient, with her big sad brown eyes and her light blue hospital gown, was looking anxiously at Shepard.

"I, uhm, don't know the answer to that, doctor."

And you fucking knew that I wouldn't know the answer.

Shepard was internally fuming, but he was able to mask it well. He had quickly learned that being a doctor meant he had to be an expert at controlling his emotions. There was a fine line he had to balance whenever he was delivering bad news. Sometimes his base instinct would have been to break down and cry right there with the patient, but he had to always separate himself from the news enough that he wouldn't be affected and yet still avoid being ice cold.

Those were the skills that kicked into high gear as Shepard stood in the center of the circle of four other residents. Nick was standing on the other side of the hospital bed, typing something out on his iPad. His face was etched in an expression Shepard couldn't read.

He assumed it was assholish satisfaction that he had successfully stumped Shepard in front of everyone.

"Right, well," Nick said in his gravelly voice. The same voice Shepard had been salivating over as he pounded him from behind. It momentarily took him back to that day in the on-call room. Where life had felt so fucking good. He was on top of the world. Not only did he have the fuck of his life, he had done it with a man who he had genuinely felt a deep connection with. Nick finished answering his own question and looked to Shepard.

"Got it," Shepard said, "I'll have to study that chapter tonight." His gaze fell down to the floor. He shouldn't have felt like a scolded child, but he did. He reverted back to being in fourth grade and getting shoved into a corner by the teacher. Sure, he may have been acting like a brat and bothering the class while they were taking a test, but that moment still had a pretty profound impact on Shepard. He remembered the awkward glances his classmates would give as he was pressed up against the corner wall, the pastel yellow walls doing nothing to soothe him. He hated that feeling of being called out and put on the spot.

This isn't fourth grade. White is testing me, that's all.

He looked back up from the floor and was surprised to

lock eyes with the doctor. There, Shepard saw the same warmth and intrigue that had captured him so powerfully in the first place. It was a momentary flash, though. Another moment later and Nick was focused in on the patient, asking more questions about the symptoms she was presenting with, his eyes no longer rooting Shepard in place.

Shepard shifted his weight, glancing down at the notes he had for the patient; Sandra O'Leary, who had come in for some intense stomach pains. His mind wanted to swirl around the image of those eyes, Nick's eyes, but he honed in on the notes, working through his mental library of gastrointestinal conditions. She had come to the emergency room for severe stomach pains along with some accompanying joint discomfort. Shepard not only wanted to help Sandra, he also wanted to get something right. He wanted to stand up to Nick and prove that he wasn't just going to sit there and take the abuse. And what better way of showing it to Nick than getting Sandra's diagnosis correct?

That was when it hit him. There was a crucial test missing in the intake chart for someone presenting with her symptoms.

"Dr. White, I'd recommend a blood test for tissue transglutaminase antibodies. I'm thinking this could be celiac disease."

Nick cocked his head, his eyes going back down to his notes and then up to Shepard. The doctor looked at him for a loaded moment, his eyes seeming to examine Shepard on the spot. Shepard felt exposed. He crossed his arms, suddenly feeling a warmth spread up his legs. Nick's face cracked into a smile. That stony jawline was highlighted by a genuine smile that warmed the doctor's face. It felt as if a proud father had just learned his son earned straight As.

"You're right, Dr. Kensworth. I'm going to have to find out who handled your intake, Sandra, because they definitely should have included that in your blood panel. Have you eaten anything with gluten recently? Pizza, pasta, a sandwich?"

"I had pizza earlier, yeah."

"Ok, that's a good thing. We want gluten in your system to provoke those antibodies into coming out. If it tests positive, we'll have to take a biopsy of your small intestine and check for any damage caused by the celiac disease. If it's there, then we'll have a diagnosis. And don't worry, the procedure is painless and outpatient." Nick looked up from Sandra, a smile still on his face. "Good job, doctors. I think we're done with rounds for the day, so just make sure to handle all your paperwork and then I'll see you all tomorrow, bright and early."

Shepard managed a smile and a nod and left the exam room, letting the other three residents walk ahead of him down the busy hospital hallway. He was thrown off by Nick's smile. It was so warm. So welcoming. Shepard had seen Nick smile before, but something in the way he looked at Shepard made this one different. Or maybe it was simply an effect from getting railroaded by a difficult question and then coming back with a proper diagnosis.

Shepard was going to go with the latter. He couldn't let himself fall for a steely doctor with an addictive smile. He knew almost nothing about Nick and had no time to try and figure him out. Between studying for the boards and getting his stress out at the gym, his free time was mostly taken up. Work and sleep took up the rest of his days.

He left the hospital still in a state of confusion. He was also feeling a kernel of frustration take root in his chest. Why couldn't Nick just admit that they had shared something that was worth following? And what had happened that changed the doctor so suddenly? They were supposed to have dinner, but Nicholas never followed up on it. Shepard was sure he wasn't the only one who felt the connection, so why was this so damn complicated? He walked to the parking garage, climbing the stairs to the third floor where his aging Honda was parked. He got in and sat at the wheel, trying to figure out whether he wanted to just head home or if he had enough energy to lift weights.

Nick's smiling face formed in his mind's eye. The frustration grew from a seed into a gigantic redwood. Fuck it, even if he didn't have the energy, he was going to head to the gym and work out this mess.

———

THE GYM WAS PACKED with people. It was the evening crowd that came in after a hard day's work. Shepard usually worked out during the mornings, before he had to make his way to Sierra View. He wasn't always a morning person but medical school changed that and now he felt weird not waking up early every day, even on the days he had off. The morning crowd at the gym was also a little easier to get around and the wait time for the machines was pretty much nonexistent. Shepard looked around the massive warehouse-turned-gym, taking stock of the situation as he walked toward the locker rooms. It seemed like most of the lower body machines were taken, and since Shepard planned on working out his legs, that made things slightly more complicated.

He turned a corner and walked down a short hallway toward the men's locker room, denoted with a neon pink arrow with 'men' scrawled across the top that seemed spray painted onto the far wall. The women's locker room was a neon blue and directly across from the men's. He followed the pink arrow and walked around a large mirror that separated the actual locker room from the outside hall. Inside, he found an empty locker and dropped his black Nike duffel bag on a silver bench. He started changing out of his scrubs, planning out his workout and doing his best to keep Dr. White out of his head.

Shepard was tying his sneakers when he heard a voice from behind that froze him. He pretended to keep tying his sneakers, meanwhile his mind was racing to try and figure out a way to sneak out of the locker room without being noticed.

What the hell? Since when does he come here?

4 NICHOLAS WHITE

Nick couldn't shake Shepard Kensworth. He was standing by the nurses' station, looking over some charts and wondering why the hell he was being such a dick, especially toward the man who had captivated him from the start. He hated himself for it.

But he also knew there was no other option, especially not right now. Nick's life had gotten infinitely more complicated a year ago, when he had opened up the floodgates for Shepard and was then told he would soon be a father (depending on the DNA test), all on the same day. His life was completely uprooted and thrashed around a bit. He didn't see himself with a daughter at thirty-two, but life had ways of twisting even the surest of plans.

The birth of his daughter, Emma, was a twist that changed Nick to the very core. He didn't think he was capable of such a sincere, powerful, deep-rooted love, but when he looked into his daughter's eyes for the first time, felt her tiny fingers wrap around his, his entire world shifted and he found an endless depth to the love. The lead-up to her birth wasn't as magical, with Anna fighting and Nick becoming overwhelmed. His frustrations were leaking out into the hospital halls. It was affecting the way he treated nurses, other doctors. He felt like he just wanted to do his job and get home, where he could be alone. He found a solace in the solitude. He wanted nothing to do with people for those nine months.

And then Emma came into his world and suddenly the thick gray clouds were shoved aside by bright beams of light, all held in her smile. He wished he could call it a day and rush home so he could hold her, smell her, feel her breathing against his chest. She was his little miracle and Nick wanted to do nothing else but hold her.

Anna was making that extremely difficult to do, and that was leading Nick back into his shell of frustration. Anna had denied the fifty-fifty custody split and went for an agreement that had Nick seeing Emma only two days a week. She argued that she would be a better fit to raise Emma for the majority of the time because Nick's schedule could get hectic. It was bullshit. As an emergency doctor, Nick knew the times he would need to be in the hospital, with only the rare moments when he would be called in if they were short on hands. That only happened if there was some kind of catastrophic disaster which involved a lot of victims. And if that were to ever happen, he had three sitters he could call at the last minute, and if that didn't work, there was a day care center in Sierra View.

Nick wanted to fight for more time with her. He was tempted to challenge the custody ruling, but it was a risk. Custody came down to the judge and he could have landed with one who just flat out didn't like him. There was even the possibility of a judge removing the two days he had already and granting sole custody to Anna. The court always leaned in the mother's favor to begin with, so he already felt like he was facing an uphill battle. Then there was the fear that Anna would get even crazier and demand that sole custody. He wouldn't put it past her to come up with more lies, or find a way to influence the judge somehow. It would completely wreck Nick. It created a huge well of frustration inside him, one that was constantly overflowing. He felt it in how he lashed out at Shepard for no reason other than that he knew Shepard could handle it. He asked him that question because he was angry he couldn't just go home, with Shepard holding his hand, where Emma would be waiting for them with that big sunshine smile of hers. That was all Nick wanted, and he was getting none of it.

Fuck.

He checked his watch. He was set to finish in ten minutes. Nick couldn't picture himself going home and doing nothing. He felt too amped up for that. He remembered he had brought his gym clothes with him and figured hitting the gym would be the best thing he could do with the feelings that were boiling inside him, creating a pent-up energy that had to be released. He wasn't a gym rat by any stretch of the imagination, but he had signed up recently, inspired by Emma's birth. The first few weeks were rough, but he was getting into it more and more as the days passed. He couldn't find time to go every day, but managed about three times a week. More than enough for now.

"Here you go, Norma." Nick closed the folder and handed it over to the nurse. She reached up and grabbed it, her bright pink scrubs engineered to put a smile on anyone's face. "Thank you, I'm going to head out. If Ms. Wilson's blood pressure drops any lower, give me a call, ok?"

"You got it, Dr. White." She opened the folder and looked over the chart. When Nick saw she didn't have any questions, he wrapped his knuckles on the counter and waved a goodbye to the other nurses. He started down the hallway toward his office. He was on the west wing of the hospital, where the hallway walls were made up of large windows that looked out at the breathtaking mountain range that surrounded Sierra View. It was already getting dark out, the sun moving down past the tall hills that cut across the sky, sending off its dying tendrils of light past the jagged cuts of the hill tops, lighting them an intense orange.

Nick had reached the end of the row of windows, about to turn when he bumped into Dean Harper, another doctor at Sierra View and one of the only ones Nick could say he considered a friend. Not that the other doctors were shit, but something about Dean really clicked with Nick. Maybe it was his crazy good lasagna or his smart humor that always put a smile on Nick's face. He wasn't always close with Dean, but after he had severed his relationship with Aaron and was constantly arguing with Anna, he found that Dean's friendship was badly needed and greatly welcomed. It took him a few weeks to open up and stop being a bit of an asshole, but Dean had managed to crack him open over a game of pool and a couple of beers.

"Hey, Nick, where you headed?" Dean was wearing a gray button-up shirt tucked into slim-fitting khakis, his white coat folded over his left arm. "Off tonight?"

"Yeah, thinking of heading to the gym for a bit. Blow some steam off."

"You look a little stressed, everything ok?"

"It's been a long day."

And week for that matter.

Dean nodded. "I get it. I had back-to-back patients all day today. I feel terrible when the appointments have to be twenty minutes, but what else are we going to do? This system, man, what a mess." Dean shook his head and ran a hand through his tangle of dark hair. It was clear he had a long day, too. "How's little Emma?"

Nick reflexively smiled at Emma's name. "She's doing great. You need to see her. She's got this mop of brunette hair that always smells like strawberries and vanilla for some reason. And that smile of hers, Dean. It's crazy." Nick grit his jaw, realizing he wouldn't be seeing her smile that night. "Anna has her for the next four days and she's not letting me see her."

"Fuck, man," Dean said. He rarely cursed. "I'm so sorry you're going through this." Dean leaned a shoulder on the wall separating two of the wide windows, his arms crossed against his chest.

Dean was one of the only people he found himself opening up to over the past year. They had become very close friends as the days passed, which surprised Nick because he knew he was ready to close himself off and push everyone away. He had suffered a huge betrayal and wasn't sure if he even knew how to trust people since. Finding out his best friend was fucking his then-wife in Nick's own house was enough to have him say he was pretty much done with the human race. He thought he'd go into work, try saving a few lives, then head home and forget about the cruel world.

Nick couldn't do that, though. He loved people too much. It was one of the reasons he had become a physician. He *wanted* to help people. He *wanted* to interact and create connections again. Especially since Emma had been on the way and he needed to make sure he was a relatively functional father for her, with friends and everything. He had put a hold on the boyfriend scenario, since that situation was infinitely more complicated, but Nick could allow

Dean in. It absolutely didn't hurt that Dean was one of the kindest, most genuine people Nick had ever come across.

"Damn it, Nick. I really wish there was something I could do for you."

"It's ok." Nick said. He wished the same thing, but understood there wasn't much anyone could do for him. "I'm thinking of taking the custody case back to court. Hoping to get a fifty-fifty split, at least." Nick didn't want to say much else about Anna or his daughter. He already felt the emotions bubbling up his chest, threatening to unload right there in the hospital hallway. He couldn't do that. He had to put on a strong face. He could break down in private, holding a picture of his daughter, desperately wanting more than just a photo.

"Hey, listen, I know this might not be the time, but... it also might be the perfect time for it. Noah and I are having a little get-together tonight and our friend, Sean, is going to be there. You guys seemed to click really well at our last Game of Thrones night, maybe you can share some mulled wine with him tonight?" Dean nudged Nick's ribs playfully with an elbow, winking the entire time.

Nick managed a smile. Dean was also one of the first people Nick had officially come out to. It helped that he knew Dean was gay so there would be absolutely zero negative reactions. He had told him and his husband, Noah, over a dinner they were having before heading to a concert. He didn't know what had pushed him into telling them he was bi at the dinner... *no*, he did know. It was the spitting image of Shepard who had been sitting at a table across from them that had inspired Nick to come out. He had left out the part about him hooking up with a resident, but he told them that there was one man in particular who had captured his atten-tion. He told them it would be too complicated of a situation and that he had to find a way to move on. Since then, Dean had been pretty persistent about setting Nick up with their close friend Sean. He seemed like an overall nice guy and everything about Sean was technically right, but he didn't spark a flame in the same way Shepard had. There was no comparison.

"Thanks, Dean, I really appreciate it, but I think I'm going to hit the gym and call it a night. I'll have to catch up on Westoros tomorrow."

"Alright, just be careful out there." Dean motioned down the hall with one arm arcing wide, like a prophet speaking about the entire world ahead of them. "There are spoilers everywhere."

Nick cracked up at the over dramatics, although Dean was right. "I'll make sure to have a social media blackout and warn any patients that come in. I can't have anyone ruining it."

"Ok, good. As long as you're aware of the perils." Dean reached out and patted Nick's arm. "See you tomorrow, then. And remember: everything is going to work out. You'll have Emma in your arms soon."

"Thanks, Dean, really. Have a great night," Nick said, feeling a little better after his chat. There was still a pain that hit him square in the chest when he remembered he wasn't seeing his daughter as soon as he would have hoped, but he knew he would see her, and he was going to fight for the right to hold on to her whenever he wanted. For now, though, all he could do was try and work out his frustrations at the gym. That way he would avoid working them out on the residents.

On Shepard Kensworth, specifically.

5 SHEPARD KENSWORTH

(Done)

Shepard hoped the voice would turn and leave so that he could sneak out of the gym unnoticed and be done with his shitty day. He'd work out in his apartment, that would be fine. A set of forty push-ups and a few workouts with the free weights he had at home and he'd be ok. There was no need to put himself in an awkward situation by working out next to his ex-boyfriend, Rick Valdez.

He hated the gym when we were together. Surprised he's even here.

Shepard finished tying his sneakers and straightened up on the steel bench. Rick was still behind him, talking excitedly about some new business venture he was working on. Back when they had dated, Rick told Shepard that he owned a booming internet marketing business and had made it seem like he was well on his way to being a thirty-year-old millionaire. It took about four months for Shepard to find out Rick had lied about all of it and was actually a sales clerk at Nordstrom without any side businesses of any kind, at least from what he could tell. Even that 'fact' had some doubt behind it. Shepard barely knew anything about the real Rick. It was clear Rick did have some kind of questionable income flow, he spent quite a bit of it on shoes and clothes, but Shepard wasn't sure if that was just part of his web of elaborate lies. The revelation had obviously shaken Shepard (regardless of how big a discount he was being offered at Nordstrom) and led to a breakup that was more dramatic than a Real Housewives reunion episode. They had yelled and Rick had cried and Shepard had wondered how the hell he had attracted such a crazy guy in the first place. Rick had spent the night camped outside of Shepard's apartment complex, waiting for a chance to make things right. When the morning came and Shepard left his apartment in his dark blue scrubs, warm coffee mug in hand, Rick had jumped onto the path in front of him and immediately started campaigning for a relationship again. Shepard was too exhausted to feel uncomfortable as Rick followed Shepard to his car, promising him that there would be no more lies from then on out. Shepard remembered scoffing and getting into his car, driving away and watching in the rearview mirror as Rick angrily kicked a concrete column and then started hopping around in pain.

"Yeah, so I should have seventy percent stake in the company by next month," he heard Rick say behind him.

"Wow, that's awesome," someone else said, sounding genuinely impressed. They must not have seen through Rick's thinly constructed veil of bullshit yet.

"For sure," Rick said, his voice sounding farther away. He must have been walking deeper into the locker rooms. Now was Shepard's chance. He grabbed his duffle bag and zipped it up. He threw the thick black strap over his shoulder, the rough fabric scratching his shoulder with how quickly he had thrown it on. He was wearing a sleeveless, light blue workout shirt so there wasn't much separating his skin from the fabric.

He hurried around the big mirror that marked the exit and out into the hallway and was almost in the clear when he saw someone else that made him freeze in his tracks. This time, though, the man who had stopped him wasn't someone he was desperate to avoid. Quite the contrary. In front of him stood Dr. Nicholas White, looking exceptionally hot in his light gray gym shorts that stopped an inch or two above his knees and a black tee that hugged his form. He wasn't overly muscular, which was exactly what Shepard was attracted to. He had a nice chest and sexy arms and a stomach Shepard wanted to run his hands over. Those legs were nothing to scoff at either. Nice meaty thighs that begged to have a bite taken out of them. It didn't hurt that the gray shorts were the perfect color in that they did nothing to hide the doctor's slight bulge.

"Oh, Dr. White," Shepard said, looking down at the floor for a moment. Not only did it allow his eyes to graze over Nick's crotch, but it also gave Shepard a moment to compose himself. The second he looked into the doctor's impossibly deep amber brown eyes, his mind was flooded with flashes of their time in the on-call room. It was a year ago and yet Shepard remembered every damn detail. From the way Nick tasted like cinnamon and coffee to the way the doctor's cock felt inside him.

"Shepard," he responded, sounding as taken aback as Shepard felt. "I... uhm, hey. Didn't know you came here."

"Yeah, usually I make it out here during the mornings, but today..."

Today you were kind of a big asshole and confused me to no end so I decided to work out twice.

Nick nodded, his eyes honing in on Shepard's. "Sometimes switching up your routine works out better."

"Yeah, looks like it did. I wouldn't have seen you here otherwise."

Whoa. What did I just say?

"You finishing up?" Nick said, a small smile cracking on his steely handsome face. He wore a five o'clock shadow like it was his job.

Shepard looked down at his duffle bag. "Oh," *shit*, "yeah. I have a lot of studying to finish up." Shepard bit on his lip. He wasn't going to say it. Wasn't going to mention what happened earlier. There was no need. "Seeing after you completely wrecked me with that question in front of everyone." Well... there it was.

Nick's eyes widened for a flash before returning to their normal, captivating state. "I'm sorry about that, Shepard. I enjoy pushing my best residents a little too hard, I'll make sure to tone it down though. It wasn't a good question at all."

Well, at least he sounds apologetic. And did he say I'm one of his best?

Shepard nodded, trying to ignore how easy it was for him to forgive Nick. Two valley girls walked down the hall, decked out in their cool Lululemon shirts with the backs cut out, blonde hair drawn up into perfect ponytails. One of them looked at Shepard as she passed and shot one of those smiles that resembled that of a lioness staring down a fawn.

"Don't worry, he's not into you," said a voice from behind Shepard. A voice that instantly made him recoil. The girl looked at the man and huffed as she kept walking, going back to hushed conversation with her friend.

"Rick," Shepard said, his head dropping before turning. Rick was already standing in front of him, arms crossed, workout gear thrown on. He looked like he hadn't gotten a haircut in months, and his beard also needed a good trim. His clothes looked brand new, though. And those sneakers were fresh off the rack.

"Wow, I didn't know you came here, Shepard." Rick looked from Shepard to Nick, his eyes narrowing. Whoever Rick had come to the gym with was standing awkwardly to the side, scrolling through his phone. Shepard considered introducing Nick but decided against it. This interaction wasn't going to last any longer than a few seconds and then none of this would matter anyway. Shepard was never, ever, coming to the gym during the evening again. Not if he was going to bump into the entire cast of *Regret- The Fucking Musical*.

"I'm actually just headed out," Shepard said.

"You haven't even broken a sweat," Rick said, suspicion clouding his features. "Are you two... running out to fuck? Wow, you moved on quick."

"Jesus." Shepard felt like simultaneously melting into the floor and punching Rick at the same time. What was he thinking?

"It's just, well, you were kind of a slut when we were going out."

Shepard's neck swiveled. He was looking at the floor before his eyes snapped to Rick. "What the — Rick, I'm leaving." Shepard was internally fuming. He couldn't blow up in front of his attending, no matter how badly he wanted to. He turned to Nicholas, who looked like he was witnessing a car wreck in the making. "Dr. White, I'm sorry you had to hear any of that. My ex is a pathological liar and clearly still has issues he needs to deal with."

"A doctor, huh?" Rick huffed. "I knew I was never good

enough for you. I knew you needed another fancy white coat."

Shepard was going to snap back, but he took a deep breath instead. This wasn't worth it. Rick was seemingly trying to sabotage a nonexistent relationship between him and Nick. He started to walk when Rick had grabbed him by his elbow and twisted him around. Shepard yanked his arm back, his face flushing red. "What are you *thinking?*" he snapped at Rick.

"Talk to me. I want you to apologize for cheating on me."

"I *didn't* cheat on you. You've completely lost it. You lied about an entire career while we were in a relationship, and then you expect me to stay with you after I find that out? Who knows what else you're hiding. I don't even know if your real name is Rick!"

Rick shook his head, a sizable crocodile tear sliding down his unkempt face. He knew damn well he was lying and yet the pathological bastard was playing up the drama. "I knew I never should have dated you." Rick looked like he was about to spit, but he threw a slur instead. "Slut." Rick had conviction in his voice when he spoke.

Shepard reeled back. He gave a surprised laugh because that was all he could do. What happened next really did surprise him.

"Back up," Nick said, his arm outstretched as he stepped up and pushed Rick aside. "And watch what you say."

Normally, Nick didn't seem intimidating in the slightest. Not in an aggressive way at least. Sexually, sure, the man would have intimidated a damn succubus. But Shepard never would have pegged him for a man to throw punches. This was different, though. The man that stood in front of Shepard had his chest puffed, his jaw tight, his knees loose. He was ready to fight, and he was doing it because he was defending Shepard.

If Shepard hadn't become so nervous, he probably would have been incredibly turned on.

"What are you going to do?" Rick was a skinny guy, tall but lanky. He definitely didn't go to the gym while he and Shepard were together, and so he really didn't look intimidating at all. Especially since, even as he was speaking, he was stepping back, away from Nick. Rick's friend no longer had his nose buried in his phone. He was now checking on his watch and pointing toward the treadmills. Without saying anything else, he left, clearly not wanting to deal with the steaming-hot batch of crazy Rick was serving up.

"Enough," Shepard stepped back in the middle before anything escalated. He didn't want any of this to happen. He looked to Nick and managed a weak smile. "Thank you," he said, before turning to Rick. "I'm done with you and this conversation. Have a good workout." And before Rick could get another word out, Shepard turned and walked out of the hallway and into the gym. He knew that Rick wouldn't instigate anything further once he was gone, and Nicholas was definitely not going to go after Rick, so he felt like removing himself was the best course of action. He shot a glance over his shoulder and saw Nick disappearing into the locker rooms while Rick was standing against the wall, head in his hands.

What a damn mess.

6 NICHOLAS WHITE

THREE DAYS LATER

Nick's office was quiet, the only sound coming from the small Zen fountain by the window, a small tower of smooth rocks rising up from the center, a wall of bamboo making up the back. His office served as a sanctuary for him in the midst of the daily chaos that was part of being an emergency doctor at Sierra View. The window looked down at the hospital's courtyard and let in plenty of sunshine throughout the day, brightening up the space and giving Nick a much needed boost of energy. He had been working through most of the night and was ready to call it a day but still had some paperwork he needed to fill out. Although, even if he had found a bed, Nick wasn't so sure he would have been able to fall asleep. There was so much going on in his life, he was having a difficult time with processing it all. From Anna being a pure monster, to the birth of his beautiful little daughter, to a man who had instantly captured his attention from the start. As he looked over the patient charts and prescription orders, his mind started drifting, away from medicine and directly toward Shepard Kensworth.

He couldn't shake it. A fucking year had passed since

Nick let his walls down and slept with Shepard, and every one of those days contained at least one passing thought about the man. Bumping into him at the gym didn't help in the slightest. Seeing him wearing a thin, sleeveless shirt and shorts gave him enough material for his spank bank to last... well, at least a week. By then he knew he would need more. Like a drug addict, he'd need another hit straight from Shepard himself. He was so taken, he had seen a flash of red when Shepard's ex started with his verbal attacks. He felt useless standing by and saying nothing, so he rode that red current and stuck up for Shepard.

Nick couldn't get him off his mind, and that was saying something, because as a newly minted father, Nick's mind was constantly full. His entire world had shifted the day Emma was born. That moment was forever cemented in Nick's heart. It didn't matter that he and Anna weren't getting along at all, Nick had left all of that at the door the moment he stepped into the hospital room. He didn't want any of that negative energy around when Emma entered the world.

Nick sighed into the empty room. He twirled his phone on his desk before pressing the button. Emma's smiling face beamed back at him, her chubby cheeks taking up the phone from side to side. She was such a pure, innocent little miracle and Nick had never felt more blessed.

The days after her birth were also magical. For a moment, Nick fooled himself into thinking that maybe he could work something out with Anna, only so that their fighting wouldn't affect Emma. Not a romantic relationship, that ship had permanently left the docks and sank somewhere in the Bermuda Triangle, but maybe they could be friends and raise Emma together. All he had to do was look into his little daughter's crystal blue eyes, and Nick would have been fine agreeing to anything, as long as it was to better her life. He was already wrapped around her finger and she couldn't even speak yet.

Teenage years are going to be rough.

He already imagined himself handing over car keys and saying yes to whatever Emma asked, all because of a bat of her eyelashes.

Those eyelashes weren't enough to stop Anna from reverting back to her old self, though. Emma was exactly a week old the night it had happened. Nick had shown up at Anna's condo, a pillowy white cake in hand, Emma White scrawled across the top in soft pink icing. He was ready to sit down with Anna and work something out. He would forget about all the times she lashed out at him, all because of her own seedy guilt. She was angry because Nick wouldn't take her back after they had verified that Emma was actually Nick's daughter and not Aaron's. Another layer of anger came from the fact that they had signed a prenup, keeping Nick's finances out of Anna's greedy fingers. Of course, Nick would send over anything if Emma needed it, but Anna wasn't getting an extra penny. That definitely left a huge thorn in her side.

She had started off gently campaigning for a relation-ship again, trying to argue that she and Aaron were a one-time flash in the pan kind of thing. Forgetting the fact that he was one of Nick's closest friends and a man that was crashing on his couch. There was no way Nick was going to get past that, and once Anna saw that, her actions escalated.

He would accept an apology for all of it, though only if it meant a shot at giving Emma a conflict-free life.

"I brought cake," Nick had said with a smile as Anna opened the door. It was six in the evening and Anna was still wearing her light blue pajamas, her hair pulled up into a sloppy ponytail, her eyes bright but the bags underneath looked heavy.

"Before you come in, I need you to be real with me, Nick." She stood in the doorway, arms crossed. "Are we ever getting back together?"

Nick's jaw had momentarily dropped before he started grinding his teeth. His jaw set, the muscles twitching. He hadn't been expecting this, and then he suddenly felt like miles and miles stretched between him and his daughter, even though he knew she was asleep only feet away. "Anna, we've already talk—"

"—I need a yes or a no."

"I've said it before, Anna. *No*. What you did shattered me. I'm *still* picking up the fucking pieces. I've been taking it out at work and I've been a complete fucking asshole to the one person that I want to be with, all because you broke me. So, no, I can never get back with you. We can work something else out. For Emma. We don't have to be friends, but we could at least be cordial."

"*Cordial?* You want me to be cordial? I want you *back*, Nick, and you don't see me getting that, do you?! Instead you're talking about someone else." She was beginning to raise her hackles.

"Why do you want me back so bad, Anna? You're the one who fucked my friend in my own house." Nick felt his anger rising. He thought of Emma. Her wide smile, her chubby little cheeks. He took a breath. "Please, Anna, let's not do this. At least let me see my daughter."

"Not tonight, Nick."

"What?" Nick had almost dropped the cake. "We decided on the fifty-fifty split. We would make it fair and do what was best for her. That was the agreement."

"Well that changes tomorrow, Nick."

"No, no it doesn't. You can't stop me from seeing Emma. She's my daughter." He remembered feeling like saying the word over and over again would hammer something into Anna's heart. It wasn't a fucking old DVD Nick was asking for. This was his *daughter*. "You have no grounds to stop me from seeing her."

"I've talked to my lawyer. Papers should be getting to your house by next week. You'll be seeing her two days a week. You aren't fit to raise her more than that."

Nick was starting to see red. He was seconds from throwing this cake across the front lawn.

"What do you mean 'not fit'? What are you talking about?"

"I'll talk to you tomorrow, Nick, when you're calmer. Please leave before I have to call the police."

Nick remembered feeling a deep swelling of hopeless desperation grow inside him in a flash. He wanted to scream, he wanted to run, he wanted to grab that dumbass stone gnome Anna thought was cute and launch it through a window. He remembered wanting to break down and cry. He saw the determination in Anna's cold eyes. She was set on keeping Nick away from Emma and she was going to do anything she could to do it, even if that meant coming up with bullshit reasons to make people think Nick wasn't fit. All he wanted was to hold his little girl in his arms and watch her fall asleep.

That had been almost two months ago and each day was a struggle. The court systems worked at a glacier pace. Nick's lawyer worked hard to prove he was more than fit to raise Emma. They provided character references, filmed interviews, requested a home-wellness visit. They did everything right. And yet, still, the court sided with Anna. Nick didn't even think it was the work schedule bullshit that did it. He knew it was that Anna actually had the balls to say "she feared for Emma living under a roof with Nick" citing the "ranges of mood he would experience when they were together, most likely because of how stressful his job was". She had turned Nick's successful career against him and left the door open for abuse. That alone had his custody rights slashed down to the two days a week Anna wanted.

It devastated him. He spent more time writing prescriptions than he did with his daughter. Nick had felt completely powerless and had fallen into a dark place for a few days. He managed to pull himself out of it after his first weekend with Emma. Her bright eyes lit something even brighter inside of Nick. The day after, he had a long sit-down with his lawyer, who ran down the entire process for him and assured Nick that he would be getting Emma back and he would have sole custody by the end of the battle. A person who went to these lengths to screw someone over — the father of her own child — should not raise a baby by herself.

That felt like ten years ago.

Nick leaned back in his big leather chair, his head dropping backward. His hands came up to rub his face, stress building up again. He tried focusing on the sound of the water running over the rocks just behind him. The bubbling and trickling centered him. The intercom buzzed and a nurse called for another doctor, throwing Nick out of his meditative state. He took a breath and checked his watch. Only two more hours until he had his little baby girl in his arms.

That was when his phone rang. It was Chris, Anna's brother. Nick reached across his desk and grabbed the vibrating phone.

"Hello?"

"Hey, Nick, thank goodness."

Nick pushed his chair back and stood up. "What's going on? Is Emma ok?" He could hear that something was off in Chris's voice, but he had no idea what.

Please be ok.

7 SHEPARD KENSWORTH

The library wasn't as full as other days. Probably because it was a sunny Sunday afternoon tailor made for beaches and outdoor malls, not for being surrounded by stacks upon stacks of medical anatomy books. It wasn't a large library, but it definitely had everything a medical student might need and it was attached to Sierra View, so they didn't need to go far to get it. Shepard glanced out of the window next to his table, which he found to be an immediate mistake. It was a beautiful day outside and the library's front lawn was filled with picnics and games and friends just hanging out. There were even a few hammocks which must have had a waiting list that stretched for days. The moment Shepard looked outside and broke his chain of attention, his mind was set free. Daydreams flooded in, pushing out the neuromuscular disease he was just learning about.

Instead, his thoughts were replaced with flashbacks from a year ago. He could see Nick's sweaty, flushed chest above him. He could see the doctor's smoldering smile, a grin that sold pure sex. Shepard could *feel* the doctor's strong hands, climbing up Shepard's stomach, grabbing at his nipples while Nick's lips wrapped around Shepard's hard, throbbing dick.

This wasn't the first time he imagined this. No, Shepard had the memories down in his mind like a grainy VHS, playing back on frequent occasions. It caused inopportune boners, that was for sure, but Shepard couldn't really control it either. He *wanted* to stop thinking about Nick, he wanted to go back to focusing on school and nothing else. But that wasn't the case. Even when Shepard was dating Rick, he would still find his mind drifting to Nicholas White.

Maybe I don't even know what I want.

Shepard sighed, realizing that even if he wanted the doctor, he would never get him. Their encounter, although spectacular and mind-blowing, was brief and never picked up for a second episode. Shepard wasn't sure what happened, but Nick immediately turned off any kind of connection they were forming and walled himself off practically the day after they had hooked up. And he cut himself off from not only Shepard, but it seemed like he distanced himself from everyone at the hospital, too. Rumors swirled around the halls of Sierra View (Shepard was thankful that his name didn't come up in any of them) but the general consensus was that something big happened in Nick's life and his new attitude was a result of it. He was still divorced, that much was obvious from the lack of the ring, but no one knew anything past that. As the days passed, he started picking on residents and became a lot icier, even when they were around patients. It confused Shepard, who had previously noted Nick's exceptional bedside manner. Shepard had considered asking him what was wrong during a visit to the doctor's office hours, and almost did, too, but Nick quickly shut down the conversation when he saw where it was headed, giving Shepard a signal to back off. It hurt, but Shepard had to listen. For some reason, maybe it was the overgrown Disney romantic in him, but he thought that he would have been able to ride in and save Nick from whatever he was going through and they would realize their love for each other in the process.

Yeah... I have to stop watching Disney movies before I go to sleep.

Shepard sighed and broke his gaze from the library's courtyard. His daydream boner had left and his mind went back to focusing on the nervous system, which was illustrated in full 3D on his iPad. He didn't even really need to be in a library since almost all of his books were e-books, but the setting definitely helped get him in the studying mood.

"Ugh," Betty groaned quietly from across the table. She crossed her arms on the table and dropped her head into the makeshift cave. "If I have to read about axons and myelin sheaths one more time, I'm going to lose it."

"I'm a chapter behind you," Shepard said. He looked at his notes, seeing a page filled with modern-day hieroglyphics. "I can't keep focused."

Betty lifted her head up. "Tell me about it," she said. "My neurons are fried." She chuckled and shook her head at her own pun. "We have to study for STEPS, plus work half the day, *annnd*, to top it off, I have to plan my sister's wedding."

"Well, not the entire thing. Just the fun stuff."

"Yeah, you would think. Being the bride of honor is no joke. I think it's harder than getting into medical school." She chuckled, her dark curly hair bouncing slightly. "It doesn't help that Selena is the *definition* of a bridezilla. I swear, I think her wedding dress even has the Godzilla spine on it. Those big triangle scales. Yep." They laughed some more before Betty added, "I mean, she can pull it off. I'm sure of it."

"Mhmm," Shepard said, smiling. He understood where the friendly sibling shade came from, seeing as he was a twin and all. "Speaking of crazy siblings getting married," Shepard glanced at his phone, "I'm expecting a call from Crow any minute now."

"Crow? Wait... your brother is getting married?!" Betty's hands came up to her mouth, covering the widening smile.

"Yep," Shepard said, matching Betty's excitement. He sat up a little straighter in the hard wooden chair. Shepard wondered if someone's job was to specifically make library chairs as uncomfortable as possible to deter from sleeping. "His boyfriend gave me the heads up."

"This is crazy," Betty's voice was getting louder. Shepard heard someone cough from across the room, on the other side of the stacks of medical books. "Crazy," Betty emphasized, lowering her voice, "So many people are getting married."

"Tell me about it," Shepard said, feeling a sting of bitterness. Growing up, he had to fight hard to stay out of his brother's shadow. Crow was always the star of the family, holding the center of attention like it was his destiny to. He knew what to do when all the eyes were on him, and he used that to his advantage. Crow was always the more popular, outgoing one of the two. Shepard found his talents manifested between books, inside libraries, studying things he didn't even need to learn about. He had simply enjoyed learning. The moment their parents realized this, they steered both children in the appropriate directions. Shepard never felt overly pressured, and thankfully he truly enjoyed being a doctor, because he was definitely prodded toward that route. He knew that if he did anything else with his life, his parents would support him, but the disappointment would be palpable. His brother, on the other hand, finished college and followed his passion for music. He was well on his way to becoming a star and was in the middle of his first national tour.

But none of that had ever made Shepard feel bad about himself. That problem never really plagued Shepard. Not until recently, at least.

Now, Shepard was feeling the bitterness spread through him as the days went on and more people settled down with the ones they loved. *That* was what made Shepard jealous. Which turned into a bitter pill because he absolutely *hated* feeling jealous. He felt like jealousy was such a terrible emotion, one that could eat at your core until there was nothing left. Some people used jealousy to drive them forward, but Shepard felt like using his own determination to better himself was more than enough fuel. All the great green monster did was make Shepard feel like shit, like he was missing out on something and quickly losing the chance to ever get it. It was an unneeded pressure. It didn't matter what anyone else had or who they were sleeping next to. All that mattered was what Shepard had in his life and that he had the means of getting whatever else he wanted.

Although... the clock *was* ticking and Shepard was nowhere closer to finding that one partner in crime he could share his life with. That was all he wanted, and he wasn't getting it.

Maybe I'm never going to find 'the one'. Maybe I'm just meant to be alone.

Betty started looking at her fingernails and pursed her

lips. "I may or may not have left a website for engagement rings open on Steve's laptop."

"You're bad," Shepard said, laughing even though the bitter blade was back again, prodding him in the ribs. Betty shrugged, wearing a playful smile, her lip gloss catching the afternoon light streaming in from the window. "I think he got the message."

"He better have."

Shepard's phone started to ring. It was Crow requesting to connect on a FaceTime call. "Oh shit, it's him." Shepard stuffed his iPad into his black backpack and got up from his seat.

"Alright, you coming back?"

Shepard shook his head. "Probably not," he said, already halfway down a stack of books, heading toward the elevators. "Sorry!" he called, a little too loudly for being in the library, smiling back at Betty, who was throwing him an under-the-table middle finger. She then blew a kiss to him as he ducked into an empty elevator that had just let out a couple of freshman, judging by their innocent faces untouched by the damages of life's major stresses. Shepard caught the kiss, turned, and slapped his butt just as the elevator doors were shutting. The phone was still vibrating in Shepard's hands, thankfully keeping the connection through the elevator ride down to the first floor. When the doors opened, he hurried out and answered the call just as he was getting out of the main doors.

His smiling twin was beaming on the screen, his eyes wet at the corners. He was definitely caught by surprise, Shepard could tell. He smiled back, already feeling emotional for his brother. He was so happy Ethan had put a ring on his finger, because they were both truly perfect for each other. Crow had desperately needed someone to ground him as his music career took off, and Ethan was exactly that. They were always such a great time to be around because of how much they loved each other. Shepard couldn't be happier to be welcoming Ethan into his family.

"Holy shit, holy shit." Crow's hands were clearly shaking as he held the phone up. They were in Paris, right in front of The Louvre, a place that couldn't be more romantic if it had tried. The day seemed perfect behind them, with only a couple of thick white clouds hanging in the light blue sky like they were painted up there with a happy little brush. Shepard could see the glass walls of the museum behind them. There was already a small crowd forming; people who must have recognized Crow and wanted a selfie with him. Crow laughed and handed the phone to Ethan, who seemed to have a steadier hold.

"Did he do it yet?!" Shepard knew it was a silly question, but he wanted to toy with his brother a bit and clue him in to the fact that he was in on the plan.

"Wait, you knew?!" Crow asked, a broad smile on his face.

"Of course!" Shepard answered, "Ethan told me like a month ago. He asked Pops, what, last week?"

"You asked our dad?" Crow turned to Ethan, his eyes wide.

"I wanted to," Ethan said, smiling. "He told me that as long as I promised to be on his team for the next Pictionary Thanksgiving marathon, then it was all good."

"Of course he would," Crow said.

"Dad gave you away for an unbeatable Pictionary teammate," Shepard teased.

"I am pretty good," Ethan added.

"Congratulations you guys! This is exactly what I

needed to hear today." Shepard moved around so that he could sit on the wooden bench just outside the library, the parking lot just across from him.

"I'm genuinely surprised you were able to hold that secret for a month," Crow said, laughing. "Check out the ring." Crow lifted his hand, showing off the classy and sleek silver band. It had a thin sapphire blue line running through the center, setting it apart from every other ring. Shepard thought it looked great over the phone but he knew it looked spectacular in person.

"He's seen it," Ethan said with a smirk. "He helped me get it fitted."

"Damn," Crow said, "you guys are *sneaks*."

"Gotta do what you gotta do," Ethan said, kissing Crow's cheek.

That was when Shepard noticed something out of the corner of his eye. Movement. But it looked like someone familiar. Shepard glanced toward the shape and saw Nick rushing down the street. It looked like he was coming from the hospital, which was right behind the library.

That was when he saw Nick trip and fall, grabbing at a parking meter next to his car but missing it and landing on his hands.

"Alright, guys, I've got to go." Shepard looked nervous but quickly adopted the big, wide smile the Kensworth brothers rocked so well.

"Everything ok?" Crow asked, sensing it.

"Yeah, yeah, I'll fill you in when you get back." Shepard hung up the call with another big congrats and then shot up from his seat, running to where Nick had fallen.

(Done)

8 NICHOLAS WHITE

"**F**uck," Nick hissed out as he fell on his hands and knees. The pavement scratched up his palms and made them pink and raw, covered with dirt and rocks. He heard footsteps running toward him. He got up before any help arrived, wiping off his hands on his black slacks, which managed to survive the fall intact.

"Dr. White, you ok?"

Nick recognized that voice. He turned around, hoping his cheeks wouldn't flush pink. Of course, out of all the people around, the cutest resident in Sierra View had to be the one to witness his fall.

"Yeah, I'm fine." Nick was short, cold. He was scared and he was angry. Scared because he was looking into Shepard's eyes and feeling something he'd never felt before. And he was angry because he didn't have Emma in his arms right that second. She shouldn't have been with Anna in the first place, not if she was feeling sick. Nick was starting to wonder if there was something going on in that house. He had no idea how to prove it, but he was growing more and more worried. If Anna was doing anything that could put Emma in harm's way— *Fuck.*

That thought alone made him want to shatter his car window with his fist.

"Shit," Shepard said, sounding surprised. Nick was instantly about to apologize for his rude behavior. He hated that he couldn't control his emotions, but when Emma was involved, all rational thinking went out the window. He looked to Shepard and realized he was looking down at the ground. Nick followed his gaze and saw what had made Shepard curse.

"Shit," Nick repeated, his shoulders slumping. It was one of those days. The entire universe felt like it was working against him. A flat tire was the last thing he needed, and sure enough, he got it.

"I'll drive, come on." Shepard rattled his keys in his scrubs' pocket. "You looked like you were in a hurry. Let's go, my car's over in that lot." Shepard pointed to the large parking lot across the street. He nodded his head in that direction and started walking. Nick was thinking of an excuse, something else, but ordering a *Lyft* would take time. He was only focused on getting to Anna's as fast as he could so he could get his daughter.

"One sec!" Nick called out. He unlocked his car and undid the car seat. Holding it under one arm, he closed and locked his car and ran over to the crosswalk where Shepard was waiting for him. A couple of nurses were standing there as well, and Nick could already tell their eyes were darting in their direction, but again, he didn't really care. All he cared about was holding his little girl.

When the crossing sign gave them the go-ahead, the two men hurried across the street.

"Everything ok?" Shepard asked. Nick's anxiety must have been palpable in the air.

"I got a call —" It was then that Nick realized just how much Shepard didn't know, and suddenly, he was... scared. He became frightened by the possibility of his own story turning Shepard away. Maybe Shepard wasn't ready to date someone with a baby? Or with a crazy ex?

Why am I even thinking of dating him?

It was a ridiculous thought and an even crazier fear. Nick worked hard to tamp it all down before it spread, like an ember catching on dry tinder and growing into a roaring wildfire. Besides, he was in no way ashamed of his daughter, and if there was a problem with her than there was a problem with him. "I have to pick up my daughter, Emma."

Nick figured he would start with a spark-noted version and unravel as time passed. It was evening already but the sun was still out, shining its last rays down on the city of angels. Nick looked at the hills ahead, already playing with the orange light of the setting sun. He could make out the houses that laid claim to the stunning views from the sides of the Hollywood Hills, their windows glittering orange and purple.

"Daughter, huh? Emma is such a beautiful name, too. Emma White. How old is she?" Shepard asked. Nick glanced to his left. He wasn't sure what he was expecting, but he was caught off guard by how wide Shepard's smile was. He expected at least a little bit of trepidation, but Shepard seemed to be a hundred percent interested in learning more about his daughter. It was a special feeling.

"She's four months old," Nick said, catching Shepard's infectious smile.

"She must be the cutest thing in the world," Shepard said, his smile practically painted on his voice. Nick liked how he didn't have to look at Shepard to know that he was smiling. "Does she have any siblings?"

"Just her," Nick said. "If there's any in the future, they aren't making a grand entrance for a little longer. How about you? Do you have any siblings?"

Shepard chuckled. "I'm guessing you're not a fan of Crow's music, then."

"Crow? Is that some trendy new boy band I should know about?"

Shepard was laughing now. "Crow Kensworth. You've probably heard one or two of his songs on the radio. He's my twin brother."

"No way," Nick said, genuinely surprised. "I had no idea."

"His billboards aren't up yet, but apparently his agent got him a few around Hollywood Boulevard, so you'll be seeing my face on your drive to work soon."

"Isn't that a little surreal?"

"I'm sure it will be," Shepard said. "I've already seen my face staring back at me from random articles on the internet, that's always a little bit of a shock. But I'm getting used to it."

"Have people started recognizing you? Thinking you're Crow?"

"It's happened once or twice, but I always have to break it to them that it's just his much-less talented brother. People are generally pretty cool about it. One girl started crying in disappointment, that was actually kind of funny."

They reached Shepard's car by then. The locks clicked open. Nick set up the car seat and took the passenger seat. Shepard pulled out of the spot as soon as they were buckled in. The radio started off playing a Lady Gaga song at full volume. Shepard laughed and lowered it, apologizing for the sudden blast of perfect singing.

"No worries," Nick said, laughing along with Shepard. "She's one of my favorites."

"Oh, really? Do you play her songs for Emma?"

"She might be a little too young to really appreciate her," Nick said, smiling from ear to ear. "Maybe I'll play her some of your brother's stuff." The immense stress he had been feeling earlier was evaporating like a puddle of water laid out under the warm sun. That was how being around Shepard felt like. He emitted a nice, comforting warmth that lowered down your walls and allowed you to relax. "I want her to love all kinds of art. From singing to theatre, she's going to be exposed to all of it. My parents never really took me to anything except a movie once a year. I don't want that for her. I want her to be immersed in culture, in art. I think that's important."

"That's incredible, is what it is," Shepard said, nodding as they pulled out of the lot. "Wait, where am I headed?"

"Oh, right." Nick took a breath, wondering in what state he was going to find Anna. Anxiety was creeping into his chest. "The Terrace Towers, the apartment building on La Brea."

"Gotcha," Shepard said, turning right onto the street. The drive would normally take ten minutes, but LA traffic never made things normal. The GPS was saying they had forty minutes of traffic to look forward to.

"Is Emma ok?" Shepard asked, looking at the time. "I'll drive between cars if I have to."

Nick chuckled. "I appreciate it, but no need to go fast and furious. Emma is ok, it's her mom that passed out. Her brother has Emma now but he says he has a flight to catch tonight."

"How's being a dad like, Dr. White?" Shepard smirked Nick's way. He seemed genuinely interested in getting to know more about Nick. It felt good to be able to open up like this. Nick hated feeling like he was carrying this entire burden by himself, and by sharing the story with Shepard, he felt like some of that weight was eased.

"Call me Nick. And being a father is incredible and crazy and frustrating and the best damn thing that's ever happened to me, along with one of the hardest things I've ever done." Nick could feel the words in his chest. He could feel the pride he held in being a father. What followed next was a moment of pure honesty. "I just wish it were different. I wish I was experiencing this with someone else. Sharing all of Emma's firsts with someone who's meant to be in our lives forever. A man that I love with my entire heart and know that he does the same, and holds that same love for my daughter." Nick took a breath. "Sorry, it's been really difficult lately."

"No need for any apologies." They pulled up to a red light. Shepard looked to the side, his face somehow looking like a damn painting with the light of the setting sun reflecting off the hood of his car. "I don't know your entire story, but I do know you're an exceptionally good man. I also know that exceptionally good things happen to exceptionally good people. Emma is one example. And you'll see that she won't be the last good thing to happen to you." The light turned green, drawing Shepard's attention in time for Nick to look away, just before a tear formed at the corner of his eye. He wasn't sure what was getting into him, but he knew that something was happening inside the confines of that little red Honda.

"It's also scary because Emma is involved." Nick was a fountain now, spilling the anxieties he had been holding inside himself. "I want the absolute best for her, and I feel like every day I spend wasting on this custody battle, every day I spend alone, every day just turns into a waste. That was all time I could have had to be holding her. It's overwhelming." Nick felt the carefully constructed barrier around himself start wavering. "And to think that Anna is assassinating my character the way she is." By the look on Shepard's face, Nick realized he had more to explain, except he started catching himself and pulling back. Shepard was an incredibly nice guy and Nick owed him for the ride, but that was all. This wasn't a date, nor was it a time to unravel completely in front of a resident. The walls started to strengthen again.

"I told you," Nick said, hoping to close off the topic, "there's way too much going on."

Shepard 'tsked' and reached across the gear shift and squeezed Nick's thigh. It was quick and reassuring and, somehow, exactly what Nick had needed. It made him feel like it would all be ok. All from a gentle squeeze. "I think what matters the most right now is that you're an incredible father and I can tell that you love your little girl with every fiber in your being. That doesn't go away. Whatever is going on with the court system, I'm sure that they'll see the love you have for her and get it sorted. They'll realize that there's no way Emma should be away from you any longer."

"Thank you," Nick said, looking out the window at the tall palm trees that seemed to be crawling along with them as the traffic moved. He knew he couldn't look into Shepard's eyes. He knew he would find too much of what he wanted staring back, and he couldn't have that. His life couldn't get anymore complicated than it already was. Maybe once the custody battle finished... *No, no. Why risk getting hurt again? Why risk bringing someone into Emma's life when it was just beginning? It can get too messy.*

Nick was resisting something magical, he could feel it and it frustrated him because he couldn't control it. He previously thought Anna hadn't caused any lasting damage to his psyche, but it seemed to be the complete opposite. It was like the dust was finally settling and the damage was now apparent. All Nick could picture was Shepard hurting him and Emma, somehow, someway. He felt like it was bound to happen. A terrible thought, but one he couldn't shake.

Shepard started with another question. "You think—"

"Let's talk about something else," Nick said, cutting in, still looking out the passenger side window. His posture straightened up on the gray-clothed seat. He flexed his neck, a few pops filling in the awkward silence. "How, uhm, how's medical school going?" Nick immediately felt bad for being cold toward Shepard. He didn't want the silence to last a second longer.

"It's going," Shepard said, an exhausted laugh slipping through. "It's easier now that I'm a resident. Those first two years were rough. It was undergrad multiplied by a thousand. Tests every single day, nights spent crashing in the library. It was rough, but it's been worth it so far."

"And it always will be," Nick assured him. "I remember those days. I was a mess, especially my first year. I was close to dropping out, actually."

"It's no joke," Shepard said.

"Nope. My dad was one of the main reasons I pushed through. He talked me off the ledge quite a few times, and when his words weren't working, I'd remember the mountain of debt I was under and I'd drop my head and bury it in the books again. You're leagues ahead of me in the academic department from when I was a resident, that's for sure."

Shepard waved his hand in the air. "I'm part of the best, right?" he asked, quickly changing his tune. The abrupt shift had them both laughing as the car inched along down Santa Monica Boulevard.

"Not just part," Nick offered. "*The* best."

"Ok, now you're just looking for a free ride, huh?"

"Free? I didn't know the meter was on."

"Oh, yeah." Shepard nodded, pursing his lips. "Mountain of debt, remember?"

Nick laughed again, relaxing back into the seat. He looked to Shepard, who was looking so damn handsome in the low light. The sun had already set and the streetlights were all on, shining down white light that illuminated Shepard's sharp features. He was definitely a looker. The kind of guy that Nick had always fantasized about. And it didn't hurt at all that he had a great sense of humor and a big heart.

How can someone with such a warm smile be capable of hurting anyone?

Nick looked away, taking a breath. Writing Shepard off was going to be way harder than Nick had thought.

9 SHEPARD KENSWORTH

(handwritten annotations:) (Done) 12/19/20 - read tonight before bed

I can't believe Dr. White is sitting in my passenger seat. And he told me to call him Nick. As if we were friends. *What the hell is going on?*

And my car is so damn dirty!

Shepard tried to ignore the graveyard of receipts he had in the central panel. He could literally spot a Starbucks receipt that was already a year old. He hoped it didn't smell weird seeing as how his air freshener gave off its last piney scents a few weeks ago and now hung from his rearview mirror serving as a basic statement piece. Nick, thankfully, didn't seem to mind the mess. Shepard wasn't normally a complete disaster, but things had been tough lately and the inside of his car was hard for him to keep up for some reason. It almost made him want to invite Nick into his bedroom simply to prove that he wasn't a total slob. His bed was made every day and his laundry was contained in a big white hamper with the word "wash" printed boldly down the side. He was actually pretty proud of how his bedroom looked, with a few oversized pillows, muted golds and browns and whites, a little fringe here and there.

He also would have invited him over simply to push him onto the bed and devour him from top to fucking bottom. The man was pure sex. It was in the way he spoke, the way he set his jaw, how he held his chest high, how his smiles always smoldered. It was in the way he simply *was*. Nick checked every single box, and Shepard was having a hard time ignoring it.

Then, Nick had started opening up to Shepard and he felt himself falling even harder. Something inside him had urged Shepard to reach out and touch Nick, and he did. He had grabbed his thigh out of a moment of pure emotion. Nothing sexual, purely supportive. And it did something to Shepard. It shifted something in his list of priorities. All he wanted to do was be able to reach out and comfort Nick whenever he needed it. He wanted to be Nick's support, he wanted to be the solid column holding him up on difficult days like these.

Jesus. I'm getting attached without even dating the guy. This isn't going to work and I need to stop fantasizing.

The same thing had happened with Rick. He had fallen hard for him before they had even gone on a date. It was months later when he realized how unhinged the man was and ended things, but he was blind to all that from the beginning. Shepard wasn't sure why, but he knew that he fell hard and fast, and he was sure it was happening all over again. But this felt different in that it felt... *worth* it. Nick was worth the fall, so long as he was around to break it.

He could also tell that Nick was done opening up. That was fine with Shepard. He understood that not everything was going to be laid out in the open. He took what he got and left it at that, wondering what Anna had done and hoping that it would all turn out as well as he said it would. Shepard was great at putting on an optimistic mask and looking toward the brighter side of things. He definitely believed that Nick loved his daughter, and hearing him talk about her... well, it definitely did something to Shepard. He wasn't sure what, but he felt it.

The rest of the drive wasn't as awkward as Shepard feared it would be. In fact, there wasn't an ounce of awkwardness to be found. Their conversation flowed as smooth as a river, the laughs as well. Shepard hadn't realized how funny Nick was, in a dry kind of way. He definitely didn't show off his humor at Sierra View, so it was really refreshing to hear him deadpan a joke about the time he was walking up a stage to give a presentation when he fell and, in his own words, "I rolled on the stage like a stunned armadillo. I don't know why I chose to roll. A backwards Willie Wonka is who I was," and Shepard laughed and laughed. Not even that the words itself were that funny, but when said by the stern doctor in his gravely voice who seemingly had the sexy ability to laugh at himself, and it was suddenly a knee-slapper. That story prompted Shepard to jump into the time he tripped and fell on a stage —his *college graduation* stage.

"No," Nick said, dread on his face. The traffic was still stop and go, so Shepard took as many chances as he could to glance over. "That's every college kid's worst fear. Well, that and your alarm not working right before a final exam."

"*Annnnd* that would be my second story."

"*Nooo*," Nick said, laughing now. "That happened to you, too?"

Shepard nodded, lips pursed into a smile. "It was for a dumb elective class, too, but without the final I would have failed the class. An easy A was going to turn into an F, sinking my GPA, and you know how important even just a decimal point in a GPA is when it comes to medical school admissions."

"So what were you doing the night before? Big party? Had a little too much to drink?" Nick winked playfully.

"I was up all night reading the last Harry Potter book."

Nick's eyebrows rose in surprise as his smile widened. "It would have been worth it then."

"Oh, totally." Shepard chuckled, remembering his time as a freshman in college.

"So did you make it to the test?"

"*Mhmm*," Shepard said, turning a left onto a quieter street with less traffic. "But, oh god, I'm not even sure I should finish this story."

"What, why?" Nick looked to Shepard, his eyes practically glowing in the dark car. "I want to hear it. Your stories help me keep my mind off things."

Shepard smiled at that, happy that he was helping out the doctor. "Ok, well, this dies in the car, ok?"

"You've got my Boy Scout's promise."

"Those are unbreakable, right?"

"Yeah, I think so."

Shepard chuckled, rolling his car to a stop at the stop sign. Apartment buildings bordered them on either side. None of them overly tall, mostly to be earthquake-safe, some of them looking newer than the others. People were just getting home from work, pulling into their garages, trudging up steps toward their homes, tired from the day. "Alright, so I was clearly in a panic when I woke up. No Time-Turner in sight, I had to throw on clothes and bolted out of my apartment. The teacher warned us he would lock us out if we were ten minutes late, giving us an automatic F. I saw my shot at medical school being destroyed. I was so dramatic. So I raced to campus and then considerably lowered my speed —those campus speed limits are no joke. I park, and I run, and I run, and I run. I had three minutes until he'd lock me out. But this was freshman year and I wasn't anywhere near being in shape back then, so I'm just this little twig fighting all the forces of the earth to get to class in time."

"Did you?" Nick was sitting on the edge of his seat.

"Yes," Shepard said proudly, before quickly deflating. "But... I also had to throw up right outside of the class." Shepard started laughing at the ridiculousness of it all, Nick quickly joining in. "I walked in and everyone was deathly silent because they already started taking the test, so they clearly heard me being a hot mess outside. I walk in, all pale and sweaty, and find the last desk open. I sit down and the teacher walks over with a test in hand. He's looking at me as if he's trying to figure out what drugs I'm on. I definitely looked like I had done peyote or something."

Nick was splitting in half with the laughter now. It was all Shepard had wanted. He wanted to hear that deep, warm laugh. It was a sound that filled Shepard was happiness, especially since it was also a sort of verification that Nick was actually having a good time. Even though shit was hitting the fan in his personal life, Shepard had the ability to take some of that away, even if only for a moment.

"Oh, oh, and get this."

Nick was trying to stop his laughs. "What?"

"I didn't bring a pencil!"

(Done)

10 NICHOLAS WHITE

Read tonight in bed

Read on 12/21/20 Monday

Nick was smiling from ear to ear, stomach hurting from laughing so hard, something he didn't expect happening on the drive to Anna's apartment. He completely expected to sit in the car, arms crossed, stern face plastered on, frustration bubbling inside him. Instead, he was relaxed and laughing and, for the first time since Emma entered his world, he felt like things were truly going to be ok. All the bullshit that had been surrounding him seemed to disappear the moment Shepard started speaking. Hell, the guy didn't even have to say a word, Nick felt calmer just having Shepard next to him.

This is dangerous.

The rest of the ride was spent with more laughs and another story. They didn't have much longer after Shepard divulged his final exam experience, but Nick had managed to squeeze in a story about his own college disaster. His happened while he was presenting to a class of about two hundred kids about the dangers of antibiotic resistant bacteria. A day when he just so happened to have felt like he was infected with one of those very same bacteria. That, mixed with the fact that

Nick naturally got nervous in front of large crowds, and well, the ending was just as pretty as Shepard's story.

"At least you showed up prepared," Shepard said, laughing with his eyebrows raised in empathy.

Nick nodded, laughing along with Shepard. "Damn right. I would have definitely mic-dropped the end of that presentation if it wasn't for my breakfast making a surprise guest appearance."

They kept talking until Shepard pulled up to the apartment building, their conversation dying off as Shepard parked at a meter right in front of the entrance. It was a decent building, but Nick preferred his house way more. He knew Emma would be better off in his house as well, with a yard big enough for a bright pink treehouse (or blue if she wanted, Nick *certainly* wasn't going to judge).

"I'll be right down; I'm just going to grab her. I live up in the hills, so not too far from here."

"No worries, I'll be parked right here."

"Thank you, Shepard." Nick held onto the door handle, his body turned toward Shepard, their eyes locking. Nick was filled with an urge to erase any distance between them. He wanted his lips on Shepard's, a reminder of the heated kiss they had shared so many months ago.

Instead, as much as it pained him, Nick smiled and opened the door. He stepped out of the car and went up into the building, climbing the dirty steps and wondering if he would ever overcome the fear of betrayal again. Maybe he was never going to lean into a kiss again. Maybe Anna had permanently broken him, the pieces of his trust unrecognizable in the rubble.

Nick pounded the secret code into the callbox to enter the building, not wanting to wait for anyone to buzz him in.

He hurried through the musty-smelling lobby with a sad blue couch pressed against a wall and stopped in front of the elevators. The button was already lit, someone must have been riding it down. Moments later, the door dinged open. Nick stepped aside, letting the passengers get off. He stepped inside when he thought he saw a face he recognized exit the elevator.

Huh... weird.

It was that Rick kid. The one from the gym, the one who had blown up on Shepard.

Maybe he lives in this building.

Nick pressed the fourth floor and took the elevator up, relieved that the guy didn't notice him. He didn't want to get into any kind of altercation moments before he was supposed to pick up his daughter. He stepped out into the dimly lit hallway, dirty green carpet stretching down the length. There was a dog barking at the farthest door, its sharp yaps loud enough to echo against the crusty walls. He walked down the hall and stopped at the third door, knocking on the cracked wood. Almost immediately, two locks unlatched from inside and the door swung open. Chris was standing there. He was the kind of guy who rarely smiled and always had a silver cross hanging around his neck. Nick barely even registered him. All he cared about was the little pink bundle of love he held in his arms. The second she made eye contact with Nick, her features lit up and her tiny body started squirming as she gurgled happily. Nick almost broke down into tears right then and there. His opened his arms and took Emma into them, holding her as close to his chest as he could, taking in her sweet scent, feeling complete with her little body against his.

"Thank you," Chris said, as though this was some kind of favor.

"Where is she?" Nick asked, looking around Chris and into the apartment. The living room was a mess, with old microwave dinner trays left out on the coffee table next to cans of soda. Nick noticed an ash tray sitting on the table. "You guys aren't smoking in there, are you?"

"Absolutely not," Chris said, stepping into the center of the doorframe, blocking out the rest of the apartment from view. "You know Emma is safe here. Anna just had a bad reaction to a flu medication and passed out. That's all."

"She didn't sound like she had the flu when we last spoke. What did she take?"

Nick was a doctor; he'd know if Chris was lying.

"She... I'm not sure, actually. But it didn't work well for her, that's all."

Something felt fishy. Emma gave a small, happy sounding chirp from his arms. "Let me see her, I'll make sure she's ok." Nick wanted to just get inside the apartment. His suspicions were growing darker and darker by the second.

"She'll be ok. She just has to sleep it off. She told me to tell you that she said thanks." Chris smiled at Emma before looking back up at Nick, the smile wavering on his face like it was being held there with old toothpicks. "She's precious. Really. God's little gift. I pray you and my sister can work something out."

Nick couldn't manage a smile in return. "I should get her to her crib," Nick said, holding Emma a little tighter. He turned and left, not waiting for Chris to say anything else. Something was going on. He could feel it. But how was he going to prove anything?

Emma gave another happy gurgle and started reaching

her tiny hands up toward his face. He managed the smile that was absent earlier. Emma would always be able to draw out his smiles. It was like a super power.

"Hi, my little angel," he said, immediately speaking in a cooing tone. "How are you? My precious baby girl. Daddy's got you now. Yes, he does. Yes, he does." She was laughing, the sound as pure as the first winter's snow. "You think I'm funny, Em? Huh?" Nick walked down the musty hall, making different faces the entire time. "And now?" His face was contorted, his eyebrows scrunched and his lips twisted. Emma laughed some more, the sound filling up the creaky elevator as they rode it down.

Outside, Shepard was waiting by his car. He looked toward Nick and Emma, lighting up the second he spotted the small pink bundle in Nick's arms.

"There's the girl I've been hearing all about." Shepard seemed like he was about to devour Emma. His grin was wide and his hands outstretched. "Mind if I hold her?"

"Of course not," Nick said, feeling a seed of nerves settle in his chest. He wasn't sure but he felt like this moment was somehow important, more important than either of the men realized. "She's a little shy around strangers," Nick said, looking down at his girl, whose big bright eyes were now looking around before settling on Shepard. Nick expected her to start crying the second he handed her off. It was her normal reaction. She didn't like being handed off to new people.

"She's beautiful," Shepard said, almost to himself. To Nick's genuine surprise (and immense relief), Emma stayed completely quiet. She wasn't laughing, but she wasn't wailing either. She was looking up at Shepard as though she were presented with a Rubik's cube she had to solve. Nick took a step back. The street was illuminated by the street lamps around them, and so Nick could make out the pure glee in Shepard's features. "Aren't you, girl? Beautiful. You already know that, huh?"

Nick crossed his arms, unable to stop from grinning at the scene. Something about this felt right. He didn't want to dwell on the thought, but he did recognize it. Maybe it was in how natural Shepard seemed as he stood there, holding an entranced Emma. Then her face cracked and Nick braced himself for a long, piercing cry. He moved forward, ready to take her back from a frightened Shepard.

Instead of channeling a banshee, Emma did the complete opposite. She started to giggle. She was looking up at Shepard and laughing. "Whoa," Nick said, surprised. "She's really taking to you. Especially since it's past her bedtime. Cranky should be her middle name right about now."

Shepard chuckled, his eyes glowing as he became hypnotized by the little girl in his hands. Nick almost pulled his phone out and snapped a picture. He wasn't sure why, but he felt a huge urge to do it. He also recognized it was probably a creepy thing to do and Shepard would most likely find it weird.

Even though I wouldn't mind a gallery full of photos of this.

The dark cloud that had been following Nick since he got that call lifted and cleared. He stood a little straighter, his arms relaxed at his side, a smile on his face. It was getting dark out, but the street lights and orange hue from the setting sun was more than enough to put a spotlight on the two in front of him. Emma started to reach up, her little fingers opening and closing in the air, her chubby cheeks pushed aside by the big smile, her dimples in full display.

"I think I'm in love," Shepard said, laughing, his eyes

still entranced with Emma's. He leaned his face down, letting Emma's fingers try to find purchase on his lip. He laughed some more, causing Emma to do the same. It was such a pure sound. Nick would never grow tired of it.

"It looks like she is, too." Nick cocked his head. "She's always a little shy around strangers, but this is the first time I've seen her so bubbly right off the bat."

"Well, we're already best friends. Aren't we? Aren't we?" Shepard's voice took on the tone Nick affectionately dubbed "the baby voice". Everyone did it whenever there was a baby around (sometimes it even applied to puppies). The universal way of dropping your voice and speaking through a huge smile, repeating things and watching the baby light up at your words. "Alright, cutie-pie, let's get you to bed." Shepard kissed her forehead and handed her back to Nick, who held her against his chest, happy to feel her soft breaths against him. She looked around, as though she were worried Shepard had disappeared, and then burst into giggles when her eyes landed on him.

"Does she just think I'm funny looking? I think that'll be the biggest heartbreak I've ever felt in my life. Finding out she only likes me because I look like a toad."

Nick laughed at that, only because Shepard looked nothing like a toad. "Please, you know you look like the prince that appears after the toad gets kissed."

Shepard smiled at that, apparently not expecting the compliment. Neither was Nick. He didn't think of how brazenly flirty it would sound until he said the words out loud. "We should get going," Nick said, feeling the moment begin to morph and shape itself into something deeper. He wasn't ready for that. He didn't want that. He was done with it all. Nick's life was going to revolve around Emma and that was it. She was the only human on the planet who

Nick trusted wouldn't hurt him. How was he going to open himself up to anyone else?

Even if that person looked so natural holding Emma. Even if that person felt so natural in Nick's arms. Even if that person could light up a room and fill Nick's heart with a simple smile.

Nope.

He wouldn't open himself up to anyone, never again. Not even if...

EMMA WAS TUCKED SAFELY in her crib, her sleeping face a picture of pure innocence. Nick found he could stare at her for the entire night and be perfectly fine. He didn't care about the lost sleep, all he wanted was the time with his daughter. She was perfect. Nick bent down and gave her a gentle kiss on the forehead, careful not to wake her. She definitely hadn't gotten Nick's finicky sleep habits. Emma seemed like she would have been able to sleep through a world war, only waking up when she was hungry again.

Nick let himself out of her room, double-checking the baby monitor worked before he closed the door so that only a crack was left open. He went back into his living room, where Shepard was standing, his hands held at his front, his posture a little awkward, as though he wasn't sure if standing or sitting was the better option. He looked so good in those scrubs. It was hard for Nick to ignore the warmth that spread from between his thighs. Nick smiled at him as he entered the open space of his living room, lit by the recessed lights above them. A fire crackled in the gray stone fireplace across from the leather couches. The scent of fresh linens filled the room as his air freshener went off and shot a puff of perfume into the air from the top of a bright blue bookshelf with glass windows set into the doors. It was a statement piece and one that was owned by Nick's grandmother, who he had a huge amount of love for.

Nick stopped a few feet from Shepard and leaned on the arm of the couch. "Thanks again, for everything. You really went out of your way to help me today." Nick was keeping his voice quiet even though he knew Emma probably wouldn't wake up.

"And thank you for letting me meet that smiling little butterball of yours." Shepard kept his voice low, too, but his *eyes*, those were bright. Loud. They were filled with an honest happiness. As though Nick had really given him a heartfelt gift by introducing Shepard to his daughter. It was touching. "I saw Rick come out of that building and thought my entire day was about to be ruined. Thankfully, he didn't spot me and kept walking. Nothing was going to rain on Emma's introduction, that was for sure."

"Emma really seemed to like you," Nick said, a smile spreading across his face. The room was dim, the lights above must not have been set to their brightest setting. Shadows flickered on the wall across from the fireplace, the wood crackling inside the orange flames. "I think she's got a good sense of people already."

"Well, I think I fell in love with her." Shadows played on the side of Shepard's face, highlighting those sharp features that drew Nick in like a moth to flames. He took a breath. Shepard continued speaking, "You're going to make an incredible father."

"Sometimes I'm positive I'm doing everything wrong, but thanks for the false sense of confidence."

"I'm serious," Shepard took a step forward, those features on his face getting sharper. Details appeared: Shepard's bitable upper lip, his sexy strong brow, the slight stubble that was much lighter than Nick's. "Don't short change yourself. I'm not sure what the entire story is, but it sounds like someone really hurt you. They did some serious damage. You wear the scars on your sleeve even though you think you have them covered."

Shit, Nick thought, *he's got me pegged.*

"You're worth so much more than that. From the second we met, I could see it. You deserve to be treated like a king, Emma a princess. I don't want you to think you should get any less, or think that no one out there is ready to do it, because I am."

That was when Shepard did something that shouldn't have surprised Nick, but did all the same. He moved in for a kiss. Nick should have let it happen. He *wanted* to. He wished he could have melted into the kiss, let it evolve into something so much bigger than either of them could ever comprehend. He should have lost himself in that moment, letting Shepard steer them both.

He didn't do any of those things. Instead, he tensed and pushed Shepard back. It wasn't hard but it was sudden and fast and seemed to have caught Shepard off guard. His eyes were wide, clearly in pain from the rejection. It was wrong and Nick immediately felt like a fucked-up dickhead.

"I'm sorry," Nick started, launching into an apology. "I've just got so much going on."

"No, that's ok." Shepard stepped back, his head dropping, his gaze breaking from Nick to look down at the floor. "I was being dumb. Got too caught up in everything. Forget it."

"Shep—"

"I should get going. Gotta be at the hospital early tomorrow morning." Shepard gave a weak wave and turned.

He grabbed his keys from the side table next to the door and unlocked it. Before stepping out, he paused for a moment. Nick took a breath, seconds from asking him to stay, from saying that he was being stupid, that he was being a *massive* fucking coward.

Shepard left before Nick could get the right words out. The door shut, leaving Nick in his empty living room, wondering what the hell he was supposed to do next.

(Done)

It was afternoon, and although a hospital was busy at all hours of the day, some times were predictably slower than others. Afternoons for some reason or another seemed to slow down at Sierra View. The halls were slightly less packed, intercom system slightly less used. It was also the time that Shepard enjoyed a routine walk with Betty toward the cafeteria. At least, they tried to make it as routine as possible. This week, they were doing rounds on the internal medicine floor which meant fewer emergencies. The week before had them in the emergency room, which had been nonstop cases that ranged from simple broken bones to complex illnesses that were far out of depth for the residents to handle alone. That was where the attendings came in. Since Sierra View was a teaching hospital, most of the doctors also worked as professors, some even going as far as holding lectures at the local universities.

All of the attendings at Sierra View were approachable, although Shepard wouldn't use the term friendly. There was always a clear hierarchy on display between the more seasoned doctors and the newer residents which kept relationships from developing.

Or at least kept them complicated.

"Have you talked to Crow?" Betty asked as they walked side by side. "I saw his Instagram blowing up after he posted a photo of the engagement ring."

"He's doing great; I don't think I've ever seen him happier. Even when he was learning about his national tour he wasn't this happy. Or, well he was, it was just a different kind of happy." Shepard glanced out of a passing window, the sun was high up in the sky and beating down on the busy LA streets outside. "They're still not sure where they want the wedding to be, but it's early, they've got time to plan it."

Even saying the word "wedding" had Shepard feeling a flash of sadness. It wasn't the expected reaction, but it was the honest one. He was definitely happy for his brother, but he also couldn't help but feel like it was another reminder of his own failed love life. There was still time to turn his love boat around and away from crashing headfirst into a cliff, but not as much time as he would have liked. He was getting older and things weren't looking any easier. If anything, things were getting more difficult. Especially if he was going to get pushed away after trying to make a move.

"And you, mister?" Betty asked, practically reading his mind. Sometimes Shepard could have sworn that his best friend was psychic.

"What about me?" Shepard knew damn well what about she was talking about.

"You've been unusually quiet in the dating department recently. Ever since Rick left the picture, it feels like you sort of threw in the towel."

"Yeah, I guess I kind of did."

"Why?"

"Because," Shepard shrugged, feeling his shoulders sag down with weight. "I just keep seeing everyone around me getting married and having kids and I'm starting to think that maybe it just won't happen for me. Even if it's all I want."

"Shep, you're only twenty-six, you've still got time."

"It still sucks. It's all I want. A husband, with a kid and a dog. Maybe a cat. Depends. But instead, I date Rick who turns out to be a whack job. And with our crazy schedules, I was lucky to have even found Rick in the first place... well, not lucky, but you know what I mean. It took enough energy back then, I don't think I could get on a dating app and play that whole game again." He was pulling excuses out of a hat like a street magician.

Betty waved it off. "You've got guys tripping over themselves getting to you."

"Eh, I don't know about that. Thankfully I haven't seen Rick again, though. Not since he blew up on me in front of Dr. White." Shepard wanted to get off the topic of his current love life.

"Ugh, what a dickwad."

"Yep," Shepard said, clapping his hands. "I sure know how to pick them, don't I?"

"For real," Betty said with a laugh before dropping her voice, "and now you're after the emotionally shut-off doctor that everyone wants to bang."

Shepard scoffed. "I'm not after him. That's done. A closed case, Watson."

"I always considered myself Sherlock, to be honest." Betty mimed using a magnifying glass on Shepard's face and being terrified by what she saw.

"Did you catch your reflection?" Shepard shot back with a smile.

"Ohh, good one." Betty laughed and playfully slapped his chest with the back of her hand. "Seriously, though, I don't know how much of a closed case it is with the way he looks at you."

Shepard almost stopped fast enough to produce a trail of smoke in the hallway. "What? Looks at me? You never told me about that."

"I thought it was obvious. He looks at you like he's ready to devour you. I mean, not all the time, but it definitely happens. Especially during our last few morning meetings."

This was new information to Shepard, who had been avoiding Nick's gaze like he was expecting the man to sprout a head of snakes. Every time he looked at Nick, he felt that little spark in his chest flare to life, threatening to catch fire and consume him. And then he would feel like a complete and total idiot all over again. The same way he felt the night he went in for a kiss and was pushed back. Rejected. It hurt. It was a feeling Shepard wasn't prepared for. He had felt comfortable around Nick. He fooled himself by thinking that day was anything more than a simple favor for Nick. It was Shepard's fault, and he wasn't going to be mad at Nick about it.

"Is it that obvious?" Shepard asked. He didn't think Nick would show any obvious sign of interest after pushing him away.

"I think I heard Lisa and Alex mention something a few days ago," Betty said. "But I don't think anyone cares as much as you expect them to. It's not like we have a full-on teacher relationship with the attendings, so he's not sexual harassing you for grades or anything. Sure, he has to write us our evaluations, but our STEPs are way more important, and there's no way those could be tampered with. *Plus*, Dr. White won't be your attending for much longer. We're done with emergency medicine."

Shepard shook his head, continuing their walk. He felt his cheeks start getting red at the simple *thought* of people knowing about him and Nick. He should have figured. How could their chemistry be invisible when Shepard constantly felt on fire around the doctor? But still, he had been trying damn hard to stifle those feelings. The failed kiss was like a burning brand seared into his brain, never fully healing, a constant throbbing that served as a reminder: *it isn't going to work.*

"Well they need to stop because nothing is ever going to happen. I don't think it's about being my attending anymore. He's got too much going on and, apparently, I'm not the person equipped to help him with it." They turned a corner then, walking into an open area of Sierra View where the ceiling was made of glass and the center of the room was taken up by a tall, stunning crystal glass sculpture of an angel with arms spread wide and wings flared. It had been donated by Harold Levy, a man with a ton of oil money who also had life-saving open-heart surgery at Sierra View. They walked past a gift shop with an assortment of different "congratulations!" balloons and cute little plush toys for newborn babies.

"Why?" Betty asked.

"Because it's not." Shepard hadn't gotten a chance to tell Betty about the almost-kiss yet. Then again, he wasn't really looking for the chance. He didn't want to talk about it, not even with his best friend. He felt embarrassed by it. He should have controlled himself and walked out, nothing else. Instead, he had let himself get carried away.

"Ok, fine…" It sounded like Betty was going to drop it but then, "What if you give it one date?"

"You're not getting it," Shepard said, his voice cut with a soft sense of sadness. "There wouldn't be a date even if I wanted one. It takes two people, he's got a lot going on, I don't see him having the time or the energy to date."

"You're making it sound like dating you is the same thing as running a marathon. I mean not that I have first-hand experience, but I still feel like I can confidently say it's not like a marathon at all. Last I checked, you're totally low maintenance. If anything, dating you is like taking a ride on the lazy river."

"Thank you?"

"It's a good thing. Who doesn't love a good lazy river? Until someone pees, then everyone's fun is ruined… Anyways, you don't need constant attention; you understand the importance of space. Plus, you've both been through medical school, you both know what being a doctor demands. He'd be the last person to ask more of you than you can handle." Betty put her hands up. "At least those are my two cents. Take 'em or leave 'em, dude."

"You're right, you're right." Shepard looked down at his black sneakers. "It's still not ideal."

"You won't know that unless you give it a shot. At least ask him out on a date. He's clearly shown interest, and sure, he has some stuff he needs to work out, but that's where you come in. You can be his antidote. Cure whatever ails him, doctor." She said that last part in an old timey accent while batting her thick eyelashes and fisting her hands to her chest.

Shepard laughed, finding truth behind his best friend's joke. Coincidentally, it also echoed the advice he had received from Crow, who he had FaceTimed a few days ago. His twin knew exactly what Shepard was feeling without Shepard even needing to finish his story. It was definitely one of those weird twin things. Before Shepard got to the part in his story where he met Emma, Crow cut in and told him to go for it. He said that it was obvious in the way Shepard spoke, there was a connection that was mutual. Even after he told the part about the rejected kiss, Crow still held the same opinion. Crow was big on taking chances and following where his heart led, and so Shepard wasn't surprised to hear his twin tell him to pursue Nick.

On the other hand, he *was* surprised Betty was also encouraging him to go after the doctor. She was a much more cautious person, reserved and thoughtful with most of her actions. They had met at the beginning of medical school and since then Betty was always the one pushing Shepard along, encouraging him and holding him accountable when it came to studying over watching TV. She had turned down plenty of relationships herself so that she could focus on school, and back then, she always advised Shepard to do the same thing. Not that he was getting a ton of offers, but when the idea did come up, Betty always served as a bit of a reality check.

She doesn't even know about the kiss. Or Emma.

"I met his daughter."

Betty's brows shot up. "Way to bury the lead, dude!" She lowered her voice as a pair of nurses walked by. "So the rumors are true, then?"

"Yep, he has a baby girl." Shepard started smiling at just thinking about Emma. "And you know me, Betty, I'm not the greatest with kids."

"Pfft, I remember what happened during our rounds on the OB/GYN floor." Betty started chuckling. "Whenever someone handed you a baby, your face would contort and you clearly looked like you were going through some inner panic."

"Ok, I wasn't *that* bad."

"You were definitely out of your element."

"I was just concentrating," Shepard said, defending himself. It was the truth, though. He had never truly felt comfortable around babies, he was never sure why. And he had even delivered a few, and those moments were absolutely magical, moments that Shepard was never going to forget. There was no better feeling in the world than delivering a baby and handing it over to their emotional parents. Shepard loved being a part of that. And yet he still felt slightly nervous around babies. "Well, that's the thing, when I met Emma, none of that happened. I wasn't terrified of holding her. She made it all click for me. It didn't feel like she was made of glass. Most of the times, I end up feeling like I'm gonna break a baby by just holding them wrong. But not Emma. I dunno... I guess it felt natural? Jesus, I've lost it."

"You might have." Betty chuckled and playfully slapped his butt. "Could be your internal clock ticking away. A constant reminder of the desolate, barren, childless future ahead if you don't get things moving soon."

"You always know exactly what to say."

"Thanks, it's a gift."

Shepard started laughing at Betty's smug expression. "She was so sweet. Probably half a year old, nonstop smiles and chubby cheeks. So cute."

"It sounds like you two hit it off," Betty nudged Shepard's side with her elbow. "You know she's the only stamp of approval her daddy is looking for."

"Please don't say daddy."

"Why?" Betty asked. "Does it turn you on?"

"Yes, you saying daddy is really revving my engines."

"Ohh... ok, Daddy." Betty said, whispering the last part even though she choked on a laugh. "You're right, you're right, I can't keep a straight face."

Shepard was laughing, but he was also thinking that what Betty said was the truth. It was obvious how much Emma meant to Nick, and that there was nothing ever coming between the two. Sure, she was a baby and probably not the best judge of character, but she was still already fond of Shepard, that had to mean something. "I already want to see that little nugget again."

"Well, maybe he needs a babysitter. There's a medical convention in Denver next month, maybe he's going to it." Emily wiggled her eyebrows. "Plus, who doesn't like a sexy babysitter."

Shepard smiled and shook his head. "That's the thing, even if I get a second job as his babysitter—which, even saying it out loud sounds crazy, as if I have the time for a second job —but, let's just say I do spend more time with them, all that's going to do is make me feel even stronger feelings in a situation where I probably won't have those feelings reciprocated. He's a new father dealing with some-thing else in the background, I don't think he's open to dating right now."

"So you *do* have feelings for him, then?" Betty was cutting right to the core of it. "Shep, I think it's worth keeping your mind open to the possibility. Maybe even push for it a little bit. Sometimes you've got to work a little harder for something that's worth it."

They turned a corner and found themselves next to the break room. Betty stopped, nodding toward the door. "Alright, this is my stop. See you later." Betty opened her arms and grabbed Shepard in a hug. "Drop by tonight if you're free. We can have some wine while we whine."

"Sounds like a plan," Shepard said. He turned to leave but Betty stopped him with a hand on his elbow. "Wait, before you go," she said. She was smiling. "Admit that you think he's hot."

"Huh?"

"I think it'll be cathartic for you. Say it. Admit he's *really* hot." She narrowed her eyes, as if she were trying to will Shepard to say it.

"Fine, yes, Dr. White is really hot."

Just then, as though it were perfectly choreographed, the door behind Betty opened and out walked the handsome devil himself in all his white-coated glory. He was looking straight ahead, smiling at the pair when he looked their way, but he kept on walking down the hallway. Shepard looked to Betty, his face immediately turning a few shades darker.

"Shit," Shepard said in a whisper as Nick walked away. "Did he hear that?"

"Absolutely not. No way," Betty said with a deep confidence. "Ok, well this therapy session is to be continued, glad I could get that off your chest." She patted Shepard's chest. "Progress."

She was laughing as she opened the door to the break room and disappeared inside. Shepard was still pink in the cheeks.

She's right. There's no way he heard.

12 NICHOLAS WHITE

(Done)

Nick heard all of it. He walked away with a small smile playing on his face. The hospital was buzzing around him as he made his way toward his office, ready to call it a day even though half of it was still left. Bumping into Shepard was a very pleasant and much-needed surprise. A part of him wanted to hit the brakes and let him know that he had heard, but there was another resident around and Nick didn't want to start any rumors (as if none already existed). Nick sighed, another part of him hating himself for walking away, for pushing Shepard away the other night. The frustration of being unable to open up was compounded with the sadness of the fact that he had to say goodbye to Emma in a few hours. A few doctors and nurses caught Nick's eyes as he walked by, offering a friendly 'hello', but Nick would simply drop his gaze and keep walking, offering a muted 'hello' in return. Needless to say, he wasn't particularly excited about the day ending, unlike the last couple of days that had him counting down the seconds until he got home and saw Emma again. Anna hadn't felt up to the task of caring for her since her incident and so she "allowed" Emma to stay with Nick. While he worked, she was with a babysitter back at Nick's home. He wished his parents lived close enough that they could bond with her but they lived six states away.

The last couple of days had been pure bliss. Sure, Emma didn't sleep a full night and she sometimes threw crying fits for no apparent reason, but none of that outweighed the absolute joy it was to hold her in his arms and feel her breathing against his chest. Hear her giggles and her chirps. He almost allowed himself to think that he'd be able to do that whenever he wanted. The unfortunate truth, reminded by a text from Anna saying that she was feeling better and wanted her baby back, was that Nick still had to fight a long and difficult battle for the right to keep her.

He made it to his office, shut the door with the lock clicking in place, and started to cry.

THE DRIVE to Anna's place felt long. Like the road stretched for miles more than it should have. Even longer than it took with Shepard, though the roads were pretty clear this late in the evening. Nick glanced up at the rearview mirror as he pulled to a stop in front of the apartment building. Emma was nodding off, her head resting against the car seat, a small string of drool dropping from her lips. He let go of a deep breath and readied himself for what was coming. He knew this wasn't going to be easy. Not only did he have to say a temporary goodbye to Emma, but he also wanted to confront Anna about what happened the other night. He wanted to make absolutely sure that

Anna wasn't doing anything sketchy that could harm his baby girl in any way.

He got out of the car, the night air particularly chilly with a gentle breeze that whipped up every now and then. Nick glanced at the white coat folded up on his passenger seat but decided against it. He didn't want to intimidate Anna, he just wanted information. He figured he already looked like he meant business in a light gray button-up and black slacks. He texted her that he was outside and then got to work on getting Emma out of the car seat. By the time he turned around, a sleepy Emma in his arms, Anna was already waiting by the entrance to the building. She looked a little exhausted but still put together in a clean black shirt and khaki shorts, her hair wet from a shower.

"Ugh," she said, as Nick climbed the steps toward her, a heavy diaper bag slung over his shoulder. "You couldn't have come earlier? I could get the cops on you, you know?" Her tone was acidic, cutting through the mood like a hot knife through butter. Nick felt himself start to boil. He focused on Emma, using her as an anchor. He couldn't fight back, even though what she had said was the truth. With their custody agreement, Nick was technically breaking the law by keeping Emma for longer than he was supposed to.

"What happened to you?" Nick was reluctant in handing Emma over to her mother. He felt like he was tearing off a limb, passing it on to a hungry scavenger. "What were you taking?" Nick was still giving Anna the benefit of the doubt, but that wasn't going to last for much longer if he didn't get any answers.

"It's ok, I'm fine now." She grabbed Emma, who was looking at Nick with soft, sad eyes. She cried for a brief moment but Anna quickly adjusted her so that Emma was facing over her shoulder, away from Nick. "Have a good night, Nicholas."

"Anna, I need answers. You're holding my daughter. If you're doing anything that could put her in danger, I'll make sure you never see her again."

Anna narrowed her eyes. This was terrible. Nick hated all of this negative energy surrounding his beautiful baby girl. She should be bathing in positivity, with all the adults around her cooing and awing. "Don't threaten me, Nicholas."

"Then answer me. Why did I see an ash tray inside the apartment? And why wouldn't Chris tell me what medicine you took? I'm a doctor for Christ's sake, I should have been the first person you called."

Anna adjusted her grip on Emma. "I don't need to tell you what I'm sick with. You're a doctor, but you aren't my doctor. You aren't *my* anything."

"I am the father of your child."

"Unfortunately."

The word cut much deeper than Nick would have expected. He felt the burn in his chest. Like a fucking molten-hot cattle brand.

That was when a hand appeared on Anna's shoulder. Rough with blunt fingers. Anna turned and stepped to the side. Chris appeared in the doorway.

"Chris," Nick said.

"I thought Anna could use a little support. Seeing as she's not getting much from you."

Nick flexed his jaw. He couldn't understand why Chris always insisted on getting involved. Since he and Anna started dating, Chris was always in the middle, starting unnecessary fights and then stepping back to watch the chaos unfold. It was like he got off on creating drama and, for some reason, Anna let it happen. The only time he wasn't concerned with Anna's relationship seemed to be when he was in church.

"You know, I've been telling Anna, she's being way too lenient with her hours. You broke up with my sister and then left her to have a baby by herself. To top it all of, I told her to never sign that prenup, but she did."

"Your sister cheated on me, which was really only the cherry on top. So yes, I divorced her, but I sure as hell am not letting her raise Emma by herself." Nick could see what Chris was trying to do, and he could see Anna start thinking about it, the cogs in her malleable brain already moving along to Chris's fucked-up beat. He wanted Anna to revoke all parental rights. He wanted it so that Nick never saw Emma again. He never liked Ethan, from the beginning, and this was only another way for Chris to show his contempt. So much for the cross that hung around his neck.

"So now you're calling my sister a liar?" Chris's face twisted with venom.

"Jesus, nothing is going to get through to you." Nick was at a loss. Emma started to whimper in Anna's arms. She turned her head and started to reach out toward Nick. It was a gesture that shattered Nick like a hammer smashing through glass. His first instinct was to reach out and grab her, but of course, that wasn't an option. Anna must have sensed it because she held Emma a little tighter and turned so that she couldn't see Nick anymore. Chris stepped forward, taking up more space in the doorway. He was a bulky guy but only because he had a little too many of those pies his church put out every month for fundraising.

"I think we're done here, thank you for taking care of her."

"We're far from done here, Chris." Nick was seeing red.

His shoes were filled with cement. They had to be. That was the only explanation as to why he wasn't just turning and walking away yet. He physically couldn't move his legs.

But he had to. And he had to keep fighting for his daughter.

He couldn't even say goodbye. He managed to move his cement-filled shoes and started his way down the hall, toward the row of elevators, every painful step taking him farther and farther from Emma.

13 SHEPARD KENSWORTH

ONE WEEK LATER

Shepard's phone had gone off at least three times while he was with a patient, the vibrations kicking off so loudly that they never failed to startle everyone in the exam room. Shepard was sufficiently embarrassed by the second time he had to quickly shove his hand in his scrubs pocket and silence the vibration. By the third, he excused himself, starting to wonder if there had been an emergency. His immediate thoughts went to his brother, who had dealt with a stalker situation that had come to a scary conclusion. Did something else happen? He stood outside the exam room and checked his phone, seeing a surprising name on his "missed calls" list.

Rick Valdez.

Shepard rolled his eyes. He couldn't help it, they practically moved on their own. What the hell was he calling for? And why so many times?

I don't have time for this.

Shepard turned his phone off.

I also don't care either.

He went back into the exam room, apologizing again

and standing aside while Terrence, another resident, went on with his questions. Shepard was good at putting aside everything he was dealing with in his personal life so that he could hone in on the patient. That exam room door was like a huge eraser, wiping away all of Shepard's baggage. He was in there for and because of whoever needed his help.

Unless he already knew what was going on. Then his mind tended to drift, out of simple human nature. In this case, the patient was presenting with classic flu symptoms and Shepard already had his plan of action in place. He knew Terrence was asking extra questions out of an over-abundance of caution. And so... his mind drifted. Rick may have started the engines, but his thoughts were driving straight toward Nicholas White. The man who proved to be incredibly elusive and extremely attractive all in one white-coated package. Shepard couldn't explain why he seemed to have lost his mind every time he was alone with the doctor, but he also couldn't deny that it happened. He never failed to transform into a horny teen, wanting to throw himself all over the man and never let go. It even went past hormones. There was something about Nick that had Shepard sprung, on all sorts of levels.

Of course, there was always one bothersome little fact: Nick clearly didn't feel the same way Shepard did. It *royally* sucked. It had Shepard confused and frustrated and sad. He didn't understand.

That all changed the day he met Emma, and then the threads of Nick's life started to tie together. Not only was Emma one of the cutest babies Shepard had ever seen, she was also Nick's entire life. And from the sounds of it, she was the only thing *in* Nick's life. Shepard hadn't gotten the full rundown but he had heard enough to know that he and his ex-wife were nowhere near speaking terms. Those factors could very well explain some of Nick's behavior. Shepard could understand why he had pushed him away that night. It was a complicated situation but it wasn't unsolvable. There had to be an answer.

I could be his answer.

...Their answer.

"Alright, Tricia," Terrence said as he glanced over his notes, "Looks like we're done with our interview."

Tricia, a woman in her midtwenties with jet black hair, managed a smile past her runny nose. "Did I get the job?"

"At Influenza Corp? You certainly did," Shepard jumped in. "Sorry, I sometimes enjoy corny jokes a little too much."

Tricia started laughing, the first time they'd seen her happy since they walked into the room. "Are you kidding me? That joke was..." Tricia paused for a moment. "*Sick.*"

This had all three of them laughing. When they all quieted down, Terrence excused them from the room. Outside, Shepard and Terrence compared their notes and agreed on one single treatment plan. They both concluded it was the flu, and so there wasn't all that much they could do besides making sure she got fluids and a dose of Tamiflu. Since it wasn't an intense case, Dr. Clark, their attending, had let them handle it while he caught up with some other things.

With the orders in the system, Terrence had looked up at the clock on the wall and pointed out that Tricia was their last patient of the day. Shepard hadn't even realized how fast the time had gone by. He took mental stock of all the patients he had seen that day, making sure that none of them had required his attention before he left for the day. He double-checked his mental notes with the physical ones on his iPad as he walked. He went through the list, happy that everyone he saw that day went home with an answer to their questions. Not all days were like that, especially when Shepard was working on the emergency floor. Those days were filled with unending questions and tragic heartbreaks from patients they couldn't save, no matter how hard they tried. It was a stark difference to the more laidback atmosphere on the family medicine floor. It gave Shepard some much needed perspective on which specialty he wanted to go into in the future. His time to make an official decision was coming soon, and then he would need to apply for a fellowship in his chosen specialty. Some doctors passed on the fellowship and started practicing as general practitioners, but Shepard knew he wanted to specialize. It meant more years of schooling, but it would be worth it. This was his career for the rest of his life, he needed to be sure he was happy doing it. Being a general practitioner wasn't his calling, and neither was being an emergency doctor. He enjoyed internal medicine but it was maybe a little *too* slow for his liking. There were still a couple of months separating him from his decision, so he pushed the thought away, already feeling his stress levels climb.

Not exactly what I need.

He had already felt himself getting overly stressed about his personal life, he didn't need his professional life contributing. Shepard had considered signing up for a yoga class, just to get his life back in balance again. Maybe it would help him control his thoughts better. He could empty out his head and stop focusing on the man who pushed him away.

Ever since he had almost kissed Nick, he couldn't stop thinking about him or about what Betty said, telling him to give it a better chance.

Well, going in for a kiss is giving it a pretty damn good chance.

Shepard only just now thought of the comeback. He shook his head, feeling like he just needed to let it go. Maybe he could dust off the ol' *Grindr* and try to find a random lay that could take his mind of Nick. He wasn't the type to have random one-night stands through an app, but desperate times called for some millennial measures. He couldn't keep thinking about a man who was clearly so unavailable.

He walked down the hall, his navy blue stethoscope bouncing against his neck, over the light blue scrubs. He pulled out his phone and went to the folder he had inconspicuously dubbed "dumb apps" thinking if anyone ever grabbed his phone, they would stray away from that folder. He popped it open and scrolled past actual dumb apps before he found the orange and black square practically smiling up at him, glowing like a tantalizing piece of lost treasure asking to be raided, and Shepard was doing the raiding. He opened the app and was immediately blasted with old messages that had been waiting to be read since the last time he used the app. He checked the timestamp on the most recent one. It was a week after he and Rick had broken up, and Shepard had actually found someone who gave him a few good nights, but nothing more.

That's all I need. A good night...

Even though Nick could give me a great one.

Shepard scrolled down the front page. There were plenty of headless torsos but there were also quite a few cuties too, smiling back at Shepard, promising the good time he thought he needed. His own profile was one of the dreaded headless-torso variety, but Shepard had a face pic at the ready if he was digging the conversation.

He realized he was walking down the halls with his head buried in his phone. He stuck close to the wall as he walked so he would bump into anyone. As he scrolled, there was one particular face that jumped out at him. Handsome guy with light eyes and dark hair, a nice smile and his first photo was of him with his golden retriever, so clearly he knew how to play the game.

Shepard clicked the profile. Ryan was only a couple of miles away and was looking for something casual, according to his byline. He also liked "Netflix and chill" and was apparently allergic to coming up with original lines.

Shepard opened up the message section and started typing something out before second-guessing himself and deleting it. His fingers went back to typing, but he didn't like his second message either so he deleted that one, too. He took a breath and decided to stop overthinking things.

"Hey, what's up?"

Ok, so Shepard wasn't exactly being very original either, but he was tired from a long day at the hospital and was not used to flirting over an app.

His phone immediately buzzed alive with another message: "Hi, hottie! Mind if I see your face?"

"Sure," Shepard replied. He sent the most flattering selfie he could find in his photo album. It took only seconds to get another reply: "Wow, you're really hot."

"Thanks, you're not so bad looking yourself," Shepard typed back. *Jesus I sound like I'm eighty-five.*

His phone buzzed with a message: "I really want you to fuck me until I can't feel my asshole. Choke me until I can't breathe and then use me as your cum dump for the week."

The message almost had Shepard's eyes pop out of his skull. He was *not* expecting things to go from Sunday

communion to Sunday sex party in a matter of seconds. He
was taken a little aback.

What the hell am I doing? I don't want this.

Shepard went back to his phone. He drafted up at least
fourteen different responses before he finally sent one that
read: "Actually, I think I'll have to rain check. Thanks,
though". He pressed send and shook his head. He didn't
even wait for a reply before he went into his phone and
deleted the app for good. He wasn't going to get what he
was looking for through a random hookup. Only one man
had the antidote to what ailed Shepard.

And he's emotionally shut down. Great.

He was reaching the elevator bay. One of the elevators
dinged open just then, letting out a stream of people.
Shepard looked at his watch and realized the final episode
of *Big Brother* was set to air in twenty minutes. If he made it
to his car in time, he could catch it live and avoid getting
spoiled by some dumb Facebook post. He hurried toward
the open elevator door, slipping his phone back in his
pocket, the door shutting as he got closer to it.

The elevator door was closing quick. Almost shut. Only
a sliver left. *Damn it.* Shepard kicked a foot between the
crack of the shutting door as if he were auditioning to be a
cancan dancer. His impromptu routine managed to trigger
the sensors. The elevator door reversed its course and
opened for Shepard. With a relieved exhale, he stepped
inside and went to press the button for the garage. He
looked up and saw Nick, his eyes pinned to the screen on
the wall displaying an ad for a nearby hotel. Shepard knew
he must have seen him come into the elevator. Why hadn't
he held the door open? Was Nick really going to try that
hard to avoid him?

"How's it going?" Shepard asked, cutting through the

tension. He was getting frustrated now. Maybe Betty and Crow were wrong this time. Maybe this wasn't meant to be.

Then, as if Shepard's question was a key that unlocked the dam, Nick turned to Shepard and looked straight into his eyes.

"Shepard, I'm sorry."

Oh.

Nick continued, the corners of his brown eyes growing wet. "I was a dick. I shouldn't have pushed you away like I did." Nick wasn't looking at Shepard anymore. No. He was looking *through* Shepard.

What the...

Shepard felt exposed. He knew he was fully clothed, but he felt like everything was suddenly out in the open, all hanging out for Nick to see. Those golden brown eyes were reflecting everything back at Shepard, sending a connection that bound the both of them together in the large elevator. The space between them felt nonexistent even though they were on opposite sides of the elevator.

"I fucked up. I've been fucking up." He took a breath, collecting his thoughts. "You scare me, Shepard. I've been married, I've been through it. And yet, I've never experienced such a powerful connection before. I look at you and I feel like coming undone. I can't stop thinking about you."

The elevator was dinging downward. They were on the twenty-third floor and no one else had called the elevator, giving them a little privacy.

"Wow," Shepard said. Then, as though his word had somehow triggered a worst-case scenario, the elevator gave a violent jerk and threw both men to the wall. Shepard gave a loud grunt as he hit the side of the elevator, the handrail jamming into his ribs. The lights flickered for a moment before staying on, but the elevator was no longer moving.

"What the fuck..." Shepard said. "Are you ok?" He looked at Nick, who was pulling himself up. He looked unharmed.

"Yeah, and you?" he asked, his eyes raking over Shepard for any sign of injury. Shepard nodded and looked around, planting his gaze on Nick. That's when he started laughing.

"I can't believe this," Shepard said, between chuckles. "Sorry, I'm a nervous laugher. But, seriously? Stuck in an elevator with you? I mean, come on."

Nick tilted his head. "Am I that bad?"

Shepard immediately realized how rude he had sounded. "Oh no, I don't mean that as a negative. I'd probably be freaking out if it were just me in here, or me and someone else I didn't know." Shepard took a breath, his laughs subsiding. "This is just very Grey's, that's all."

"Which one of us is McSteamy?"

"I'll take McDreamy," Shepard said. His heart was racing but his smile was wide. For all intents and purposes, he should have been jammed in a corner, freaking out about the situation. Shepard was never a big fan of enclosed spaces, and the elevator had suddenly become a locked steel box around them. The thought would have unraveled Shepard, but Nick was there, and Shepard felt invincible with him around. It was an odd feeling, and one he hadn't thought would be so powerful, strong enough to override one of Shepard's most basic and primal fears.

"Fine," Nick said, smiling. Thankfully, the lights hadn't gone out, so Shepard could focus on Nick's handsome face. That was when Nick went to the panel on the wall and pressed the emergency button. It connected them with the fire department, who assured them that everything would be ok and that there was already a team on the way.

"You're shaking," Nick pointed out, his eyes looking

down at Shepard's hands, which did, to Shepard's surprise, have a slight tremble.

"Oh, heh, look at that." Shepard's breathing started picking up in pace. Nick must have noticed. He moved next to Shepard and put an arm across his shoulder, his hand massaging Shepard's tense neck.

"We're ok, Shep, nothing to worry about."

"*Pfft*, I'm not worried. Just upset I'll miss Big Brother, that's all." Shepard started to sound worried. He could hear it in his own voice. The tiny tremble in his throat that was difficult to conceal. The fear was beginning to claw past Nick's assuring presence. He wanted to put on a strong front, especially since he didn't want to break down in front of Nick, but Shepard was feeling the silver walls get tighter and tighter.

"Here, sit down with me, that helps." Nick grabbed Shepard's hand and pulled him down to the floor, where they both sat, Nick's hand still encasing Shepard's. It was so natural; a perfect fit. Nick's thumb slowly traced circles, the touch pushing away the anxiety. Shepard was feeling more grounded. Not completely comfortable, but better. Sitting definitely helped, but Nick holding his hand was what really did it.

"Don't worry, I'm sure we'll be out of here in five minutes tops," Nick said and Shepard believed him.

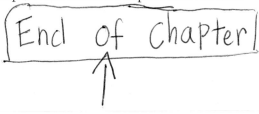

14 NICHOLAS WHITE

(Done)

Twenty minutes had passed since the elevator jerked them to a stop. Twenty minutes of Nicholas trying to avoid looking into Shepard's eyes for longer than necessary. Twenty minutes of Nicholas trying not to think about how good the man smelled. Like pine, and sex, and coffee. Twenty minutes of Nicholas fighting a deep and powerful urge to spin Shepard around and pin him against the elevator wall, where he could devour him with his mouth, encasing him in his arms. He had already gotten the apology off his chest, which made him feel better but still not great. He held onto the regret of pushing Shepard away that night, and that was something Nick hated. He tried his damndest to avoid living with the spiny specter of regret hovering over him. He even managed to move past the initial regret he felt over allowing himself to settle into a toxic relationship with Anna. He saw now that it was necessary to move him to a better point in his life. It also gave him one of the greatest gifts of his life: his baby girl, Emma.

Rejecting Shepard was different. That didn't feel like a move that was supposed to enhance Nick's life. There were no blessings or gifts coming from that. He couldn't see any logical reason he could have had to push him off that night, except for the fear that had stolen the wheel driving his actions. A kiss wasn't a binding contract. He wouldn't have been forced to automatically tie Shepard to his and Emma's lives, and yet there he had been, open to the potential but too scared to take the chance.

Thankfully, the twenty minutes were passing by with some good conversation. Shepard's nerves seemed to have completely subsided, especially after they had a chance to speak to the fire department and moved down to sit on the floor. Nick didn't even think about it before his hand had moved to hold onto Shepard's. He wanted to make sure Shepard was comfortable, and sure enough, he seemed to have been very comforted by Nick's presence. That was something Nick couldn't ignore. He felt the same way, using Shepard as an anchor. He was definitely scared, but he was better able to keep his anxiety at bay. He knew that Shepard needed a solid support. If they both started freaking out, then things would have been exponentially worse. Instead, they were sitting on the floor, cross-legged, their backs against the wall behind them, Nick's knee gently touching Shepard's. They were in a deep discussion about the drawbacks of putting pineapple on a pizza. Thankfully, they were both in agreement about it being a *huge* no-no.

"Seriously," Shepard said, "I'll inhale a can of cold, sliced pineapples, but don't put those things on my cheesy, meat-covered dream of a pizza. The sweetness and the texture." Shepard shook his shoulders. "Ugh, the worst."

"How about mushrooms?"

"Meh, I can handle a few. But I'll pick them off most of the time."

Shepard kicked his legs out, his scrubs drawing up so

that more of his legs showed. "I gotta stretch." He pushed up from the floor and started stretching his arms, twisting his body, rolling his neck, pushing his shoulders back. Nick thought he should do the same. He got up and dropped his head, letting his body bend inward, down toward the floor, getting the blood flowing again. The fire department had already arrived and were busy trying to get the elevator to work through mechanical means before they moved on to their plan B. Since the elevator had stopped between floors, they couldn't just pry the doors open and have them walk out, so things got a little more complicated. Both of their phones didn't have any signal so they used the emergency phone to communicate with the fire department.

For now, though, it was just the two of them in a tin can suspended above fourteen floors.

"Do you ever think about what happened between us? Back in the on-call room?" Nick wasn't sure where the question came from, but all he knew was that he had to ask it.

Shepard took a moment to answer, sucking in his bottom lip as he thought. "Every day," he said, honesty clear in his voice. "You left your mark on me, Nick. Since before we even did anything. You had me feeling all kinds of things. I thought I'd get over it by dating someone else, by forgetting about us altogether." Shepard chuckled sadly. "But that's something I just can't forget."

"Neither can I," Nick said, feeling himself opening up like a flower toward the sun. "You weren't the only one walking away with a mark that day." Nick moved closer to Shepard. "And then when you met Emma, suddenly that mark you gave me turned into a crater-sized impression. You seemed so natural holding her. And she seemed so happy, too."

"I was nervous. I thought things weren't going to go as well as they did. And I know how important she is to you."

"I never saw that meeting going any other way." Nick took a few steps forward. Shepard licked his lips. "Although it really did put me on a different level, seeing you holding her. It was definitely one of the sweetest things I've ever seen." Nick's face broke into a grin. "You also looked pretty hot holding a baby."

"Oh, I did?" Shepard teased. It was his turn to take a few steps forward. There wasn't much space between them anymore. Nick could practically feel the heat coming off through Shepard's thin scrubs. His dick shifted in his scrubs, reminding him just how badly he wanted this. The fire spread through him at a furious pace. "I guess dad is a good look on me. Although you've got that look down to a science."

"All it requires is a decent five o'clock shadow and a body that balances the tight rope between doughy and muscular like a drunken Cirque Du Soleil performer."

Shepard cracked up at that line. Nick joined in. Then, from one moment to the next, Shepard was in Nick's arms. It was as natural as breathing. And it happened that smoothly as well. Nick almost hadn't realized what was happening until his lips were inches from Shepard's. This time, there was no pushing away. Nick wanted it all, and he was the one initiating it. For a second, he was nervous Shepard would push him off, a bitter sliver of the karmic pie, but that immediately subsided the moment Shepard lifted his hands and encased Nick's head as their kiss deepened.

It went on for a few more minutes. Nick stumbled backward until he felt his back hit the cool steel wall, the elevator slightly shaking with the impact.

Both of their bodies were pressed together now, and the scrubs they had on might as well have been see-through. The fabric was so thin, Nick could feel everything and it was fucking magical. He could feel Shepard's muscular body against him. And that wasn't all he could feel that was hard. Unless Shepard carried an extra stethoscope in his pocket, he was pretty sure that Shepard was rock hard and, *damn*, was he packing. It felt like a third leg pressing against Nick, which only made him start kissing Shepard even harder. Their tongues lashed together, probing one another, hands gliding over each other, squeezing and kneading and tugging. This was the accumulation of a year's worth of fantasizing. It was boiling over, the passion so intense, Nick was already feeling his balls tighten with a need to release. He was close to coming and he hadn't even taken his clothes off yet.

This guy is something else.

Shepard pulled back for a breath. He glanced down with a sexy grin. Nick was hard, that part was obvious from the thick outline against his dark blue scrub pants. The thin fabric looked like it was close to tearing. He licked his lips and came in for another kiss, pushing Nick back onto the elevator wall, rubbing his body against Nick's. Both of their hard cocks pressed together through their scrubs, the heat and friction between them threatening to start a fucking bonfire.

"You feel so good against me," Nick groaned, low and deep, his hands roaming over and under Shepard's scrubs, feeling his smooth, warm skin. He ran his hands up over Shepard's strong chest, feeling a slight covering of fur around his pebbled nipples. Shepard gave off a delicious moan the moment Nick started to play with his nipples, teasing them between his fingers, tugging at them while his tongue went back to probing Shepard's mouth, swallowing the moans. Nick's hips pushed forward, pressing his cock harder against Shepard's, relishing in the sensation he felt knowing that Shepard was just as hard as he was. He glanced down and almost came undone right then and there. Shepard's cock had been aimed up so that the head was pressed against his light blue scrubs, which were darkened from the precome spilling out of Shepard's dick.

"Fuck," Nick growled. He wasn't sure what had come over him, but he knew he needed to have a taste. Maybe it was his way of making up for being such a dick over the past months, maybe he just needed to suck Shepard's dick and it would cancel everything else.

Shepard's eyes widened in surprise as Nick made quick work of untying the knot that held Shepard's scrubs around his waist. He looked up, a sultry grin on his face as he kissed at Shepard's bulge through his already wet briefs. Nick mouthed it, going up and down, rubbing it with his hand while making sure his gaze stayed locked with Shepard. He was looking down, a trance falling over him as his eyes glazed and his fingers knotted in Nick's hair. That had the effect of driving Nick crazy. He loved having his head played with, his hair tugged. He felt his cock give a pulse against his briefs, aching to break free, an urgent need to release coming over him.

He ignored it all. Nick put all his focus on Shepard and his pleasure. He wanted to give the man an orgasm that would rock him to the core. He wanted to do it by worshipping every single fucking centimeter of Shepard's body, starting with his rock-hard dick. Nick smiled up at Shepard as he pulled the scrubs down, tugging them down over Shepard's massive bulge. His black Calvins were easier to pull down, which was good because Nick was ready to tear the briefs apart if it took another second longer.

He was rewarded by the sight of a fucking magnificent cock bouncing out into freedom. Perfect. Nick didn't realize dicks could look so damn good. He'd really only seen his own in real life, in a sexual setting and not in the exam room, and the last and only time he and Shepard hooked up, it was in a dimly lit room and went by in a flash because of how much passion had been pent up between them. This time, though, the elevator was *very* well lit and Nick was down on his knees, at eye level with the magnificent specimen of a dick. He had the best seats in the damn house.

"*Fucckk,*" Nick hissed, grabbing the base with one hand, which didn't even cover the whole thing. He grabbed the rest with the other hand, feeling the velvety warmth that radiated across his palms. He fucking loved it. He could feel Shepard pulsing in his grip, his fingers tightening in his hair, pulling him closer. Nick was in heaven. He opened his mouth and took the head in, immediately tasting the salty sweetness of Shepard's excitement. He couldn't help but compare it to the times he'd go down on Anna, and already, he knew which one he preferred. His tongue swirled around the crown. The taste was intoxicating. Nick loved it. He moved a hand down from the base to play with Shepard's tight balls. He enjoyed the weight of them in his hand as he gently applied pressure, all while his lips moved further down Shepard's dick. It was definitely a mouthful, and one Nick was going to need to practice at swallowing.

I'm always up for a challenge.

Nick managed to fit more of Shepard down his throat than he was expecting, the moans coming from Shepard only encouraging him to go even farther. He was about halfway before he had to come back up for air. He used his hand to stroke up and down the wet length, rubbing his thumb over the tip and causing Shepard's knees to shake. "Oh, fuck," he said from above, his voice taking on a tone Nick had only heard from him once before. "I'm so close already."

This drove Nick wild. He wanted to make Shepard blow, and he wanted to take it all. He went back to working Shepard's stiff cock with his mouth, licking up and down the sides before popping the head back in between his lips, sucking and slurping and slipping a hand down, past his balls, pressing on the sensitive stretch of skin between his cock and his ass. This had Shepard shaking. His fingers twined tighter in Nick's hair. His moans grew to grunts. Hips started to thrust. Nick took as much of Shepard's cock as he could, opening his mouth wide and readying himself for Shepard's release. He could feel Shepard tensing, his thrusts becoming erratic. His grunts turned to words that became tangled on his tongue. "*Fuuck*, coming," Shepard managed to moan out. He moved to pull his cock out but Nick grabbed onto his thighs and held him in place, looking up as Shepard blew his load down Nick's throat. He swallowed every last drop, honestly, a little surprised at how much he liked it. He licked Shepard's twitching cock and got back up on his feet, his lips shiny and plump. Shepard looked spent but also like he had just won the fucking lottery. He had a goofy grin on his face that quickly warmed up back to smoldering-hot levels as he reached down and started grabbing Nick's hard cock. They came in for a kiss, their tongues swirling, Shepard surely tasting himself on Nick. The thought almost made Nick come right then and there, with Shepard palming his hard-on over his scrubs.

Then, as if someone was waiting for a cue, the elevator suddenly jerked downward as the motor started up again.

This had both of them scrambling to look presentable and hide the fact that they had just raised the temperature in the elevator by at least a hundred degrees. Nick was beginning to think that a cloud of steam would float out as the elevator doors dinged open again.

"Guess they fixed the technical issue," Nick said, breathless as he ran a hand through his hair, hoping to make it look less like sex-hair and more like mess-hair. Shepard let out a laugh as he tied a knot on the front of his scrubs. He was flushed and still had that "cloud-nine" quality to him. The kind of look someone got just after they had their world rocked by an orgasm.

"I'm upset I didn't get to return the favor," Shepard said, smiling.

"So am I," Nick toyed. He had tucked his boner into the waistband of his scrubs so that he wasn't pitching a visible tent for whenever those elevator doors opened, but he was definitely still rock hard. "I've got Emma for the next couple of days. Let's meet up on Friday. We can spend the day at Griffith Park and see where the night takes us." It was still a few days away, and the wait was going to be brutal, but Nick knew it would be so damn worth it.

"That sounds absolutely perfect."

The elevator stopped on the ground floor, the doors sliding open to a crowd of people clapping and cheering. Nurses, other doctors, patients, residents, even a couple of firefighters.

If I knew I'd get this reception every time I swallowed, I would have started sucking dick much sooner.

End of chapter

(15) SHEPARD KENSWORTH

The doorbell rang through Shepard's apartment. He lived in a newly constructed building on the top floor, with some really nice views of the Hollywood Hills that surrounded him. It wasn't big in space, but it was definitely big in character. He had a little bit of an eclectic taste when it came to furnishings, using old but well-kept hand-me-downs alongside brand new and much more modern pieces. Like the classic leather couch his parents had given him next to a Ferrari red side table that was held up by a small white marble column. The photos he had hung were all taken by himself, and may not have exactly been National Geographic cover worthy, but definitely went with the flow of the apartment. He had a huge black and white shot of the canals in Venice Beach hanging above the couch, adding some depth to the living room without using the typical Ikea-bought cityscape shots. He always thought that if medical school hadn't worked out, he would have really enjoyed life as a photographer. He liked learning about cameras and different photographic techniques in his spare time, and he always loved a good golden hour; when the light was perfect and the photos were guaranteed to come out as showstoppers.

Shepard walked toward the door, pushing his sneakers to the side. Another knock. "I'm coming, I'm coming." He unlocked the door and opened, revealing a smiling Betty holding two pints of ice cream and a bottle of wine.

"Hurry, I think the goods are melting."

"Come on in," Shepard said, grabbing the bottle of wine so that Betty could free up a hand. She kicked off her sandals and hurried to the kitchen, where she popped the pints into the refrigerator. She turned around, smiling, still wearing her scrubs, her curly hair drawn up into a ponytail. "Tell me everything."

Shepard laughed, not even sure where to start the story.

"I CAN'T BELIEVE you were locked inside of an elevator," Betty said, digging her spoon into the confetti-covered ice cream. They had decided to crack them open while the ice cream was still soft, moving to the living room where they sat on the couch. "With the doctor of your dreams," Betty continued, a smirk playing on her face, "Did he ask you to bend over and cough?"

"Yes," Shepard deadpanned. "I had him perform an entire physical in there, actually."

"Well," Betty said, waving her spoon in the air, "at least no one can ever accuse you two of being inefficient. Might as well get checked while you've got nothing else to do."

"Priorities."

"Exactly."

Shepard laughed before digging into his own pint of ice cream. Instead of birthday cake, he went for the mint pistachio flavor. He loved how it tasted like those little chocolates hotels sometimes leave on the pillow. The ones in the green wrappers that were way more addicting than they had any right to be.

"You know I found his Instagram account, right?" Betty was waving her phone in the air, biting her lip mischievously.

"You did? How?"

"I've got my ways." Betty shrugged. "I know how to hack into the mainframe and pull up the entire NSA directory."

"Yeah, ok, and I know how to conjure up a patronus."

Betty laughed at that. "He showed up on my 'recommended friends' list or whatever the hell they call that. We probably have a few mutual friends, I'm sure the nurses all follow him. His page is the definition of a *thirst trap*."

"What's on it?" Shepard quickly put his hands up. "Not that I'm all that interested in it."

"Mhmm," Betty said, smiling as she tossed her phone across the couch, Shepard catching it midair. Nick's page was already open, and wow, was Betty right. Nick wasn't only good at saving lives. The man was *great* at taking photos. They were all effortlessly sexy, too. Like the one of him and his daughter, playing together on the floor, his face wearing a huge smile, his butt looking very nice with him laying on the floor the way he was. And then another photo of him coming out of a pool, dripping wet and smirking like he was told he was auditioning for a Bond movie.

"Don't get any drool on my phone. I know it's water-proof now, but still, that's gross."

Shepard stuck his tongue out and motioned that he was going to lick the screen. Betty snatched her phone back, smiling as she closed Nick's page. Shepard had memorized the username for... well, for research purposes obviously.

"Seriously, though," Betty said. "What happened in the elevator?"

Shepard already felt himself going pink in the cheeks. Betty wasn't one to let the details slip her by. Her eyebrows shot up, her quick mind already putting two and two together. "You hooked up with him." She said it like she had uncovered the answer to one of those popular true crime documentaries.

Shepard couldn't deny it. *Physically*, he just couldn't do anything about it. He was a terrible liar. Even if he wanted to hide it, he would have given it away through one of his many tells, all of which Betty already knew by heart. So, he just spilled it: "Yeah, things got hot in there."

"Get it!" Betty almost dropped her pint of ice cream. "Oh, shoot," she said, managing to catch it before it landed on her lap. They were sitting in Shepard's living room, on his parents' old leather couch. Even if it had fallen, leather and hardwood floors would have made cleaning up ice cream a breeze.

"I didn't announce a pregnancy, calm down."

Betty cracked up at that. "I feel like you just did, though. I've been waiting on the edge of my seat for weeks now, wanting this to happen. It's like you just walked out of the bathroom with a smiley face on your pee-stick!"

"Pee-stick, huh? Is that the terminology you use with patients?"

"Obviously," Betty said, digging her spoon into the ice cream. "I say, 'mam, can you please go to the wee-wee room and do number one on this pee-pee stick, pweaty pwease?'"

Now it was Shepard's turn to crack up. He was glad Betty had come over because if she hadn't, he knew he would have stayed up all night obsessing over what had happened in the elevator and what it meant. They still hadn't talked about anything serious, but Shepard wasn't going to deny that what happened in the elevator wasn't just a random hookup. It felt like more than that. Something that definitely needed to be continued, but also something that was cementing them together. The way Nick looked into his eyes, there was something there. Something powerful. It felt meant to be. Shepard wasn't exactly the type to believe in "meant to be", but he just couldn't deny it. He had never felt it, either. Not with Rick, not with the few random hookups he'd had, not with *anyone*.

"Ok, so back to your elevator rendezvous. Did you guy's touch pee-pees?" Betty could barely keep a straight face by the time she finished her question.

"Please stop," Shepard said, practically choking on a laugh. "No. Dicks did not touch."

"Whoa, that word sounds so aggressive now."

"Ok, fine. No '*cocks*' touched. Better?" Shepard was smiling as he took another bite of his mint pistachio ice cream.

"Yes, much," Betty said, smiling, sarcasm coloring her tone. "So no cocks touched, then. What did you do in there? Play Monopoly?"

Shepard laughed, dropping his head as he felt a blush coming on. "Let's just say Nick would definitely pass an oral exam."

Betty nodded her head, eyebrow arched. "You dirty, dirty dog." She playfully punched Shepard's shoulder. "I'm so proud of you. Did he bring up that time you called him 'really hot' in the hospital halls?"

Shepard snorted at that. "No. What a mess. Of course I'd say it right as he's walking out of the break room."

"I may or may not have heard him coming from behind the door."

"So you knew he was about to walk out?"

"It was either him or Ralph from Radiology, and I was *really* hoping it wasn't Ralph."

"You're ridiculous," Shepard said, laughing along with his friend. He was once again glad he had her around to distract him from replaying his elevator rendezvous over and over again. He would have spent the night playing with his dick, and with the way Nick had him, he was a little scared he'd get one of those "it's been four hours you should probably see someone about this" kind of boner. "I'm glad it wasn't Radiology Ralph either." Shepard shook his shoulders. "He always does that weird breathing thing whenever he's talking to me. Like he's trying really hard to smell me without being obvious about it. Except... it's definitely obvious."

"Yeah, and he doesn't do that with me, so it's clearly not an obstructed airway issue."

Shepard chuckled, leaning back into the couch. "I can't believe how crazy this has all been. And I haven't even told you the best part yet."

"You mean there's something better than getting oral from the man of your dreams?!" Betty sounded genuinely shocked.

"Yes. The possibility of it happening again."

"You're seeing him again?" Betty's eyes were wide. "Please tell me you're both taking the stairs wherever you go."

"Yeah, we have a date. He asked me right when we got out of the elevator."

"Holy shit, way to bury the lead!" Betty was all smiles. She knew how badly Shepard wanted to connect with someone. A blow job was all well and good, but now there was the potential for so much more.

The doorbell rang just then. Shepard lived in a one-bedroom apartment and wasn't really used to random visitors, especially not at eight-thirty at night. Maybe if he had roommates, he would have figured it was for one of them, but the doorbell ringing that late at his place felt weird. He looked at Betty, who didn't seem to be as jumpy. "Expecting anyone?" she asked, not looking away from the television.

"Nope," Shepard said, playing it cool. He didn't want to freak Betty out for no reason. Maybe it was just one of his neighbors. He lived next to a friendly gay couple that always liked to point out how "they didn't own their husky, their husky owned them". On his other side was another couple who looked like they were fresh out of college and were always reminded the husky owners that they were allergic to all animals.

More knocks. Harder now. Shepard stepped to the door, holding his phone in his hand, ready to call the cops. A face peered back at him through the peephole. One he instantly recognized.

Oh, shit.

"It's Rick," he said in a hushed voice. Betty immediately sat up on the couch, setting aside her ice cream on the coffee table.

"Now? Here? What does he want?"

"I don't know," Shepard said, shaking his head. "Do I open?"

Sharp knocks punctuated his question.

"Uhmm," Betty was scratching her head. Neither of them knew what to do and Rick was only knocking harder and harder.

Shit.

(End of Chapter —Turn Page)

16 NICHOLAS WHITE

(Done)

The crying pierced through his dream like a dart flying through a balloon. Images of a naked Shepard were blown to dust as he woke up. The alarm clock on the night stand glowed a soft blue, telling him it was four-thirty in the morning. Instinctively, he grabbed his phone and rolled out of bed on auto-pilot mode, pulling on his loose gray shorts and walking over to Emma's room, rubbing his chest as he walked, yawning half the way. He already felt pretty programed to waking up for Emma's cries, but he was also still human and exhaustion wasn't anyone's friend.

Her room was right next to Nick's. It used to be his home office, but he had emptied it a few months before Emma came around and completely converted it into a little girl's paradise. The walls were a calming pale yellow, with a few inspirational quotes scrawled in a smooth white script across the walls. There was a nook that had a window facing the backyard which Nick had turned into a little mini-castle, which Emma was too young to appreciate but was bound to like once her imagination kicked in. There were shelves holding a variety of different toys and dolls, from a collectible Wonder Woman figurine one of Nick's patient's had gifted him to an old black and pink Furby Nick had found in the closet. Admittedly, the Furby was a little aged. Thankfully, the batteries had died long ago and there were no more random calls for food or whatever else that thing needed. Possibly the souls of little children. Nick just thought it was kind of cool and a bit of an antique. There was also a tall, beautiful white bookshelf already holding a ton of children's books, their colorful spines coming together to create a vibrant collage.

Emma's room was dark when Nick stepped in. There was some moonlight coming in through the window, enough for him to make his way to the crib. The nightlight shaped like fairy wings helped as well, casting a soft orange glow on the scene. "Hey, baby," Nick said softly, cooing as he got closer. Emma immediately fell silent when she realized her dad was in the room. She started to gurgle, the cries already forgotten. No matter how tired Nick had been, her little noises would always put a smile on his face. He looked over the crib, seeing her looking up, her bright eyes catching the moonlight. They had a slight blue hue to them, most likely set to turn into the same light brown her dad had. She already had a beautiful head of brown hair, straight and soft and perfect to kiss. She was perfect in everyway. Nick's pride and joy. The absolute best thing he had ever done in the world.

She started to cry again. Not as loud as she had been, but it was climbing in intensity. Nick knew she was hungry and his presence could only go so far in that department. He gently picked her up and held her to his chest, gently bouncing her as he walked, cooing into the air, talking gibberish to her but making sure that she heard his voice, that she felt the vibrations in his chest as he spoke, that she smelled his scent and knew who her dad was. It meant all the more since Nick knew he wasn't always at the liberty to pick her up and walk around with her. His days were counted, and that hurt him to no end.

But for now, he was going to pretend like nothing else was going on in his life. He held Emma tight and carried her out of the bedroom, her cries getting a little more insistent. She was definitely going to be someone who knew what she wanted and how to get it. Nick couldn't help but smile, even with the cries ringing in his ears. He grabbed some premade formula and waited for it to get warm. While he waited, he pulled a chair out from his dining room table and sat down. He bounced Emma on his thighs, her cries morphing into giggles. It was only a momentary distraction, though. She was sharp. She realized what Nick was trying to do and stopped her giggles, her smile flipping upside down, her forehead wrinkles scrunching together and her cheeks drawing up. She let out another wail. Louder this time. Nick relented and got up, testing the temperature with a drop of the formula on his wrist before deciding if it was ok, although he had a feeling Emma would have downed anything at that point, whether it was ice cold or not. Her eyes took on a whole new level of brightness when she saw the bottle.

"Wow, if only you looked at your dad like that," Nick said, chuckling as he went back into her room with the bottle in one hand and a hungry Emma cradled in his other arm. He went to the rocking chair and got set up so he could feed her without losing feeling in his arms. She looked like the happiest little bundle of cheeks on earth the second her gums clamped around the rubber nipple. Nick looked down at her, love clear on his face. It was still dim in the room, but he could make out each one of her features like there was a spotlight on them. She definitely had his nose. And his eyes. And his lips.

"You're beautiful, Emma," he whispered into the night, leaning down and kissing her soft head of hair, taking in her sweet scent. It struck him then, a stab of emotion that brought uncontrolled tears to his eyes. He was hit with a dose of reality. Anna could still be trying to block all custody rights from Nick and he wouldn't have known until it was too late. He had hope that the court system wasn't as fucked up as some of the stories he had heard. He knew that the decision ultimately came down to a judge who didn't know him or Emma and wasn't personally involved in the situation. His only hope was to find something on Anna that would prove she was the unstable one. He wished he had documented the couple of times she had lost complete control in his house, but he had no way of proving anything.

"I'm fighting so hard for you, Emma." He was still whispering. He started rocking back and forth as Emma drank her fill. Time passed as the bottle emptied, the rocking motion putting both of them in a calm state. Nick's mind started to wander in the direction of Shepard Kensworth, the man who had captured his complete and total attention. His thoughts went back to their elevator ride earlier in the day. He knew that getting stuck in that elevator was an extremely happy coincidence. At first he was worried he would be stuck in an awkward situation with no way out, but of course, things were never awkward with Shepard. He definitely wasn't expecting to drop to his knees while they were stuck in a floating steel room, but he also *definitely* didn't regret doing it. In fact, he couldn't wait until he could do it again. He was hung up on the guy and everything about him. He could feel himself finally admitting it. All it took was getting stuck in an elevator and saying an impulsive and heartfelt apology for Nick to realize that something could actually work between them. Shepard was not only a looker, but he was also incredibly smart and had a *hugggee...* heart (where did you think that was going? Get your mind out of the gutter).

He also had a big dick, which was great, too.

Everything about him was perfect. Nick had been scared for no solid reason, and he realized that. There was nothing Shepard did that had ever thrown up a red flag. It was the complete opposite. Nick saw Shepard at work, saving patients' lives on a daily basis, having a positive impact on countless number of people. Of course he would trust Shepard with Emma. And from their first meeting, it seemed like Emma had already staked her claim on Shepard. He knew he was a great role model and Shepard clearly loved his daughter, everything about it was right.

Nick was smiling. He felt like things were all lining up the way they should be. Emma was finishing up the bottle, her eyelids already gaining some weight as they dragged down. He held her a little tighter, absolutely loving the warmth that was coming off of her tiny body. She was an angel in his hands. Nick got up and rested her against his shoulder, where he could pat out whatever burps she was brewing before putting her back to bed. He slowly paced around the room, hoping that his life stayed on this upward trajectory. All he needed next was for the court to settle his custody rights and give him a full fifty-fifty split. Then he could feel much more at ease.

Emma rocked the side of his head with two powerful burps. "Nice ones," he complimented her before going back to the rocking chair. He didn't want to put her down in the crib just yet. He wanted to keep her in his arms for as long as he could. He sat down and started rocking, singing

"Twinkle Twinkle Little Star" to her. He definitely didn't have a singing voice to write home about, but he could hold a note in a karaoke bar pretty well. Emma didn't seem to be complaining. She was looking up at her dad with tired but hypnotized eyes.

Nick was rocking slowly back and forth on the rocking chair, the gentle sound of the wood creaking filled Emma's room. A sliver of moonlight was cutting in through an opening in the curtains, but Emma didn't seem to mind and Nick found it comforting. That was when another source of light lit up the room. It was his phone, vibrating slightly against the top of the sturdy white dresser next to them. It was a notification letting him know that someone liked one of his Instagram photos. Nick looked a little closer and saw it was Shepard's username on the screen.

Maybe he was in too relaxed of a state. Maybe that was what had him opening up his private messages on Instagram and searching for Shepard's username. Maybe it was because he was sleep-deprived, maybe that's why he was typing away with one hand, sending a message to Shepard that read: "What are you doing up so late, Shep?". Emma was already nodding off against his chest, the sudden vibration and light not bothering her. He could feel the beginnings of a drool puddle forming.

He wasn't really expecting an answer. It could have been a glitch in the notifications. Shepard probably liked the post earlier in the day and it was just showing up now.

Oh, shit. This sounds like a booty call, especially at this time. He might think I'm looking for a quick late-night hookup.

Nick entered into a mini-panic mode. He would have hated to give off the wrong impression, especially seeing how he already had to apologize once about being a complete dick toward Shepard. He didn't want Shepard to think he was in it just for the sex and nothing else. He pulled up his messages again and typed up another one: "Not that this is a booty call or anything. Emma woke me up. Putting her back to bed now."

His head fell back on the soft cushioned back of the rocking chair, his neck cracking in the process. "Your daddy's a buffoon," Nick whispered into the night, wondering how dumb he was going to feel in the morning, when there would still be no response and he would have to see Shepard in the halls of Sierra View.

Fuck it. I'll just forget this ever happened. Won't even bring it u—

His phone buzzed in his hand. He looked at it, squinting in the darkness, the brightness set on the lowest setting so that Emma wouldn't get bothered. It was a reply.

"Having some trouble sleeping. Bit of drama earlier. And lol, I didn't think it was a booty call."

His phone buzzed again.

"Although, I mean, if it were... ;)"

Another buzz.

"Lol jk." And then a gif of Buffy the Vampire Slayer jumping backwards into the night.

It cracked Nick up. He had to keep his laughter contained, though. Emma wasn't completely asleep yet. Once she was knocked out, he could be as loud as he wanted and she would have most likely slept through it all.

"Everything ok?" Nick managed to type out. He was able to maneuver himself so he could use two hands without bothering Emma.

Shepard responded almost instantly. "Eh, it's too long to type out over text."

Nick chewed at his lip. He considered a few different

options in terms of replying. He initially wanted to use that as an invitation for Shepard to call him, because hearing his voice was always a treat. But he wasn't sure if that was too old-timey for him. Shepard was a good amount of years younger than Nick was, who at thirty-two was a little more comfortable using the phone as a communication device and nothing else. Now, things were a little different. Calls were only made when you had a problem with your internet provider, everything else was done through texts.

Maybe I can just reply with a gif. A funny one.

Wait, no that could be insensitive.

But, maybe not. Maybe he'll find it funny. Relatable.

Jesus, when did this get so difficult?

Nick was overthinking it. He could feel himself turning over every single pebble in his brain. Looking for a right answer even though nothing was clearly labeled. He put the phone down and got up from the rocking chair, holding Emma tight and making sure she didn't feel any of the movement. He slowly walked with her to her crib, where he gently placed her down under the plush light blue blanket. She looked like a bite-sized snack in her cotton-candy pink onesie.

"Night, baby girl."

He left the room, leaving the door cracked open again. He decided to stop overthinking things. He opened his phone and typed up a message, hitting send before he could second-guess himself.

Well, there it is. I asked him to call me. Ball's in his court.

A few moments later his phone was ringing.

"Hello?"

"Hey, Nick, it's Shepard." His voice was just as smooth as it sounded in person. Even with the exhaustion that comes with being up at four in the morning, Shepard sounded like he was ready to headline a concert. "Sorry, I really shouldn't be calling you at this time. This was dumb. Thanks for asking me to call you—"

"What's going on?" Nick asked, cutting Shepard off. He didn't want him to hang up. He wanted Shepard to know that he wasn't bothered in the slightest by the call. In fact, it was the total opposite, Nick wanted this. He wanted to be there for Shepard when he needed someone to talk to. "What has you up this late?"

Shepard stayed silent for a bit. Nick could hear the rustling of bed sheets in the background. He suddenly pictured himself between those bed sheets, legs tangled with Shepard's. "My ex," Shepard started. It sounded like he had gotten up out of bed. "He showed up today. Completely by surprise. Started knocking like crazy, then he must have heard me because he started saying that he knew I was inside and that all he wanted to do was talk. He wanted to apologize and he said he wanted to make things right. That was when I told him to leave or that I'd have to call the cops. I never opened the door, just yelled from behind it. He still didn't leave, even with me threatening to call the police. He kept banging on the door, saying that I was making a mistake."

"Shit," Nick said during a brief pause in Shepard's story.

"Yeah, it was getting scary. He kept saying I wouldn't call the cops on him. He was almost trying to guilt trip me at one point. The knockings got louder and I could hear a neighbor come out to complain. That was when I knew I had to do something. I went through with my threat and called the police. He must have seen the cop lights from a hallway window because he gave one last kick against the door and ran off before the officers showed up."

"Were the cops able to do anything?"

"I filed a restraining order, and I really don't think he's a guy who fucks with the law, so I'm thinking it'll be enough to keep him off my doorstep in the future."

Nick was in his bedroom, standing by a window that looked out onto his backyard, which was being bathed in white star light. He was one of the lucky ones who had some extra space in the crammed city. It was a good-sized yard, too, with a concrete porch big enough to hold a table and seating for five along with a quality barbeque. Then there was the grass portion, that stretched further out, leading to a perfectly maintained desert garden that lined the wooden fence. It was a river of white and beige rocks with bright green cacti and succulents sprouting up from them. There was a hammock held between two tall palm trees growing at the far side of his yard. He wished he could bring Shepard over. That way he could hold him, make him feel safe. He could lie with him in the hammock and watch the sunrise, seeing as that was happening in a couple of hours anyway.

"He wasn't himself, either, at least it wasn't the Rick I remember dating." Shepard continued, sounding shaken. "I looked through the peephole and he looked strung out on something. I've never seen him like that. His eyes were bloodshot and his pupils blown. He was fidgeting. Something was up."

"Well, you did the right thing. Sounds like someone you don't need in your life anymore."

"Not at all." Shepard gave a deep sigh. "What a terrible way to end the night, huh?"

"Tell me a story, then. One with a happy ending." Nick

was smiling. There was a slight moment of silence. He knew he caught Shepard off guard on the other end of the line.

"I, uh, I don't know. A story?" Shepard asked. "Like... read you a fairy tale?"

"No," Nick said, unable to hold back a laugh.

"Oh, good." Shepard sounded quite relieved. "I was worried you were into some *weird shit*. Not that I judge or anything... but, fairy tales. Man, that would have been a hard one to get over."

Nick couldn't stop laughing. "I'm sure that's a real kink," he managed to say when he caught his breath.

"Oh, for sure," Shepard agreed. "And I'm sure they have a fondness for Pinocchio's story."

Nick's stomach hurt from laughing, which he was trying to suppress as much he could. "What I meant was: tell me one of *your* stories."

AN HOUR later and Nick was wide awake and totally wrapped up in his conversation with Shepard. Time had completely flown by. One second, Nick was dragging himself out of bed, and the next he was sitting on the edge of it, an uncontrollable smile on his face as Shepard recounted the time he swam with manatees and was hit in the face by a big floating "poo ball". Literally, just a big ball of manatee poop floating through the water.

Nick felt bad laughing, but he just couldn't stop when Shepard was recounting the story. Nick hadn't laughed that much in a long time, and it felt *really* damn good. "That has to mean you got good luck," Nick said.

"I did win twenty dollars off a scratcher two days later... *hmm*, maybe you're onto something."

Nick chuckled. He got up off the bed and started walking around his bedroom. "Let's open up an online shop where we sell manatee poo lucky charms?"

"Honestly... I totally think that would sell like hotcakes. Like hot poo cakes."

"You're something else."

"I'm just saying," Shepard was laughing, too, "I think we've got a billion-dollar idea here. It's going to be the next big thing. Move over rabbit feet, you've hogged the lucky charm spotlight for *far* too long."

A few more minutes of this and both of them seemed to crash simultaneously, both men giving off equally impressive yawns, both at the same time.

"Did you just yawn at the same time as me? Did we transmit yawns without even seeing each other?"

"I think we did," Nick said, smiling at Shepard's playful enthusiasm.

"Interesting... very interesting."

"Why?"

"No reason, just that I think it means we're meant for each other. But yeah, no big deal."

"Not a big deal at all," Nick said. He could tell Shepard was joking, but wasn't there always supposed to be some kernel of truth inside every joke?

"Alright, I'll let you get some rest. You don't work today, do you?"

"No, I'm off." Nick didn't want this to end, but he logically knew they both needed at least a couple of hours of sleep. It was going to be hard shutting off when he was already so wired up from talking with Shepard. That's when

Nick got an idea. He may not have been able to extend their phone conversation, but he could set something up for a few hours from now. "I'm taking Emma to the park for a stroll tomorrow. Or, well, I guess it's in a few hours now." Nick was pacing a circle into his soft beige carpet, the light color turning a darker shade around the path he had been taking. "Want to meet us? Thinking of going to Griffith Park."

There was barely a second of silence. No hesitation. Shepard immediately answered with a "that sounds great". It was genuine excitement and it was infectious. It pushed away the nerves Nick had been feeling.

"Ok, great," Nick said, sounding a little more relieved than he had intended. He caught his reflection in the mirror he had propped against the wall. He was smiling.

"Cool."

It was that time at the end of every phone call you made to your high school crush. The dreaded "hang up" moment. Who would be the first to do it? Both at the same time? Maybe don't even hang up at all? Falling asleep with the phone next to you isn't so bad, kind of like those meditative ocean soundtracks, instead of the waves crashing on shore, you get the gentle breathing of you —

"Talk soon," Shepard said and hung up.

Or, maybe one of you is mature enough to take the lead and hang up the damn phone.

"Well, there's that," Nick said. He laughed, his stomach still hurting. He closed his bedroom door and went to his bed, throwing the soft gray blanket to the side, pulling his shorts off and climbing in, grabbing the blanket and tugging it over him.

He started wondering how it would feel if Shepard were lying next to him, sleeping under the same blanket.

I think it'd feel pretty damn great.

T he day couldn't have been better for a stroll around the park. Shepard had been nervous it would be too hot for them to walk around, especially with the changing weather that had brought more and more wild fires to the surrounding areas. Thankfully, though, the heat wasn't record-breaking. No eggs were being fried on the pavement and no one was seemingly melting down into the ground. The complete opposite, actually. There was a gentle breeze that kept the intense heat at bay. Shepard was wearing a thin green workout shirt and black shorts that ended above his knees, the perfect outfit to spend time outside in. Plus, he didn't mind showing off a little bit of leg. He knew Nick was so used to seeing him covered up in scrubs, he figured Nick would appreciate some skin. Especially since Shepard *never* skipped leg day.

Griffith Park was massive. It was filled with a ton of hiking trails: some that led up to the iconic Hollywood Sign, others that led into more forested areas, and a few regular parks scattered around with swings and seesaws and monkey bars. There was the Griffith Observatory, which boasted some of the best views of Los Angeles, from the coast to the hills and everything in between. It was especially impressive when the morning smog cleared and the sun was shining down on a cloudless city of angels. Shepard considered making that their meeting spot, but parking was a mess and it wasn't exactly an hours-long activity, and Shepard wanted to make sure that he spent as much time with Nick and his daughter as possible. Plus, he knew Emma wasn't really old enough to appreciate the stunning views. So instead, they had decided to meet at a popular café near one of the entrances to Griffith. It wasn't uncommon to spot a celebrity or two having their morning breakfast on the quaint wooden patio before taking off up one of the hiking trails, phones at the ready to Instagram their hike at a moment's notice. Because, if a celebrity hikes and doesn't take a selfie, did they even hike at all?

"Shepard, hey."

The voice came from behind him. Shepard felt himself lighting up before he even turned around, his face already breaking into a smile. He turned and, sure enough, it was Nick, pushing a big stroller with a black hood drawn over the top, protecting a bubbly little bundle of smiles from the sun. Shepard smiled at Nick, who was looking like an absolute *snack* in his black Nike shorts and white T-shirt, the collar of the shirt dipping low enough to reveal the glint of a rose gold necklace underneath.

"I was scared you'd sleep all day," Shepard said.

"You kidding me? She wouldn't allow that," Nick said. He opened his arms and took Shepard in for one of the best hugs of his entire damn life. And sure, that may have been hard to really measure, but damn it, Shepard felt it. He let go and looked down at Emma, who was so cute in a blue polka-dotted shirt and tiny khaki shorts, all while rocking a white bonnet that had Shepard involuntarily saying "*awwww*," for far longer than he should have.

"She's so precious," Shepard said, reaching his hand out so Emma could grab at his fingers. She was giving a big gummy smile and a few random gurgles that told Shepard he was more than welcome to come hike with them.

"She woke up two hours after we hung up," Nick said. Shepard looked up, his forehead wrinkling as he gave an apologetic look. "Oh, no, it's fine," Nick said, waving a hand, "I can run well on two hours. After a few days I need a good nap, though."

"I feel like medical school trained me to work on barely any sleep, too. I used to get *soo* cranky when I missed even an hour out of seven. But after my first month in med school, things changed *real quick*." Shepard spoke up to Nick while his finger was being held onto by Emma.

"It's a good trait to have as a dad, too."

"I bet." Shepard had to look away from Nick and back down at Emma. He was finding that looking up at Nick was doing things to his body he couldn't control.

"Do you want anything from the café? I'm thinking of getting some iced coffee."

"I'll take one, too. Vanilla latte if they have."

"Nice choice, although I'm more of a mocha man myself." Nick was beaming down at them. "I'll leave Emma here with you." He walked around them and up the wooden steps that led to the café. It was a cute little spot with a painted white wooden fence surrounding the path that led up to the entrance. The name was hand painted on a slab of wood and hung over the door.

"You're such a cutie and you know it," Shepard said to Emma, who was looking at his finger like it was an alien puzzle she was destined to solve. She had a strong grip, too. Shepard was impressed. She was either going to be a future president or a world-renown arm wrestler.

Potentially both.

Nick came back with their coffee a few minutes later. He playfully tapped the cold drink against the back of Shepard's neck. Shepard flinched forward and looked up, smiling at Nick as he handed him the coffee. He got up off his knees and reached for his phone. "How much was it? I can send you the money."

"Don't worry about it."

"You sure?"

"I mean, we'll have to get by on eating old hot pockets for a few days, but I think we'll be ok."

Shepard gave a sarcastic smirk as they started their hike, iced coffees in hand, Emma getting pushed in her mobile throne by a very sexy Nick. Shepard had underestimated how good fatherhood looked on the man.

About half an hour later they were already reaching the peak of the hike. The trail wasn't meant to lead them all the way up to the Hollywood Sign. This one instead ending at a beautiful outcropping of rock playfully named Lover's Lookout. It boasted a stunning view of the surrounding hills and looked down on a small lake that frequently attracted families of deer and goats and some-times coyotes. It was also a shorter hike and wasn't as steep, so pushing Emma in her stroller wasn't a Herculean feat after a while.

"So you'd prefer going to a play than a movie?" Shepard asked, taking the last sip of his coffee, sucking up through the straw.

"Yeah, there's just something about live theatre. When it goes right, it goes *right*. Obviously, not all of them are great, but you could say the same about films. There's been plenty of movies that I've wanted to walk out of."

"I guess I haven't been to many good shows, then." Shepard was hoping Nick would take the bait and invite him to a show, but it seemed to have floated right over his head.

"I've been to a few crappy ones, but I'll never forget the great ones."

They turned a corner. Shepard didn't notice the woman at first, but she was hard to miss as she got closer. Running down the path was Lisa Flynn, a resident in his same year with a big golden mane that reflected the sun. Her face was a cherry pink with sweat dotting her forehead. That was when Shepard became hyperaware of Nick walking by his side, pushing his daughter along with them. Shepard immediately felt self-conscious, almost uncomfortable. There were no legal ramifications for a resident dating an attending, but it wasn't exactly a common thing either. Shepard was lucky in that Nick already handed in the evaluation every attending needed to give whenever the residents moved on to another floor. Shepard's evaluation was turned in a couple of weeks ago. But still, people talked and shit spread. The last thing Shepard wanted was for Nick to get into any hot water if other residents even sniffed out something that felt unfair. To add to Shepard's stress, he and Lisa have never exactly been friends. They got along well enough, but Lisa was extremely high-strung and had problems with Betty from the start. He considered himself extremely loyal and he certainly wasn't going to get close to anyone that had an issue with his best friend.

So Lisa was maybe one of the last residents Shepard would have hoped to randomly see out on a hike.

He glanced down at his watch, hoping that would

obscure his face and stop Lisa from recognizing him. Nick was at his side, talking about his love for *Wicked*, completely oblivious to the familiar face getting closer to them. It didn't help that the path was getting narrower, forcing them on an even tighter trajectory.

"I love pretty much any Broadway show. I don't think I've ever been disappointed. *Book of Mormon*, that one has to be one of my favor—"

"Dr. White!" The voice was loud and excited and a little out of breath. This was a *code red*, worst-case scenario for Shepard. He would have been fine if she simply recognized them and kept on with her jog. Then he could go on with his life, and hope Lisa would do the same, maybe second-guessing herself by the end of her jog and deciding it wasn't even them in the first place.

"Lisa! Hey, how are you?" Nick sounded happy. *Too* happy, but then again Shepard was already a little on edge, maybe he was just being overly sensitive. That's when he remembered Betty mentioning something about Lisa already talking about him and Nick being together. Shepard wasn't entirely sure why it bothered him so much. He wished he had more of a "fuck it" attitude but in reality Shepard cared way too much about what other people were thinking and saying. He knew he had to get over it, but it was just going to take some more time.

They moved to the side so that other joggers had a clear path. The view where they stood was already beautiful and they hadn't even reached the top yet. The side of the hill was clear of trees and looked out to even higher hills, the sides rocky and brown, dotted with green from the trees that survived the desert-like conditions. The city seemed like such a distant thing, even though they would be able to see it when they followed the bend in the path.

"I'm great, just getting some opioid peptides pumping before heading into Sierra View." That was when Shepard noticed Lisa's gaze was practically devouring Nick. She barely even acknowledged Shepard, who managed to say hi even past his dry mouth.

Opioid peptides? Did she really just use the chemical family instead of just saying endorphins like a normal person?

Shepard felt like giving an audible "*pfft*". He sucked air and ice water through his straw instead.

"Looks like someone's been focusing their study time on the nervous system," Nick halfheartedly joked. He didn't seem that impressed either.

"Oh, I've got all the systems down." She wiped her forehead with a pink towel she had wrapped around her wrist. "And who's this?" Lisa said, turning her attention down toward Emma.

"My little girl, Emma." Nick puffed his chest out a little bit. Shepard wondered if Nick realized just how proud he was of his daughter.

"What a cutie!" Lisa bent down to say hello. Shepard couldn't see Emma since the stroller's hood was covering her, but he could hear her and she didn't sound very happy. Her gurgles were much different compared to the ones she gave Shepard earlier. These sounded angry. "Oh, she must be tired," Lisa said.

I know I am.

I'm tired of you.

Shepard was feeling salty. He suddenly transformed into an insecure housewife bumping into their sexy nanny out in public. It was probably the lack of sleep. Had to be. He knew it was irrational, but he couldn't help it. The way Lisa was bending over to see Emma was doing everything to highlight her boobs that threatened to burst out of her neon pink sports bra. And she was clearly focused in on the doctor and wanted nothing to do with Shepard. That part was clear as she stood back up, keeping her eyes pinned on Nick's lips.

(End of chapter)

(finished)

Nick could feel Lisa's eyes peeling back the layers of his clothes as he stood on the hiking trail. He threw a glance toward Shepard, who was standing to the side and keeping pretty quiet for someone who just bumped into their classmate. That's when he realized Shepard must have been internally freaking out. Even though Lisa seemed to be oblivious to the fact that Nick was there on a date with Shepard, she still could put two and two together and then spread the word around to the other residents. She could have also been playing dumb and have known exactly what was going on between Nick and Shepard. He remembered what it was like when he was going through his residency, and it was definitely no walk in the park. He also remembered how other residents in his class loved to talk, turning the hospital into a mini soap opera where the season never seemed to end. Thankfully, Nick stopped caring about what others thought pretty quickly. He didn't think Shepard had that same ability, yet. Being able to give no fucks was basically a superpower and Shepard was just starting on his origin story.

"Alright, well, it was great seeing you, Lisa," Nick said, wanting to end things so that Shepard wouldn't feel uncomfortable any longer.

A wave of disappointment flashed across Lisa's flushed face. Her eyes bounced from Nick to Shepard. He could practically see the wheels start turning underneath that bright blonde crown of hair. "Oh, right, got it," Lisa said, smiling at them both. She suddenly seemed to be paying way more attention to Shepard now. "Ok, well, see you both at work."

"See yah," Shepard said. Before leaving, Lisa crouched down and said goodbye to Emma, who sounded a little less cranky but still not as bubbly as when Shepard popped up in front of her. Nick knew that his daughter wasn't the be-all and end-all of moral tests, but he did like how she seemed to have really clicked with Shepard from the second she saw him.

Lisa left with another wave. She took off running, leaving Nick and Shepard standing in silence. Nick looked to Shepard, eyebrows raised. "That was kind of weird. I've barely ever talked to her before and today she seemed so interested in me."

"You weren't her attending?"

"No, she was with Dr. Torrez."

"Hmm," Shepard said, glancing down at Nick's legs. "Must have been the shorts, then."

"My shorts?!" Nick looked down at himself. "What's wrong with them?"

"Absolutely nothing," Shepard said, smiling as he started walking. "Come on, let's get to the lookout spot."

"Are they too short?" Nick asked, pushing the stroller and following Shepard. "I bought them thinking they might be a little sho—"

Wait, I'm supposed to not give a fuck.

Shepard had Nick all kinds of messed up.

"The shorts are the perfect length," Shepard said, slowing his pace so that he was next to Nick again. Nick looked down again. They were definitely on the shorter side, ending midway down his thigh, but he didn't mind the skin, and Shepard clearly didn't either.

"Perfect length, huh?"

"Ok, now you're just fishing for compliments."

"How about my butt? I don't think it looks good in these." Nick gave a playful bump of his hip against Shepard and stopped so he could lean on one leg and prop his butt out. "Right? I'm just not feeling it," Nick said, smiling, looking down at his butt (which actually looked pretty fucking great, if he did say so himself). Shepard was smiling, too, catching onto the game, his eyes darting back and forth, doing that thing where he tried not to stare at Nick's butt yet couldn't help himself.

"Nope, doesn't look good at all," Shepard said, giving it a slap, the sting surprising Nick. Another thing that surprised Nick? How good he felt around Shepard. How comfortable he felt just walking with him through the Hollywood Hills. This was technically their first date, and Nick had expected a much more awkward encounter. He wasn't sure why, but he just felt like it was what was supposed to happen. He didn't expect to gel with Shepard so well that he would be letting him slap his ass in the middle of a public hiking trail. Clearly it was all fun and games, but still, Nick was feeling very relaxed around Shepard and that meant something.

They continued on the path, Nick pushing the stroller ahead of him. They kept talking the entire way, about whatever struck them. The conversation was easy and the company was exceptional. Nick had become a little winded the past few times he went with Emma on a hike (pushing a stroller could be a workout even when there wasn't an incline involved), but this time around, Nick didn't even think about feeling tired. Even with his two hours of sleep, Nick had never felt more alive. He was pushing his baby up the Hollywood Hills, beautiful views around every corner, with a beautiful man at his side. What else could he ask for?

It didn't take them much longer to reach the spot they both wanted to see: Lover's Lookout. If Nick were with anyone else, he might have cringed at the potential level of corniness involved with the location's name. But with Shepard, nothing else could have suited the spot better. It really was a stunning spot that held a special charm to it. It marked the end of the trail, where the gravel and rocks and dirty turned into a well-taken care of stone path. The big, smooth, multicolored rocks led the way toward a large, rustic-feeling gazebo, its light gray paint chipping off at the sides, a trail of dark green moss growing up one of the columns. A bench sat in the center of the gazebo, painted white and looking straight out over the breathtaking valley. The recent rains had allowed most of the flowers to bloom, making the place look like an explosion of color. It was a rare sight in Los Angeles, where the dry climate usually had all the plants withered down to brown husks.

"Wow," Nick said as they walked toward the bench, the view of the valley below them becoming clearer. Thankfully, no one else had been struck with the idea of stopping at Lover's Lookout. The spot wasn't in any of the big tourist websites and the trail was popular with runners but mostly left alone by everyone else. They had the place all to themselves. Shepard walked close to the edge of the cliff but didn't step too close. Nick hung further back with Emma, admiring not only the view of the valley but also Shepard's back side. Even his damn back was sexy. He could almost make out the powerful muscles moving underneath Shepard's shirt whenever he moved.

"Beautiful," Shepard said, almost to himself. He turned around and walked to the bench, where Nick was parking the stroller next to. He unbuckled Emma from her stroller. She always got antsy whenever the stroller stopped moving. Her eyes were wide as she was taking in everything around them. Nick couldn't control the smile that crept on his face from just looking down at his daughter, her soft brown hair getting lifted by the gentle breeze. She looked away from a nearby tree and up at Nick and broke out into giggles.

"What's going on over here?" Shepard asked playfully as he joined Nick next to the stroller. Emma looked toward Shepard and kept her giggles going. She was so happy, and that made Nick even happier. He pulled her out of her seat and cradled her in his arms so that she could look up at Nick and Shepard, both craning their heads down at her and making kissy-faces. This went on for a few more minutes, both men completely entranced by the baby who was staking a claim on both their hearts.

"Come on," Nick said between goo-goo ga-ga's, "let's sit down."

They moved to the bench, sitting down without any space between them. The wood creaked as they sat, the sound mixing with the rustling of leaves and the chirping of a nearby robin. They both stayed quiet for a little bit, taking in the moment. Even Emma was looking out at the view as if she were pondering all her big life choices. Nick looked down at her, feeling an immense explosion of love rock him to the core. It was one of those moments where everything clicks and you're reminded of exactly just how lucky you are. The gratitude and love that comes flooding in after that realization could almost be overwhelming. Nick felt moisture prick at the corners of his eyes. He wished he could do this whenever he wanted. He wished he could grab Shepard's hand and walk out of the house with him, Emma in the stroller, and they could do whatever they wanted, whenever they wanted. But that wasn't the case. Nick had Emma on counted time, and Shepard wasn't even anything official to Nick. He was letting himself get carried away. He had to pull it back. He couldn't let emotions control him, not when the stakes were so high. He had to have a clear head.

Nick looked to Shepard, their eyes locking, and any chance of having a clear head was gone.

"You're so handsome," Nick said, a twinge of disbelief in his tone. "How are you so good looking?"

"Stop," Shepard said, a slight blush creeping onto his cheeks. "But also keep going."

They laughed at that. Even Emma joined in, giggling as she bounced on Nick's chest with his laughs. "You're something else," Nick said.

Shepard simply smiled. It was enough to unravel all of Nick's tensions. He couldn't help himself. He leaned sideways and planted his lips on Shepard's. It was short but, *damn*, was it passionate. Everything that was boiling up beneath them came shooting up to the surface in just seconds worth of kissing. Nick leaned back on the seat, his eyes glazed over with a starry quality to them. Shepard looked equally affected. He was still smiling, just wider now. Nick was, too. Emma was still giggling, oblivious to the powerful connection that was solidifying between the two men. Nick didn't even care that they were out in public. All the residents could have been standing around them in a circle and he *still* would have gone in for that kiss.

They went back to enjoying the moment, neither of them saying much. It was special.

Emma broke the silence with a loud gurgle. She gave a little bit of a whine, which told Nick that she was getting hungry. He checked his watch and, sure enough, it was time for her bottle. He reached to the side and grabbed the diaper bag from underneath her stroller. "Can you grab the bottle of milk from in here?" Nick asked Shepard, handing him the heavy green bag. Shepard unzipped it and dug inside, finding the bottle and taking the cover off the nipple. Emma lit up the second she saw the bottle.

"She's knows what she wants and how to get it," Nick said. He held the bottle up for her as she went to town, sucking down the milk like it was the last water bottle in the desert.

"Just like her dad," Shepard said playfully. "How's her mom?" he asked, almost nonchalantly. He had no idea how badly that relationship was fractured. "Her name's Anna, right?"

"Yep, Anna," Nick said. The next thing that came out of his mouth was meant as a joke but definitely carried a hint of truth; "Also known as the Antichrist."

Shepard huffed a laugh. "That bad, huh?"

"Pretty bad."

"What happened? If you don't mind telling me."

"Not at all." The truth was, Nick would tell Shepard whatever he wanted to know. He felt himself becoming an open book around Shepard. A sense of honesty overcame him, one he had never really felt before. Not that he was a frequent liar or anything, he just wasn't always fond of being open about things. That was one of the main reasons he didn't tell anyone in the hospital about his relationship troubles. He had friends, he just didn't really talk about himself to anyone. Especially not after Anna had wrecked him.

But with Shepard it was different. It was always so different with him. "Her brother called me saying she was sick and had a bad reaction to something so he wanted me to pick Emma up. When I got there, I noticed an ash tray in the background. She wasn't a smoker when we were together, but I definitely don't want anyone smoking around Emma. And then Chris's behavior was weird when I asked him to tell me what was going on. He was never friendly with me, but he was definitely holding something back. I'm just worried something is going on in there. I don't know how to prove anything, though."

"Have you thought of using a private investigator?" Shepard asked.

Nick cocked his head. "Not really, no. I didn't think it would ever get to this point, but maybe that's the route I should go down." Nick shook his head. "I could call the cops, but I don't have any solid proof of anything going on. I don't want to call them and lose credibility when they show up and nothing's happening. Who knows if Anna could even take that to court and have them take all my parental rights away. I wouldn't put it past her to say she was being harassed by me."

"She'd do that?"

"I didn't think she'd ever fuck my best friend and end up having me take a paternity test because Emma could have been his, but people surprise you, I guess."

Shepard's brows rose before he composed him. "Jesus. I'm sorry you had to go through that." Shepard reached over and placed his hand on Nick's shoulder. There was an immediate and welcome soothing affect, like rubbing cool aloe vera gel on a burn. Nick took a breath and looked out from Lover's Lookout, seeing the birds dipping down on a draft of wind out on the horizon. Emma was finishing up her meal. Nick took the bottle back and wiped her mouth with a soft terry cloth.

"I found out the same day we first got together," Nick said, moving so that he could burp Emma. "I found out she was pregnant that same day you and I shared something special. Only thing was, I had no idea if it was mine or my friend's, the man she cheated on me with."

Shepard swallowed hard. "That's why..."

"I shouldn't have pushed you away so hard. I'm always pushing, aren't I?" Nick shook his head, feeling regret spread over him like a poisonous gas. "Hell, you were probably the only one who could have helped me during that time. Instead, I cut myself off and acted like a dick."

"I mean, I can't imagine how big of a hit that was to your trust. Fuck."

"Yup." The wind filled in the silence, whistling softly around them, shaking a few branches nearby. Another advantage to this trail was that it was much less traveled, so they were the only ones standing at the peak. It felt like there was no one else for miles and miles around, even though the city was just around a bend in the trail.

"Well, then I definitely think you should talk to my cousin. He's the owner of Stonewall Investigations. It's a detective agency with a focus toward working with the LGBTQ community. My cousin, Zane, started it because he used to work in law enforcement and saw some of the discrimination going on. Lots of queer people don't even report crimes because they're scared. I think he can help figure out what's going on."

Nick appreciated Shepard trying to help him. "Sounds like he's my best bet. And he sounds like a great guy, too."

"He is," Shepard said. He looked out over the valley that was laid out in front of them like a painting. Emma was dozing off against Nick's chest. "We grew up together. He's like another brother. Poor guy's had a rough road, but he's turned dirt into diamonds. Things that would have crushed me only made him stronger."

"I'll check him out, then," Nick said. "Anyone recommended by you should be golden."

"Only trying to help," Shepard said, a soft smile playing on his face. "I really wish I could do more. I can't imagine the amount of anxiety that comes with all of this. She's so precious, she deserves that perfect life you can give her, twenty-four seven. And you deserve to be able to hold her whenever you want to." Shepard looked away from the pair. His hand came up to his face for a quick moment before falling back down on his lap.

"Let's talk about some lighter stuff," Nick said, feeling bad that he was bringing over a big gray cloud on their date. He would meet with Shepard's cousin and hopefully figure out what was going on with Anna. He hoped that would be enough to prove that she wasn't fit to raise Emma. Nick didn't want to take Emma completely away from Anna, but if she was going to fight tooth and nail to take Emma away from him, then he wasn't going to back down.

"Ok, let's," Shepard said, sitting up a little straighter on the bench.

(End of chapter)

19 SHEPARD KENSWORTH

(finished)

The date couldn't have been going any better. Shepard could have found out he won the damn Powerball and he still wouldn't have felt the peaks he had when everything simply fell into place between him and Nick. It was magic. Everything about the day had a certain glow to it. As if it were all pulled straight from a fairy tale. *Especially* when they got to Lover's Lookout, which was aptly named, Shepard decided. It was totally and effortlessly romantic. It was also empty, so they had it all to themselves. The three of them couldn't have looked more picturesque if they tried to; Shepard and Nick sitting on the bench, smiles on their faces, knees touching, Emma sleeping on Shepard's chest after he had asked Nick if he could hold her. At first, Shepard had been nervous to even speak in case he woke her up, but Nick quickly explained how his daughter could sleep through most anything. Shepard found that to be the truth after he couldn't hold back his laughter when Nick told him the story about the time he ripped his pants while presenting in front of two hundred other medical residents.

"Yeah," Nick said, dropping his head and shaking it, the

smile still obvious in his tone, "Thankfully, I had a sweater with me which I wrapped around my waist faster than I would have done with a life vest on a drowning ship. And I obviously have terrible luck giving presentations."

Shepard laughed some more, this time being able to contain most of the loud laughs. "Please tell me you hadn't decided to go comm—"

"*Yuuup,*" Nick answered before Shepard could even finish. This had Shepard's eyebrows shooting up.

"*Nooo,*" Shepard said, secretly wishing he was sitting front row and center for that presentation. Nick was smiling, a slight pink blush coloring his cheeks underneath his light scruff. "Well, at least you bared it all for that class. I hope you got an A."

"Pfft, A-plus," Nick said. It was his turn to hold in the laughs. He dropped his head back and looked up at the clear crystal blue sky, not a cloud in sight. Shepard glanced toward him, taking in how sexy his neck looked.

Everything about him is sexy. No wonder he got an A-plus.

"What was the presentation on?"

"The uses of CRISPR in cutting and reassembling genes in order to battle genetic conditions."

"Cutting jeans, huh?" Shepard couldn't help it. "That's some serious foreshadowing," he said with a chuckle. Emma squirmed on that one but didn't open her eyes.

"I should have seen it coming," Nick said, smiling a wide grin, pearly white teeth on full display.

"You know what I never saw coming?" Shepard said, "This."

"Honestly, neither did I." Nick was looking at Shepard now. "I mean, I desperately wanted it. I wanted to see you holding my little baby girl, I want to see you falling hard for me, the same way I was doing for you, just from afar." Nick licked his lips. He shook his head. "I wanted it, but I never thought I'd get it. I never saw it coming."

"I was so hung up on you, Nick." Shepard was feeling himself fall into Nick's gaze. It was like chugging down a bottle filled with truth serum. Everything was bubbling up to the surface. Unfiltered and completely raw. "I wanted you. Bad. I saw you in the hospital, and I would have to turn down a different hall because I had trouble looking at you. I'd lose focus and think about you all day. And then, finally, all my dreams came true when we landed in that on-call room. We had talked before then, you were my attending and so I knew you, but I didn't know you how I wanted to. Until the on-call room." Shepard felt his body heat up just thinking about that day. "And then you barely even looked at me after. I see why, because you were clearly going through things. And I get it. And so I had to figure something out. Find someone to get you out of my head. That's when I met Rick. He was great at first, but I kept thinking about you. Like a boomerang. I couldn't stop, my thoughts kept circling back around to your face, your voice, your presence. And it's not until now that I realize how heartbroken I was back then, I was just trying to cover it up with this fake love I found for Rick."

"And I was such an ass to you." Nick's eyes broke their connection, looking down before looking back up at Shepard. His eyes were misty. "I'm sorry. I don't know how many times I can say it, but I'm going to try to hit the limit. I should have opened up to you from the start. I knew that what we shared was something strong, from that day we first connected. It was something I never felt with anyone, ever before. And I was scared of it. Then I was scared of potentially being a father, then I was scared of *actually being* a father. There was a lot of fear in my life. All while I had to keep things solid for my patients. Every time I put on that white coat, I tried to separate all my anxieties and fears from my life and leave them outside the hospital." Nick's eyes looked bright in the sunlight. "The only problem was one of my biggest fears was inside the hospital with me."

"The call's coming from inside the hospital," Shepard chimed in with a small smile. This had Nick chuckling. He reached his hand out and placed it on Shepard's thigh. His hand was big, fingers softly gripping the side of Shepard's thigh, his palm warm on Shepard's skin.

"Especially after what Anna had done to me. You scared me so damn much. Because I already felt so strongly toward you, that only meant you had all the more power to hurt me."

"I just want to state for the record: I'd *never* hurt you."

"And I believe that. A hundred percent."

Shepard matched the growing smile that was on Nick's face. Emma moved slightly against his chest before settling back in. It was a reminder of the small miracle Shepard was holding in his arms. Another reason why he would never be able to hurt Nick. Because that meant he would be hurting Emma as well. That was a hard no, full stop, brakes-screeching kind of thing.

"How have you been dealing with the difference in equipment between Anna and me?" Shepard looked toward Nick, who managed to crack a smile.

"I enjoy driving stick way more than I enjoy fingering the ignition."

Shepard cocked his head. "Odd analogy, but I get it."

They both laughed at that. Nick looked like he was totally relaxed, and that made Shepard feel good. They weren't exactly talking about simple things like the weather and baseball. These were hard-hitting topics that not a lot of people would talk about with someone they weren't comfortable with.

"I've obviously always known I was interested in men, but I grew up wanting to be as damn heteronormative as possible. I felt like I would be a disappointment to my parents and I couldn't live with that. They had talked about my gay uncle and nice words were never said. I knew they wouldn't have had an easy time accepting me, so I told myself I was just confused and that I could be fine with women. Nowadays, I'm much better at saying "fuck it" and just going with things because they feel right for me. I've learned that I can't live my life to other people's expectations or wants. There are bigger things to think about in this world. You're holding one of those things." *And you are one of those things.* "But back then I was even fooling myself. I dated a few girls in high school but never got to any of the bases past first. Then I met Anna and things were easy with her. Not in the romantic way, just easy in the simplest sense of the word. Plus, medical school was going to brutalize me and so easy was good for me back then. I also did start developing feelings for Anna. Strong ones. She was supportive of me in the beginning. I guess she saw me going through medical school and figured I was an investment. I thought I could see the rest of my life with her. I thought that I'd be fine without ever exploring the side of me that held the most truth." Nick shook his head. "Thankfully, I didn't stay the rest of my life with her, because looking back on it now, I could see it was all so empty. I've felt happier here with you over the past few hours than I ever had throughout my entire relationship with Anna." Nick huffed a breath. "How sad is that?"

"It's not sad, especially if you consider that it was all

paving the path for this moment. I don't want to get sappy and cliché, but I really do think that things happen for a reason. If you hadn't settled with Anna, you never would have gotten Emma."

Nick nodded at that, his expression turning lighter, his smile growing larger. "You're right. Who knows, without Anna in my life I could have found someone else, a bad influence. Maybe I wouldn't have even graduated med school. Maybe I would have never met you."

"Exactly," Shepard said. "That's what I mean. You can't look back and think your past is sad. It's beautiful. It's a huge mural with pieces all fitting together to create a breathtaking image. And it just keeps growing larger and larger, pieces being added with every life event. Sure, some of those pieces come from negative experiences, but if you zoom out, you can see that the entire mural still fits together and creates something beautiful."

Nick was looking deep into Shepard's gaze. "You've got a lot of wisdom for not even hitting your thirties yet."

"It could be all the time I spent on *Tumblr* in college," Shepard said, smiling, chuckling. Emma moved against his chest again. This time it felt like she was waking up. Her fingers opened and closed around a bundle of Shepard's shirt, her eyes slowly working themselves open. "Looks like someone is waking up from her nap."

Nick softly brushed a strand of light brown hair away from Emma's face. She rubbed her eyes and looked to her dad and started to gurgle for him. Shepard was glad she wasn't a big crier. He was getting way more comfortable around babies, but he still got nervous when they cried. He handed her back to Nick before she got anymore upset. As soon as she was back in his arms, she settled down.

"What are you doing later today?" Nick asked.

You.

Was what Shepard *wanted* to say, but that would have felt way too forward. "Nothing. Day is pretty open. Got all my studying for the week finished up yesterday and work isn't until tomorrow."

"Spend the day with us," Nick said, almost as if there wasn't an option to say no, which Shepard wasn't going to be saying anyway. "Let's start walking down and we can take this little party to my place. I can cook us lunch and you can watch Emma while I nap." Nick was smirking now.

"I'm not all that sure about the last part," Shepard said with a laugh. He knew Nick was joking, but he also would have been totally cool with actually doing it. He liked helping Nick, in whatever way he could, whether it was through babysitting or lapsitting, Shepard would always be an eager volunteer.

Especially for lapsitting.

End of Chapter

[handwritten annotations: "stopped here:", "Read tonight", "(Done)", "6 or 7pm : DR MOLOD"]

"**A**nd she'll sleep through the night?" Shepard whispered as Nick shut the door to Emma's room.

"She's been close to sleeping the entire night, but not just yet." He checked the baby monitor in his hand, making sure the volume was set on the highest level. "Although after the day we had today, I have a feeling tonight might be the first night she sleeps through." He walked with Shepard down his hallway, back into the living room. The sun had disappeared behind the hills, leaving the recessed lighting above them. Nick had just bought a roll of cinnamon sticks and had placed them in a tall glass vase in the corner of the room, which was enough to fill the room with a pleasant, sweet scent that didn't overwhelm anyone. Especially since it was beginning to transition from summer to fall and Nick really enjoyed celebrating those different changes. He liked buying different flowers for his house whenever the seasons changed, along with different decorations that switched up the color palettes in his home.

"Thanks for this incredible day," Shepard said as he sat down on the couch. Nick walked over to his wet bar. He opened up the wine fridge and grabbed a bottle of pinot noir he had been saving for a special occasion. The label was all black with one single silver leaf emblazoned into the center with a rose gold outline. 'He grabbed the bottle opener and uncorked the wine with a loud pop.

"Are you kidding me? Thank you," Nick said. He grabbed two thin-stemmed wine glasses and started to pour. "I was able to take a thirty-minute nap because of you. That's *huge*. That never happens when Emma's around."

Shepard was grinning. "I'd babysit her all day if you ever needed me to. She's a joy."

Nick walked over with the glasses, both holding generous pours of the red wine inside. He handed one to Shepard and sat down right next to him. He lifted his glass up and locked eyes with Shepard. "To new beginnings."

"To new beginnings."

Their wine glasses clinked. Nick drank, not taking his eyes off Shepard. He looked so damn sexy in the dim light. Nick had turned on a couple of candles, which had orange light dancing off of Shepard's defined cheek bones.

They sat for a while, enjoying the silence between them, enjoying the fruity bitterness of the wine, enjoying each other. Nick couldn't remember a time he ever felt so comfortable sitting in silence next to someone else. Even with Anna, he felt like there always had to be something going on unless they were sleeping. It never felt right to just sit there and relax with her. Shepard was different, though, in every sense of the word.

They drank for a little while longer. At one point, they talked about wanting to go camping sometime in the future. Then their conversation took a random turn into what kind of cartoons they watched as kids. From there, they started talking about what kind of superpowers they would have, and as a twist, they had to choose superpowers that were rejected by everyone else.

"So like..." Nick said, thinking of shitty powers as an example, "I dunno, say you have to choose between growing your body hair super fast or you could turn your feet into Jell-O molds."

Shepard snorted at that. "Well, I guess the body hair. I'd never get cold... wait can I degrow it too? Or do I have to shave it all off?"

"Shave."

"Fine, I'll go with the Jell-O."

"Thought so," Nick said, laughing. "At least you'll be great at parties."

"Perfect," Shepard said. At some point during the night, Nick's arm landed across Shepard's shoulder. He played gently with the side of Shepard's head; rubbing the ridge of his ear, massaging his temple. Shepard leaned into the touch, clearly enjoying it.

When they had finished up their glasses of wine, Nick offered to get up and get some more. He went to his kitchen, the ivory white cabinets had shadows dancing on them from the candle light. He hadn't had a chance to turn the light on. He moved to the switch when he stopped, seeing Shepard walking into the kitchen with a smile on his face. The candle was one of those wick candles, so the sound of crackling wood filled the room, along with the scent of an evergreen forest. Crisp. Warm. In that moment, Nick felt all his walls come tumbling down. All he had to do was look into Shepard's eyes to know that he wanted to be nowhere else, looking at no one else, moving toward no one else. He reached out before he even realized what he was doing, his hands closing around Shepard's hips, drawing him in. *Breathing* him in. His hands gripped a little tighter as their faces hovered inches apart.

"Shep," he said, looking deeply into those calming hazel pools, "I want this. I want you."

Shepard smiled. It was a grin too good to pass up. Nick pushed in for a kiss that turned a hundred degrees hotter in seconds. Their tongues started slow and steady, running over the other, slowly probing deeper, more aggressive, soon their tongues were more desperate, their faces moving, their hips grinding together.

When Shepard broke for breath, his lips wet and plump, he was still smiling. "I want this, too. I want to be here with you. And with Emma. I'd never hurt either of you."

Nick believed it. He felt it, deep down.

He also felt something else deep down. And it was getting harder.

Nick thought this was the perfect time to move things to the bedroom. He grabbed Shepard's hand and walked with him to his room. He shut the door, glancing at the baby monitor before turning his complete attention toward the hunk of a man who was currently running his hands all over Nick's body. His back was getting rubbed while his front was getting squeezed and his tongue was getting tied by a kiss. Nick could barely even realize what was going on before he was standing there completely naked, hard dick jutting out into the air.

"How are you so hot?" Shepard said, smiling as he pushed Nick back onto the bed. He was still completely dressed when he moved to suck on Nick's hard cock.

Nick stopped him. "No, sir." His eyes were lit with a fire that started in his groin. "Strip for me first."

Shepard looked like he was up for the challenge. He

stepped back and smiled as he started to slowly gyrate his hips. They didn't even need music. Shepard could move to the beat of their passion, it was practically thrumming audibly in the air around them.

Nick sat there on the edge of his king-sized bed, his legs wide open, his thick cock hanging between his thighs like a third fucking leg. Shepard eyed him with lust in his gaze, his lips slightly parted. Nick trailed a hand down his own body, slowly, feeling himself as he grabbed his dick, the meaty size barely able to fit in his grasp. He squeezed and tugged and watched as Shepard undressed slowly in front of him. It was tantalizing. A silent picture that had Nick glued to the screen. His cock swelled in his grip, pushing against his hand. He squeezed harder. Shepard was moving his hips now, slowly, working his jeans off, throwing his shirt in the corner. Shepard was already hard, his briefs doing nothing in terms of hiding his impressive bulge. That only made Nick even more turned on. He felt it in his gut. A feeling that spread through him, warming his every muscle. He was entranced by the man in front of him. Completely and totally enraptured. He started stroking himself as Shepard tossed his jeans aside and began palming his own erection over his briefs. Shepard's head dipped back and he let out a groan. Another wave of heat shot through Nick. His cock pulsed in his grip, leaking precome at the tip. He thumbed it, spreading it on himself, his gaze still fixated on Shepard. Like a hungry lion staring down its prey. This wasn't the first time he had seen Shepard naked, but this was the first time he could openly appreciate him, devour him, totally and completely consume him. He wanted all of Shepard.

"You're so sexy," Nick growled, as Shepard tugged his briefs down over his hard cock. A tuft of soft brown hair revealed itself, marking the exact spot Nick wanted to kiss.

He could barely contain himself. He wanted to launch off the bed and throw Shepard to the floor, where he could make him his with his mouth alone.

"Yeah?" Shepard asked, knowing damn well what the answer was. His six-pack rippled when he moved, his cock bouncing in the air as he stepped toward Nick. Shepard grabbed himself by the base of his dick, aiming it forward, the tip glistening, and stepped closer. Nick reached out and grabbed Shepard's thighs, unable to wait any longer. He pulled the man toward his mouth, his lips parting for Shepard once again. Nick took him in between his warm, wet lips, immediately drawing a delicious moan from Shepard. He felt Shepard's hands lose themselves in his hair, the spot Nick fucking loved to be grabbed. He felt his own body relax another degree as Shepard steered his head, moving Nick's mouth further down his cock. At one point, Nick had to pull back for a breath, but wasn't tapped out of the ring for long. Nick didn't want to spend another second without tasting Shepard. Without serving him. Giving him a pleasure so intense, his balls were already drawing up and his grip was getting tighter in Nick's hair. Nick still had a hold of Shepard's muscular thighs, squeezing them and pulling them forward as Shepard pulled back. Nick looked up and squeezed his thighs tighter. Shepard picked up the pace, thrusting his hips now, burying his cock deeper and deeper down Nick's willing throat. He wanted to go all the fucking way. He wanted Shepard to disappear down his mouth. It was definitely a lofty goal, considering how big Shepard was, but Nick was never one to turn down a challenge. *Especially* not when it tasted this good.

"Oh fuck," Shepard hissed, his hips moving faster, pushing his hard cock even further. Nick closed his eyes, relishing in the feeling. He let every muscle in his body relax as Shepard took over. He could feel his own hard dick aching for attention, but all Nick wanted to do was focus on Shepard. He wanted to give that man all of himself, beginning with his face.

"So," Shepard grunted, "Fucking," Shepard moaned, "Good," Shepard twitched above Nick. He was getting close.

21 SHEPARD KENSWORTH

(finished)

S hepard's entire body was tingling. From his toes, which were currently curling into the soft plush beige carpet, to his fingers, which were trying to find purchase in Nick's messy hair, to his fucking earlobes. He was like a live wire, exposed and bare and sparking, ready to explode at a moment's notice. He glanced down at the unbelievably handsome man who was swallowing his dick down to the balls, a feat that was not only incredibly hot, but also incredibly impressive. Shepard looked down even further, at Nick's cock, jutting out from between his thighs, the head slick with precome, showing off just how turned on the man was. That was when Nick's tongue gave a soft swirl over Shepard's shaft, tickling at his balls, sending more electric shocks coursing through his body. Shepard gave another moan, one that came from deep in his chest, one he couldn't hold back even if he wanted to. Nick was making him lose control of his body in more ways than one. Shepard wasn't even sure if he could stay standing any longer.

"Mhmm, come, let me lie down," Shepard said. "It's hard for me to come standing up," said playfully.

"Who said I wanted you to come yet?" Nick said, grinning as he took Shepard's cock back in his mouth and kept him standing.

"Ohh, fuck," Shepard said, "maybe I can come standing up."

Nick smiled around his dick, his tongue working its magic along Shepard's shaft. Shepard never felt so comfortable before. Especially not while he was naked. He worked hard to have a nice body, but that didn't mean he was immune to feeling vulnerable when someone else had his cock balls deep down his throat. But with Nick, he wasn't only harder than steel, but he felt like he was Play-Doh in Nick's grip, too.

"*Fuuuck,* that feels so good," Shepard said, as Nick moaned around his cock, the entire thing slick with his spit. He could practically feel himself pulsing in Nick's warm mouth. It was bliss. Shepard couldn't imagine anything better. Not only was the feeling intense, but the view was incredible. Having Nick look up at him with those captivating light brown eyes, mouth full of cock, smile on his lips. It was enough to make Shepard's knees tremble. When he was able to steady himself, he grabbed onto Nick's chin and lifted him up off his knees. His lips were wet and puffy and exactly what Shepard wanted against his own. He went in for a kiss, tasting himself on Nick's tongue, melting into Nick's body. They both moaned as Shepard led them backward toward the bed. Or, at least he thought it was toward the bed. Ten seconds later and Nick moved forward with a surprised grunt.

"Oh, sorry," Shepard said, realizing he had steered them toward the dresser, which had rudely interrupted them by jabbing Nick in the ass with a corner.

"I think I just lost my virginity," Nick said, rubbing his

butt with a flushed face. They both started cracking up at that. Shepard went back in for kisses, but the laughs were almost too much.

"I hope the dresser was a gentle lover, at least," Shepard toyed as he led them toward the bed, his eyes open this time.

"Oh, it knew what it was doing."

This had Shepard laughing even more. He couldn't believe he was almost in tears while his cock was functioning as a fucking flag pole, sticking out into the air and bouncing with his laughs.

"Alright, get down on that bed," Nick said, his tone growing a little heavier. He still had a smile on his face, but it was quickly evolving into a hungry smirk. The kind he gave when he was attempting to swallow Shepard moments earlier. It was so damn sexy. Shepard felt the mattress against the back of his knees. He sat down and moved back on the bed, bringing his feet up, moving the pillow up with him so he could lean on the headboard. He opened his legs wide as Nick climbed on, his own cock hard and leaking. Shepard loved seeing him on all fours, moving toward him. He couldn't get enough of how hot Nick was, *especially* when he was rock hard.

Nick leaned down and licked Shepard's balls while his cock bounced on his taut stomach. Nick grabbed Shepard's tight balls in his hands and lifted, exposing the sensitive skin underneath. Nick went to town and Shepard was seeing stars. He lifted his legs up higher in the air, giving Nick's tongue a little more access. He fisted his own cock, squeezing out a rope of precome as Nick continued working wonders with his tongue. It was like he was casting a damn spell, Shepard completely and totally entranced. Nick could have asked Shepard to do anything in that moment and he would have done it without a question asked

"Fuck, Nick, I'm so close," Shepard groaned into the dark bedroom. He could feel himself getting tighter, his body ready for the pending explosion. His toes were curling as Nick licked his way back up to the swollen head of Shepard's cock. He popped it back into his mouth, the heat immediately consuming Shepard. He couldn't take it. He was going to blow.

"That's it, that's it," Shepard said, his eyes already beginning to roll back. "I'm gonna—" Shepard couldn't finish his sentence. His cock erupted down Nick's throat as his entire body tensed, his legs kicked out straight, his toes curled, his fingers dug into the mattress, his hips twitched and spasmed. He could see stars. He was scared he had passed out for a second.

"Oh my god," Shepard said on an exhale, his head body shifting back into that Play-Doh state. He tried moving his arms, but they lay useless at his sides. Nick came up from between Shepard's thighs, a smile on his face. He kissed his way up to Shepard's lips, spending a few extra moments on Shepard's pebbled nipples. By the time Nick made it up to Shepard's lips, Shepard thought he was ready to go again. His dick had barely gotten any softer, even after he just finished blowing his load.

"I want you," Shepard whispered, nibbling on Nick's earlobe as he pulled back. He grabbed Nick's head in his hands and steered them together for another kiss. The overhead lights were set on their dimmest setting. Shepard pulled back, finding Nick's glowing eyes in the soft light. His lips were still wet from the kiss, catching Shepard's eyes for a moment before they flitted back up to Nick's. "I want you to fuck me."

They had already done this once before, but this time, things felt so much more potent. There was way more involved. The stakes were so much higher. A year ago, back in the on-call room, Shepard felt like he was simply living out a fantasy. As much as he daydreamed about the sexy, elusive doctor, he felt as though them being together had as much chance of happening as him being killed by a falling toilet seat. It was a good thing he wasn't a betting man, because those odds weren't as skewed as he once assumed. Now, being with Nick felt almost like a certainty. Something that was bound to happen, woven into the fabric of their destinies. They worked too well together, their chemistry never flickering and their feelings already knowing no bounds.

And so this felt very different to the first time they hooked up.

Nick didn't need much more encouragement. He reached over to his nightstand and opened the drawer, pulling out a small bottle of lube and a condom. He got to work with the rubber while Shepard squeezed a dime-sized amount of lube on his palm. He rubbed it on his still-hard dick before slipping his lubed fingers down past his balls and over his hole. He pressed two fingers against his ass, slipping inside and getting himself ready for Nick. He bit his lower lip as he pushed his fingers in a little deeper. He took a breath, working them farther. Nick was now standing at the edge of the bed, watching Shepard finger himself. Shepard enjoyed putting on a show. He lifted his ass off the bed so Nick could have a better view as Shepard found his swollen P-spot and started massaging it, his head falling back and his eyes closing with the pleasure.

Shepard felt the bed sink. He opened his eyes and saw Nick sitting on his knees, his hard cock sticking up straight. He reached for the bottle of lube and squirted some in his hands, which he rubbed over his dick as Shepard continued to probe himself. With Nick all lubed up, he grabbed Shepard's wrist and pulled him out slowly, his fingers coming out with a small pop. Shepard moaned, immediately feeling a sense of emptiness that had to be filled, and he knew exactly how he wanted it to be filled.

Nick grabbed Shepard's ankles and lifted him up, exposing his tight ass. He held his feet up in the air as he maneuvered his hips so that the head of his cock was pressing up against Shepard's ready hole. Shepard took a breath and relaxed even further, granting Nick full access. He felt Nick's cock push past the tight ring of muscle. A sharp sting coursed through him. Shepard winced slightly, causing Nick to freeze in his tracks.

"You ok?" Nick asked, the head of his cock successfully buried in Shepard's ass.

"More than ok," Shepard encouraged. He knew some slight discomfort came with the territory, and that it would quickly give way to intense pleasure. He reached up and grabbed Nick's shoulders, pulling him down for another kiss. This spurred Nick on. He pushed in a little deeper. He was slow, tender. Shepard loved it. He loved feeling Nick slowly enter him, giving him that sweet sensation of being filled with his lover's cock.

"Right there," Shepard said as Nick hit his spot.

"Yeah?" Nick asked, grinning as he picked up his pace. He pulled almost completely out before sinking back in, still slow but working in deeper now. Shepard's fingernails dug into Nick's broad shoulders. Nick was thrusting faster now. He was entirely inside of Shepard, his cock stretching Shepard in a way that made him forget the fucking English language. Shepard's brain turned to mush as Nick started to pound at his ass. Shepard's legs were still high up in the air, held onto by Nick, who began to kiss his ankles as he continued to fuck him. Harder. Faster. Shepard opened his eyes and saw a completely different Nick. One that was filled to the brim with a heated passion, it burned in his gaze. Shepard couldn't even jerk himself off, even though his cock was still hard and bouncing against his stomach. He was so overwhelmed with pleasure, he just lay there and took it all. Everything that Nick was giving, he was a receptive vessel.

"Fuck, you're so hot," Nick said over the sounds of his thighs slapping against Shepard's ass.

"Keep going," Shepard was able to say, past the stars that clouded his brain. He reached a hand up and grabbed Nick's chest, feeling the soft hair on his palm, the hard nipples, the fast heartbeat. Everything that reminded Shepard he was with his perfect man. "You're going to make me come again," Shepard said, a little surprised at how good Nick was at fucking him. He never came twice, and not in such a quic—

"Oh, fuck, fuck," Shepard said, feeling his cock erupt again. It was a hands-free orgasm, something else that never happened to Shepard. His cock jerked against his stomach as it emptied his balls. His ass clenched around Nick with every orgasmic wave.

"*Fuuuck*," Nick said, running his hand over the puddle of come Shepard had created around his belly button. He spread it over Shepard's chest as he continued to fuck him. "I'm going to come," Nick warned.

"Keep fucking me," Shepard said, his cock now softening but his body still ready for more. Nick listened to Shepard, continuing to drive his thickness into Shepard's ass. A few more thrusts, and Nick dropped his head and tightened his grip around Shepard's ankles. His hips gave three twitches, each one a shot of come into the condom.

When everything was over, a sweaty and breathless Nick pulled out of Shepard, threw out the condom, and collapsed onto the bed. Shepard was equally sweaty and breathless. They both chuckled as the postorgasmic bliss started to take over. Shepard rolled on his side and threw an arm over Nick's chest, enjoying the feeling of his chest rising and falling with his breaths.

"That was... something else," Shepard said.

"I'm honestly speechless," Nick replied with another laugh.

"I've never came twice like that before." Shepard sounded clearly impressed. Nick looked his way and smiled.

"Want to make it three times?"

(End of chapter)

22 NICHOLAS WHITE

(finished)

Once morning arrived, Shepard had to get to the hospital. It was the first time Shepard had slept over, and Nick could feel himself already addicted to the feeling of having him under the bed sheets. He hadn't woken up so happy in months. He woke up a little earlier than Shepard's alarm so that he could whip him up some pancakes and a nice cup of coffee. Emma was awake by that time, too, so Nick had her in the kitchen while he cooked. It was the perfect morning, and Nick was excited to continue the trend. They had already set another date at an outdoor mall next to Santa Monica beach in a couple of days, and Nick couldn't wait.

But the day also brought with it other things. He knew he had to see Shepard's cousin at the detective agency and he had to do it as soon as possible. Once they had their breakfast, he dropped Emma off at Anna's place and drove to the location Shepard had given him. Nick walked up to the red-bricked two-story building, a wall of dark green ivy climbing up the left side and reaching toward the center, where a sign read "Stonewall Investigations". It felt like a building picked up from the New York streets of *Gossip Girls* and dropped into the middle of Los Angeles, on a residential street in Century City. There was a subtle rainbow crossing through the center of the sign above the door, adding a touch that Nick appreciated. He understood that gay rights and LGBTQ people were more and more accepted as each day passed, but that didn't mean he still wasn't nervous about negative interactions, especially in businesses that were centered around revealing information and seeing the entire story. It certainly didn't help that he already had an incredibly negative reaction coming from his dad, whom he had never had an issue with growing up. The last thing he wanted was to meet with a private detective who held some kind of secret bigotry and ended up sabotaging Nick's case. This felt like his last resort. If he couldn't prove that Anna was doing something shady, then he'd be stuck seeing Emma two days for the rest of his life, with the possibility of Anna doing something shady and trying for sole custody. He'd be devastated. He hoped that even if he didn't find anything on Anna, that it wouldn't come to him losing complete custody, but he had no idea what she was up to and he had stayed up way too late on quite a few nights, reading various different horror stories of parents losing their kids to a terrible spouse. Nick wanted to cover all the bases and make sure the judge was on his side. Besides, Nick wasn't fine with the arrangement they had. Two days a week was nothing. It had to be changed to at least a fifty-fifty split.

Nick opened the heavy red wooden door, pulling on the white door handle. The exterior was all pretty picturesque, and the inside of the building didn't disappoint either. He was expecting to step into a typical lobby, but instead Nick walked into a foyer that was furnished like someone was expecting to land the cover of a home and garden magazine. The floors were freshly polished dark wood. The walls were an extension of the exterior, wallpaper peeling away in strategic areas to reveal the red bricks underneath. There was a cozy feeling to the place that Nick enjoyed.

Am I even in the right place?

For a second, Nick forgot about the sign outside and thought he had strolled into some random (and beautifully decorated) house. Before he had time to question it any further, he was greeted by a bubbly guy wearing a casual gray sport jacket over a simple white shirt and jeans. He bounced more so than walked, a hand extended out for Nick to grab, which he did.

"You must be Dr. Nicholas White?"

"You can call me Nick," he answered.

"Great to meet you, Nick! I'm Andrew, the office manager slash receptionist slash janitor slash assistant to Zane. He's upstairs in his office," Andrew turned on his heel and started walking. "Right this way." Andrew led Nick through the hall, past a couple other rooms with their doors closed, name badges marking the detectives that worked inside each office. Nick liked the feeling he was more inside someone's home than in the hub for detective work. It gave a kind of undercover feel to the place, like they were a secret operation inside of a spy film.

Zane's office was on the top floor, reached after climbing the spiral staircase and walking a short distance down another hallway, toward a dark blue door that was left partly open. There was sunlight streaming in from behind, lighting up the hallway, the sunlight bouncing off the shiny floors. There were picture frames hanging on the walls, stylized photos of different city skylines held within each frame.

Andrew knocked on the door before he opened it further. "Hey, Zane, I've got Dr. White here to see you."

"Perfect, thank you, Andrew." The voice was deep, commanding. Nick smiled a thank you to Andrew as he stepped aside so that Nick could enter. Zane's office carried a similar style to the rest of the building; classic, cozy, but with some modern touches to it. The floor changed to a gray concrete and the wall was mostly just exposed red brick. Picture frames also hung in this room, but they were all black and white photos of an extremely photogenic bulldog. There was a tall green plant growing out from a marble pot set next to a floor-to-ceiling window. Zane's desk was against the side of the room. He sat behind it in a leather chair. As soon as Nick stepped into the room, he stood up and walked around the glass desk. He had a strong—almost intimidating— look to him, but his warm green eyes balanced out that powerful square jaw and prominent, stern brow.

"Hi, Zane. I'm Nick, nice to finally meet you."

They had talked a bit through email, where Nick had given him some slim details on what was going on.

"I'm looking forward to helping you get to the bottom of things," Zane said, taking Nick's hand in both of his. His grip was firm, his hands strong, his eyes were honest. Nick was getting a military vibe from him. From the way he stood, shoulders stiff and back straight, to the way he spoke.

"Let's get things started so we don't waste any time," Zane said, letting go of Nick's hand and motioning to the comfortable-looking white chair set in front of his desk. Nick pulled the chair out and sat, the soft cushions shaping to his body. He brought a small folder with him holding some documents he thought could be important. There weren't many things to collect, but he wanted to be prepared for anything. Mostly, though, it was filled with notes about his relationship with Anna and what he thought could be happening. He set the black folder down on the desk and looked to Zane, who was pulling out a much-larger binder from a bookshelf.

"Ok, so, this is the preliminary information I was able to pull up." Zane put the binder on the desk and pushed it over to Nick, who grabbed it, in awe of the weight.

"Preliminary? You mean there's more?"

That got a laugh out of Zane. Nick could already tell those laughs weren't given out freely, so he gladly took it.

"Oh, yeah," Zane said, turning to his computer. He moved the mouse around to wake the screen up. "That's just things we could pull off her public social accounts, along with a couple other things that have deeper sources."

"Deeper sources?" Nick opened the binder, looking down at a cover page with his case number printed across the front. Case Number Seventy-Seven. He considered seven to be his lucky number.

"Don't worry, everything we do is clean." Zane said that in a way that made Nick wonder if he purposefully didn't use the word "legal". "We have connections with local law enforcement wherever we're working. Our main headquarters are based out in New York. This is our second biggest location."

"Do you normally work out here on the west coast?"

"I actually live in New York, but I read your email and knew I had to fly out and take your case."

"Wow, thank you." Nick felt good about that. Not only about the fact that he had the owner of the entire detective agency working on his case, but also that Zane cared enough to put everything on pause back in New York so he could travel across the country and help Nick secure Emma's future.

"Of course," Zane said. He wasn't a man of frequent laughs, nor of frequent smiles, but he cracked one for Nick. "So inside that binder, I'm pretty sure you'll see all things that you already know about Anna. And obviously, we can't bring her in for questioning since we don't have the full power of the law behind us like detectives on the police force do, but I can ask you some questions and use those just the same."

"I'll try to answer the best I can."

"Alright, so about Anna, from everything I found, she seems pretty clean. She works as a receptionist at a local gym and is working toward her associates degree in public relations. She was married once to you and hasn't had any obvious relationships since then. That all sound right?"

"Yeah," Nick said, looking up from a photo of a smiling Anna holding Emma in her arms. Nick recognized it as her profile picture.

"Ok, but there were some gaps that I need you to fill in. Her associates degree. Was she pursuing it when she was with you?"

"No, she was never interested in going back to school. She was happy living off having a doctor as a husband. I didn't even know she was going back to school."

"That's the first red flag." Zane typed something into his computer. "I found this conversation," Zane tilted the computer so that Nick could read the screen, "where she tells one of her CPS case workers that she's been studying for three years now and sent them a schedule, clearly to show that she's responsible. I looked closer at the schedule and realized there was a subtle difference between the font of Anna's name and the rest of the schedule. I went to the college's website and contacted the administrator, asking them to send me whatever font they had coded into the webpage. Sure enough, it was different."

"Holy shit," Nick said, "Shepard was right. You are good."

Zane smiled again. Each smile felt like a badge of honor that Nick could wear proudly on his chest. "The last piece of that puzzle was asking you, who would have known her at the time she said she enrolled. So we've definitely got something going on."

"Is that enough? Falsifying documents?"

"Unfortunately, no. The judge is going to be hyper focused on Emma and what would directly affect her, not a bad Photoshop job. Not just one, at least. I could see a lawyer swinging that so it would seem like she was a mother doing anything she could to protect her daughter.

"Wait a second," Nick hadn't even realized that he was looking at one of Anna's private emails on the screen. "Where did you get this? How do we know it's real?"

Zane looked to Nick, his green eyes as bright as the sunlight that was streaming in from the huge window. "Trust me, it's real. And as for our source, unfortunately there are some things I need to keep quiet about. But again, I have full confidence that this is real and a sign of something going on."

Nick had no choice but to trust Zane. In the short amount of time he had been in Zane's office, he was already closer to figuring out what was going on with Anna than he ever would have been if he was going at it by himself. This guy knew what he was doing, and there was still more to dig up.

"How do you know my cousin?" Zane asked, turning the computer back toward his own eyes only.

"Shepard?" Nick stumbled on the name. He felt silly getting nervous, but he couldn't help it. His heart started to flutter and his hands got a bit cooler than normal. They hadn't really labeled themselves yet, which made questions like these extra awkward. Did he say boyfriend or did that sound too clingy? He definitely felt like one. Or maybe he was overthinking the entire thing. "He's uh, well, we're together."

Zane smiled again. This one was the biggest of them all. "I'm joking, I already knew." He looked past his computer screen to Nick. "What kind of detective would I be if I didn't know you were dating someone in my own family?"

THE REST of the meeting with Zane was extremely productive and had Nick feeling much better. He was getting closer to an answer. He left the office and all he could think about was holding his baby girl. Unfortunately, it wasn't his day so he wasn't legally allowed to. He walked to his car, wondering if maybe he could get Anna to agree to a couple of hours with Emma. It was still early afternoon so it wasn't like he was taking her anywhere when it was getting dark out.

As if that should matter. I'm her fucking father.

The thought punched him in the gut. He suddenly wished Shepard was waiting in the passenger seat as he got into his car. He knew he'd be able to get some support from Shepard, who had even offered to come with him to Stonewall Investigations. A last-minute change in shifts had

Shepard working the morning in the hospital, though, so Nick had gone alone.

Before even pulling out of his parking spot, Nick grabbed his phone from the pocket of his jeans and called Anna. It rang and rang and rang until the voicemail came on. Nick assumed she was probably changing Emma's diapers or maybe feeding her. It was around that time of the day when Emma would have been crying for a bottle as though the world would end if she didn't get one immediately. He gave her a couple more minutes, still sitting in his car. He scrolled through Twitter to try and take his mind off it, but it was no use. He called Anna again and got the same result.

One more time.

Ring until the voicemail.

Nick sighed. This was rare, but it happened before. Once, Anna said she had lost her phone and found it a day later. The second time she said she had broken her phone and didn't fix it for a week, only contacting Nick through Chris's phone twice. The third time she didn't even bother giving an excuse. Nick was documenting every missed call, but he wasn't sure if they would even make a difference. He knew it stressed him out to no end, but would a judge care?

He called one more time. It rang five times before it was finally answered. "Hello?"

"Chris?" Nick clearly sounded confused. He looked at the screen, double-checking to make sure he had dialed Anna's number.

"Yeah, it's me." He could hear a children's television show in the background. If he listened real close, he could hear Emma talking in her baby-gibberish to it.

"What's going on? Why isn't Anna answering? Where is she?"

"Oh, she's ok," Chris said. Then he turned his attention to Emma and started baby-talking to her, as if the conversation with Nick was over.

"Where is she?" Nick asked again, more pointedly this time.

"She has a migraine. She's locked up in her room trying to sleep it off. Happy?" Chris sounded annoyed. He went back to baby-talking to Emma.

Nick exhaled. "I want to see Emma. Just for an hour." He felt himself lay it all on the line with his statement. He felt like a tightrope walker, tiptoeing across a rope that was swaying dangerously in the wind.

"No," Chris said, pushing Nick off the tightrope and sending him falling down a hundred stories. "Sorry, Nick. It's not your weekend. It'll confuse her. I'm taking great care of her. Isn't that right, Emma? Isn't it right? Huh? Yes, it is, Emma."

Nick was white-knuckling his steering wheel. His grip was so tight he was scared he would snap the wheel. "My own daughter won't be confused by seeing me. Chris, let me come by. I'm only asking for an hour. That's it." Nick wanted more. He wanted so much more than just an hour, but he knew he was bargaining and Chris had the most bargaining chips.

"I'm sorry, Nick."

"No, you're not, Chris. Don't give me that crap."

"I really am. I wish you hadn't cheated on my sist—"

"For fucks sake, I didn't cheat on her. *She* cheated on *me*! With one of my closest friends. I get it, she's your sister, you're going to want to take her side, but open up your eyes, Chris. Your sister has issues and I think something else is going on. She needs help, Chris, not a blind hype-girl that's going to cheer on whatever lies she keeps spouting out."

The outburst came from deep inside Nick. He was so sick and tired of Anna smearing his name with lies, just so that she could come out as the victim in the entire situation when the whole time she was the one wearing the clown paint and holding a fucking red balloon in her hand. *She* was the monster, not Nick, and she was the main reason why he couldn't hold his daughter.

Turn Page for next Ch.

Question — (Emma's Anna's new "boyfriend)

Why won't Chris let **Nick** See Emma? (his daughter) The story continues...

(End of chapter)

23 SHEPARD KENSWORTH

Third Street Promenade was bustling with people, shopping bags in hands, sunglasses and caps obscuring faces. It was a beautiful stretch of shops that took up about five large blocks, just a few minutes away from the world famous Santa Monica Pier. The street was closed off to traffic, so people spilled out from the sidewalk and made their way down the center path. There were street performers working for their tips; from a singing duet made up of teenage twins to a slightly disturbing clown blowing up balloons and taking requests, there was something for everyone. And if the street performers didn't do it, tourists could spend their day sitting on a bench and watching celebrities pass by, some trying to be as discreet as they could while others seemed to wear a glowing neon sign that said they were famous.

It was the perfect place for a date. There was so much to see and talk about, even if the conversation was dying down (which, let's be real, Shepard was not expecting that to happen) there would be plenty to point out. It was also later in the evening, so there was a little bit of cloud cover and a refreshing wind that blew in from the ocean nearby. The cool temperature allowed Shepard to dress up a little fancier than he was expecting. He thought he'd have to wear a damn speedo with how hot it was getting in Los Angeles, but thankfully the past few weeks had been blessed with cooler weather. Shepard had on a pair of fitted jeans and a long-sleeved button-up shirt that had the first couple of buttons popped open, showing off a bit of his chest and the glint of a rose gold necklace.

He was waiting by the triceratops fountain. It was definitely an interesting piece, with the dinosaur covered in dark green leaves, a stream of water shooting from its open mouth. Across from it was a t-rex doing the same thing. As Shepard was wondering how high the designer had to be to commission two dinosaurs made out of hedges for an outdoor mall, he felt a hand fall on his shoulder. He had been sitting on the edge of the fountain with his back turned to one of the main entrances. He wasn't sure which way Nick would be coming.

"Hey, Shep," Nick said as Shepard got up from his seat. He was already smiling wide as Nick opened his arms for a hug. Shepard already had trouble letting go. There was just something about Nick's big arms wrapped around him that made Shepard feel giddy. Like a kid on Christmas, except Nick was the gift that seemed to never stop giving.

"You look great," Shepard said as they separated. And he honestly did. Nick was wearing a sleek pair of navy slacks and light brown shoes that seemed like they were freshly shined. His white shirt, tucked in underneath a belt that matched the shoes, was rolled up at the sleeves, giving him a little bit of a more casual look and showing off those sexy forearms that Shepard couldn't get enough of. He was beginning to realize just how much a white coat ended up covering. Then again, if Nick looked like that every time he stepped into the hospital, Shepard would have had a very tough time concentrating on his patients. Hell, he was sure the patients would join him in his gawking.

"I knew you'd come here looking like a model, so I thought I should step things up a little bit."

"Oh, stop," Shepard said, dropping his head to the side. "A model, huh? What else you got?"

Nick laughed, dropping his head slightly. Shepard stood there, waiting for more compliments, a smile on his face.

"Let's go before I inflate your ego so much you end up floating away."

THEIR DATE WAS PERFECT. Shepard could walk for hours with Nick at his side and never get bored. They always had something to point out or joke about. And even when there wasn't any conversation, Nick's presence alone was enough for Shepard to have a good time. He couldn't help but compare it to the early days he was dating Rick. Hindsight was twenty-twenty. He never felt anywhere near as happy with Rick as he felt with Nick. He thought he had felt the big L-word for Rick, but he could see that he wasn't anywhere close to loving Rick. To *really* loving him. He dated him and had decent sex, but he never felt the kind of connection that was obvious between him and Nick.

"So have you given your specialty any more thought? Residents have to apply for fellowships soon, don't they?" Nick asked. They had been talking about Nick's decision to work in emergency medicine.

"Soonish, yeah," Shepard said. They walked past a Starbucks, the scent of coffee drifting out from the open door.

The patio was filled with people sitting underneath the green umbrellas, some with their laptops opened, most likely all working on a screenplay of some kind.

"I've been pretty lost since I got into medical school," Shepard said, "I thought I wanted to do surgery, but thinking about the hours and lifestyle make me want to drown in a puddle of my own tears. So that quickly got scratched off the list. I thought, ok maybe I can do emergency medicine like you. It keeps me on my toes and I could still have decent hours. I just don't want to be a slave to Sierra View, either. I want to be able to enjoy time off so I could spend it with family and not worry about being on-call all the time."

"Good thinking," Nick said. "I sense a 'but' coming."

"But," Shepard said with a wink, "I'm hesitant about that because I really enjoy connecting with patients. I like how family medicine doctors practically grow up with their patients. Emergency doctors like you save lives on the daily, but you don't really create deep connections with patients, do you?"

Nick shook his head. "Not really, no. There's definitely a connection that comes with saving someone's life, but it's not like I see every milestone in their lives or anything like that. It's what had drawn me to emergency medicine in the first place." Nick laughed at how opposite the two seemed in terms of their wants for a medical specialty. "The energy in an emergency room also really called to me."

"Which is *also* why I can't do family medicine. It's too slow for me." They reached the part of the street where the mall ended and regular business resumed. Cars stopped as the crosswalk lit up across the way, releasing a flood of pedestrians. Nick and Shepard jumped into the flow. They hadn't really talked about what they were doing after the walk around the mall, but it felt like they were naturally headed toward the Santa Monica Pier. "So I was actually pretty stressed about it until a few days ago."

"What happened a few days ago?"

"Emma," Shepard said, with the same reverence as if he had discovered the cure to the common flu.

"Did she tell you what she thought was best? I mean, I trust her opinion, but she is just a baby."

"Well, that's the thing, she's a baby." Shepard's pearly white teeth caught the sun as he smiled. "I was always uncomfortable around kids and babies, but after being with Emma, I think that's all gone away. I think I know what I want to do for the rest of my life." He was beaming, from the inside out. "I think I want to be a pediatrician. I really want to help kids, I want to see them grow up and know that I'm helping keep them healthy and safe. I want to connect with the parents and help them keep calm through whatever comes up. I know I'd be happy. I get I wouldn't be making a dermatologist's salary, but I'm totally fine with that."

Nick looked just as happy as Shepard felt. "That's incredible. I think you'd make a great pediatrician. Especially since it's obvious you really want to do it. And yeah, kids can be scary at first, but remember you've always got the upper hand."

"Sometimes, I'm not so sure about that," Shepard said with a laugh. "I'd probably be better if my mom had given me the little sister I was begging for back in middle school. I thought it'd be so cool to brush her hair." Shepard smiled fondly at the memory of a simpler time, when his biggest problem in the world was that he didn't have a sister to groom.

"You're an only child, right?" Shepard asked as they

walked away from the promenade and toward the beach. The ocean breeze started getting stronger as they got closer to the beach.

"Yep, just me. I think I asked for a little brother once, and my mom shut me down *real* quick. I do have a half-sister, though. My mom had her with her new husband."

"Oh, wow, I didn't know you had a sister. How old is she?"

"Twelve, her name's Megan. She's a sweetheart. Super smart, too. Says she wants to be a doctor."

"Must be your mom's genes then."

"Oh, for sure," Nick said. "All I got from my father was his oversized nose."

"Your nose is the perfect size," Shepard said, playfully bumping into his side with a shoulder. They crossed the street, the salty sweet scent of the water becoming stronger. They could see the pier stretching out into the ocean, the huge Ferris wheel spinning right next to a small roller coaster, both set at the middle of the pier. "Everything you've got is sized perfectly." Shepard smirked toward Nick.

Nick laughed. He surprised Shepard by grabbing his hand. It was such a smooth move, Shepard barely noticed until a few moments after his fingers were entwined with Nick. He had a second when his thoughts flashed to "oh shit, what if someone from the hospital sees us" but he quickly pushed those thoughts away and focused on just how happy holding Nick's hand made him. That was the important part. Not what other residents would say if they saw them. That stuff didn't matter anymore. It was all about how good he felt with Nick at his side.

"You know," Nick said as they walked, their steps in sync, "I've never held a man's hand in public before."

"It takes a little bit to get used to the random stares, but you learn to ignore them. Besides, we're in Los Angeles, I feel like the majority of people here are fine with two men holding hands. It does suck though, how it feels like it puts a spotlight on you. You'd think we were about to stick each other's dicks in our mouths. Why does anyone care whose hand I hold?"

"Because of the children," Nick joked, changing his tone to sound like an old handmaid, "What ever will we explain to them?"

"Oh, dearie me, you *are* right," Shepard said, joining the game. "We mustn't spoil their innocence with thoughts of love. The *homosexual* kind!"

"So stupid," Nick said, laughing. "There are people out there who seriously can't sit down with their kids for five minutes and explain what love is. Crazy what unfounded fear and prejudice can do to someone." Nick's hand squeezed a little tighter. Shepard loved it. He knew Nick must have been a little on edge, he certainly was when he held Rick's hand in public for the first time, but that feeling would soon go away. Things were changing. There was still a long way to go, but holding Nick's hand for everyone to see would only push things forward, not back.

Neither of them noticed the portly man who walked out of his church service a few feet behind them. He noticed them, though, his phone in his grubby hand, his camera open and aimed at the two men. He got his photos and walked the other way.

Nick and Shepard reached a set of stairs that led down toward the beach. They decided to skip the tourist packed pier and chose to sit on a bench by the beach instead. Shepard remembered finding the seat a few months ago, when he was determined to study outside. It was a bit of a secret spot, hidden from the main beach by a large outcropping of rock. Shepard led the way down the stairs. When they reached the bottom, they both took their shoes off so they could walk barefooted through the warm sand.

"Have you come out yet? To your parents? Friends?" Shepard watched Nick's reaction closely. He knew that Nick had been married to a woman, and clearly got things to work at least once. Shepard also knew that Nick got it to work with him way more than just once. So there was a little bit of a question mark in Shepard's head, clouded by some fear as well. Shepard was nervous to see how Nick would handle being with a man when it came to his family. Shepard's parents were hippy liberals who completely accepted their twins coming out as gay, but Shepard knew that everyone's experience was different. They reached the bench then, both sitting down.

Nick's reaction was composed. A sad smile crept onto his lips. One that was pursed and hung half-crooked on his sculpted face.

"I told my father, and he, well, uhm," the smile disappeared altogether. "He cut things off." Nick's voice choked at the end. Shepard squeezed Nick's hand, which was still holding his and resting on Nick's thigh. The fresh ocean breeze drifted in as waves crashed feet ahead of them. The bench wasn't located on the sand, but instead on a small island of concrete. The breeze felt cool, a contrast to the warm sadness that was filling Shepard. He held onto Nick's hand, letting him compose his thoughts and figure out how best to keep talking. "I told him about two weeks ago. Told him that after a year of being alone, I found someone I think is really special. Someone who's worth letting into Emma's life. Someone whose reminding me that not everyone is out to destroy me. I told him I think I found the one. I told him that person was you."

Shepard felt his breath hitch. He was filled with an even deeper sadness. A moment that should have been filled with smiles — *he thinks I could be the one* — instead turned out to be a moment anchored by guilt. He shouldn't have felt guilty for what happened between Nick and his father, but Shepard couldn't help it. He was the reason the man was turning away from his son and granddaughter. All because he was a man and not a woman.

"It's tough," Nick continued. Shepard could almost see the bricks holding up Nick's walls come tumbling down, in the way his neck moved, his jaw twitched. In his eyes, which looked up from his toes to stay on Shepard's gaze. There was sadness, but also an honesty that Shepard hadn't really seen before. Nick was allowing him past another layer, and it seemed as though they both realized how powerful that was. "I just want what's best for my daughter." Nick took another moment, taking a deep breath. "I want her to grow up with grandparents that spoil her, with a father that loves her unconditionally, with another who does the same. I want her to grow without a care in the world. Plus, I was close to my dad. He pushed me through medical school when I needed it." Nick shook his head. Shepard squeezed his hand a little tighter, his thumb rubbing circles over Nick's soft skin. He wished he could just reach inside of Nick and take whatever pain he was feeling. He could see how big of an effect this had on Nick. It hurt them both. "Instead, I'm going to need to explain why her grandfather refuses to talk to his own son, cutting her off as well. She'll see the world for what it is, way too soon, much earlier than I'd ever want her to. I wanted to protect her from all the fucked up shit for as long as I possibly could."

"You can't hold your dad's decision over yourself,"

Shepard said, speaking over the gust of sea breeze. "And you can't assume you know how this is going to impact Emma. I hear you, I wish there was something I could do to protect that little smiling cinnamon roll—" Nick chuckled at that, "—but the thing is, the world was going to show its teeth eventually. At least this way, you still have some control over how she receives the info. She'll clearly still love you endlessly and she'll just be a little more aware of how people are acting. I think something like that could make her wise beyond her years, and that's nothing negative. She already looks like she's ready to run a Fortune 500 company all before nap time hits. She's got those sharp eyes. She'll be just fine."

Nick was smiling. The mask of sadness he had suddenly donned was discarded. This was the Nick that Shepard wanted to see. The man whose smile could headline a damn Super Bowl half-time show.

"She does have that look, doesn't she?"

"Yep. It's almost intimidating, if I'm being honest."

Nick laughed, the sound mixing with the crash of the waves. "Thank you, Shep. You know exactly what to say. I've been feeling like shit, honestly, feeling almost like I'm supposed to be mourning my father, mourning the world I brought my daughter into, but then I'm reminded that there's so much more to be happy about, and it all starts with you. Who knows, maybe he'll come around one day, but even he doesn't, looking into your eyes is going to remind me that I did the right thing."

"Of course you did. It took courage and it took strength. It's weird. I mean, we're obviously both two grown—*grown*," Shepard emphasized with a wink and a quick glance down at Nick's lap, a chuckle coming from them both, "men, but in a position like coming out to your parents, it doesn't matter what age you are, you're suddenly transported back to being twelve and vulnerable and *scared*. You've got this big secret, which shouldn't even be that huge of a deal in the first place, and suddenly the entire world hinges on someone else's reaction to it. It's hard. But you did it, because you knew you wouldn't be happy otherwise. If that's not role model material, I don't know what is."

"On the upside, my mom took it in much better stride. She was caught off guard when I told her I was with a man, and even more surprised when I told her I was feeling something special for you. I don't think she was expecting me to find anything very serious after Anna, but the second she realized how much you mean to me, she broke into a teary smile and hugged the air out of my lungs. Said she could see how happy I was and that was all she ever wanted."

Shepard smiled at that. There was a kite shaped like a cartoon dragon cutting through the wind in the distance, its long green tail whipping back and forth with the shifting ocean winds, the clawed hands coming up and down and the face showing its teeth as the jaw flapped open and shut. "She sounds like a great person."

"She is. She got divorced from my dad back when I was in high school. I didn't understand it back then, but I see it now. They were just never a good match. From the start, it wasn't meant to work. My mom explained that she had fallen into a routine with my father, but that the routine was all it was. There was zero passion, and that was really hurting her. When she left, he went deep down a religious rabbit hole, coming out as a born-again Christian."

Shepard nodded. "That explains things."

"Yep."

"Well, I think he'll come around," Shepard said. "I think you're too important of a person to completely shut out of anyone's life. And Emma, there's no way anyone can stay away from her for too long."

"She's something else, isn't she?" Nick was looking out toward the waves. Shepard put a hand on his thigh. He was feeling more and more connected to Nick as the seconds passed, as the stories unraveled, as they both opened up in ways neither expected.

"With you as her father, she's bound to be."

(End of chapter)

24 NICHOLAS WHITE

Nick was baring it all. Everything was getting dumped on the table. He felt vulnerable. It scared him. Shepard could have easily thought it was too much drama and walked away from it all. From him. He wouldn't have been able to blame him, either. It was just a man running from a burning building instead of into it. Nick wasn't only dealing with a messy divorce and a nasty custody battle, but now he had a father who wanted nothing to do with him. His life was falling apart, as if he had picked up a handful of sand and let all the grains run through his parted fingers. All that was keeping him solid was Shepard. He was keeping him from thinking about everything else going on his life. He offered a moment of peace and serenity that not even the beach could give him, and Nick used to love coming out to the beach. He always found a way to relax when the ocean was feet away, whether it was by just letting his toes sink into the sand or grabbing a board and catching a wave. He hadn't surfed in a long time, but he remembered it being a great stress reliever back in college.

Now, it felt like he was being swallowed by a monster

wave every single day. Then Shepard came along with the life vest, ready to pull him to shore. He looked away from the foamy waters and to Shepard. He was looking incredibly handsome, with hair that was slightly mussed up from the wind, and cheeks that were tanned from the sun. It was a moment he couldn't resist. He leaned in for a kiss. Their lips were already familiar, parting almost instantly, their tongues dancing together. Nick brought a hand up and grabbed the back of Shepard's head, feeling his fingers slide through his hair, grabbing at it as they kissed harder.

"You're an incredible kisser," Shepard said when they separated, sounding a little out of breath.

"It takes two to tango," Nick replied. His smile matched Shepard's. He had to go back in for another kiss. He felt the urge rise through him. Their lips met again, their tongues going back to business. A soft moan rose from Nick's throat. The sound of the ocean surrounded them. From the slapping of waves on shore, to the gulls that squawked nearby, to the wind that swirled around the rock formation that bordered them.

When they separated again, Nick couldn't help but notice the front of Shepard's pants were looking fuller. Nick didn't have to look down at his own lap to know he was the same. Shepard bit on his lower lip. It was a move that drove Nick wild. He thought Shepard already looked sexy when he was doing regular things, so when he started doing sexy things, Nick was taken to another level. A level where his reason and logic were a little blurred and his brain would hand the wheel over to less thoughtful command centers. His dick twitched in his briefs.

He was feeling risky. There was no one on the stretch of beach in front of them, and everyone by the pier was obscured from view by the huge dark black rock that sat next to the bench. Nick reached down and grabbed the growing bulge in Shepard's pants. He smiled as he pushed in for another kiss. This one hotter than the last. Nick could feel Shepard growing in his hand, his cock pushing up against the zipper of his jeans, aching to break free.

I'd hate for him to break his jeans, guess my only option is unzipping them.

Nick's thoughts were hazy but his senses sharpened as he grabbed the zipper and tugged it down. He was hearing the ocean cheering them on, but he was also listening for the sounds of anyone approaching. They were conccaled from the popular section of the beach, but people could still walk down the shore and pass by their hidden little bench as they collected seashells. They would have no trouble seeing Nick collecting his own conch shell.

Shepard looked around, his eyes a little wider than usual. He looked down at Nick's hand, which had already pulled down his zipper.

"Right now?" Shepard asked, a little sheepishly. It turned Nick's body ten degrees warmer. He reached into Shepard's jeans and gave him his answer. Yes. Right now. He licked his lips and bent down as he pulled Shepard's hard cock and balls from the front of his briefs. He didn't pull anything down in case they needed to make a hasty exit. Nick was feeling daring. Not only were his hormones raging, but his adrenaline was pumping, creating a rush that was intoxicating. Shepard was already leaking a clear drop of precome. Nick licked it up, and then ran his tongue down Shepard's shaft. He looked up at Shepard, who appeared to have worked past any nerves he had been feeling. He lifted his ass off the bench, pushing his hard dick deeper into Nick's mouth. Nick couldn't get enough. He opened wide and went down farther, gripping the base with his hand, saliva dripping down, blotting the gray briefs Shepard was wearing.

He kept blowing him for a few more minutes, curling his toes into the sand as he tried to deep-throat Shepard. He came up for breath, the bright sun causing him to squint his eyes. He glanced around, making sure no one had snuck up on them. Shepard looked like he was in another world, a sexy grin on his face, his eyes locked on Nick's as Nick continued to hold Shepard's throbbing cock in his hand. He used his free hand to pull down the zipper on his own pants. Unlike Shepard, Nick had decided to go commando (he never learned his lesson from that one presentation). He pulled his cock out from the front of his jeans. Now both men were exposed, the ocean breeze caressing both of their hard dicks.

"My turn," Shepard said, licking his lips as he leaned down. He took Nick in his mouth and went to fucking town. He worked up a lather, spitting on Nick's cock and using it as lube while he stroked the lower half of his shaft with his hand and worked the top half with his lips. Nick was in heaven. He kept his eyes open, just in case someone walked by, but all he wanted to do was shut them and let his body float away with the pleasure.

Shepard's tongue swirled around the head as he continued to apply pressure with his hand to the base. Nick was getting closer. He could feel his core tightening.

"Come up," Nick said.

"Is there someone coming?" Shepard asked, sounding a little concerned, his hand moving to cover his dick.

"No, no," Nick assured him. "I just want to jerk you off."

"Oh, well in that case," Shepard said, grinning. He opened his legs more and pushed his cock out into the air, as if saying "come and get it" without opening his mouth. Nick spat in his palm and grabbed the velvet-soft length. Shepard did the same, spitting in his hand and reaching over to grab Nick's cock. They started off slow, their hands acting as though they were memorizing each other by touch alone. Nick leaned in and kiss Shepard, their strokes becoming faster. Nick tightened his grip. He knew exactly what he liked when he was jerking himself off, so he figured Shepard would like it, too.

And it seemed to be working. Shepard was grunting, his ass lifting from the bench, thrusting his cock harder into Nick's closed fist. Nick did the same. Shepard's hands knew exactly what to do. He was throbbing in the man's grip. They were both getting so close. Nick squeezed his grip a little tighter. Shepard had his eyes closed now. Nick could tell he was about to come. He aimed his cock out toward the sand, and sure enough, Shepard blew. He moaned as his cock pulsed in Nick's grip, blowing rope after rope of come out onto the sand. All the while, he kept his hand on Nick's hard cock.

Nick was pushed over the edge as soon as Shepard finished, returning back to his strokes. The sensation was all too much. Nick leaned forward and aimed his dick at the sand, coming an equally impressive amount at his feet, grunting and moaning and twitching all the while Shepard still had his hand tight around Nick's dick.

"Wow," Nick said, leaning back on the hard wooden bench.

"So is that why the ocean's so salty?"

The question caught Nick off guard and drew a big laugh out of him. "Yes, I think that's exactly why."

"Gross," Shepard said, laughing along with Nick. They stuffed themselves back into their pants and zipped up.

Shepard leaned over and rested his head on Nick's shoulder. Nick couldn't believe what he had just done, and how fucking hot it was. They stayed quiet for a few moments, taking it all in, watching the ocean waves rise and crash on the shore. A seagull swooped down into the ocean in front of them, cutting its beak across the water, coming up empty. Still, no one walked by them. It felt like they had taken a mini-trip to a secluded paradise, even though Nick could still hear the occasional "ding ding ding" of people winning prizes on the pier.

Shepard lifted his head off Nick's shoulder. "I love you," Shepard said. The words almost mixed in with the sounds of the ocean and yet sounded worlds apart at the same time. Nick wasn't expecting it, but he could also see how it was also the perfect time to say it.

Nick felt Shepard tense for a moment. He realized that the words most likely slipped through Shepard's lips without much thought behind them. A spur of the moment thing, reflecting the deepest feelings Shepard had.

"I love you, too," Nick said into Shepard's ear, giving him another kiss on the cheek before turning him around so they were face to face. Shepard looked part relieved and part in shock. He was smiling, which only made Nick want to kiss him even more. He pulled him in tighter and brought their lips together. Nick may not have been planning on falling this hard, this fast, but life rarely ever followed the plans. In fact, he was quickly learning that the best things in his life happened because life bucked the plans. Emma was unexpected and also the light of Nick's life. Hell, even medical school wasn't even in the plans, not until his third year of university when it was almost too late. And of course there was Shepard, a man who came barreling into his life from left field. He defied the plans and opened Nick up again to love. He knew he felt it from the moment he laid eyes on Shepard. It was dimmer back then, easily pushed aside and attributed to devilish good looks. But Nick had known there was something much deeper than that, and he wondered if that was what caused him to initially fight it off. He hated to think of how close he had been to pushing Shepard away permanently. From picking on him with dumb questions to physically pushing him away, when all Nick had really wanted to do that night was pull him in and never let him go.

It was all fear. And he was letting it all go. Like an anchor dropped into the waves, the rope getting cut free, the weight disappearing from Nick's shoulders. He was no longer scared. He knew that Shepard was the one. He could trust him with Emma, he could see Shepard raising her right alongside him. It was something he had been thinking about for weeks now. And there were some days when the fear had been stronger, gripping at his throat, threatening to overtake him and cause him to shut down again. But that never happened, because what they had was so much stronger than a baseless fear.

It was love. They had pure, unadulterated love.

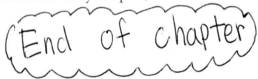

25 SHEPARD KENSWORTH

THREE DAYS LATER

(Done reading)

Shepard sat on the couch with Emma bouncing on his lap, her chubby cheeks pushed up into the biggest of smiles, her one lone tooth breaking through and leading the way for the rest. She was currently being endlessly entertained by Shepard, who found out he had a knack for making funny faces. He had a few he just kept on rotation and was switching between those; his lips twisting and eyebrows scrunching and forehead wrinkling, all with his eyes crossing.

"Be careful," Nick said, sitting down next to Shepard, setting two glasses of ice cold water down on stone coasters, "Your face could get stuck like that."

"No joke," Shepard said, "I was actually scared of that as a kid. That and swallowing a watermelon seed. Have you ever seen that *Rugrats* episode?!"

Nick laughed, the sound filling his living room. The window was open so the sound of birds mixed with the city drifted in, along with a cool breeze. "I think I know which one you're talking about. Where Chuckie swallowed the watermelon seed and so the babies shrunk themselves to get it out."

"Yeah, and then Angelica starts watering the seed, making it explode inside Chukie."

"...That's messed up. And that was a *kid's* show?"

They both started cracking up. "I wonder if that's what inspired me to go to medical school, now that I think about it," Nick said, catching his breath.

"I grew out of the goofy-face paralysis, but I'm still a little suspicious around watermelons if I'm being honest." Shepard twisted his face again and looked to Emma. "Don't you agree? Yes, you do, don't you?" He looked to Nick, "She said she does."

"Oh, you speak baby now?"

"Quite fluently, yes. Have anything you want me to tell her?"

"That I love her very much."

Shepard turned to Emma, whose big eyes were fixated on Shepard's face. "Googagoo, googity-goo. Love, uh, goo, ga. Ok? Ok." Shepard broke into a laugh, matching Nick's. Emma was equally entertained, although who knew exactly why. She was adorable in a light blue onesie with a cartoon stethoscope stitched on the front. Shepard had bought her the onesie a couple of days ago. He had seen it online and knew he needed to buy it.

Emma mumbled something that sounded suspiciously like "daddy". She looked to Nick and burst into another fit of giggles. It filled Shepard with a joy he didn't think possible. The sound was so innocent, so *pure*.

"Did you ever think about having kids?" Nick asked. The question didn't catch Shepard off guard. He had been thinking about it, and knew it was something that should be discussed.

"Definitely," Shepard answered without a moment's hesitation. "I've always seen myself with kids down the line. I was never sure at what point they'd come, but I knew it was something I really wanted."

Nick looked happy at that. He was about to respond when his cell started going off. The ringtone wasn't like his regular ringtone. This one sounded like a damn tornado alarm. It made Shepard jump a little bit, startling Emma, who was looking around the room for the source of the abrasive sound.

"Shit, sorry." Nick jumped up from the couch and grabbed his phone off the table. "It's the hospital." Nick answered the call and walked a few feet away. Shepard turned back to Emma, trying to calm her down. She still looked a little spooked but didn't cry, which Shepard was thankful for.

Nick finished the call and hurried to his room, calling behind his shoulder, "There was a bus crash and they're low on hands in the OR." Less than a minute later, Nick was back in the living room, wearing his scrubs and holding his white coat. "Do you mind watching her for the next few hours?"

"Absolutely not," Shepard said.

"Ok, great. You know where all her things are. I should hopefully be back before midnight." Nick leaned down and kissed the top of Emma's head. From there, he moved for a quick kiss from Shepard and turned to run out the door.

"Well," Shepard said, looking down at a still-smiling Emma, "looks like it's just you and me, girl."

AN HOUR WAS all it took for Shepard to experience

some more of the joys and terrors of having a baby around. He was having the time of his life, but he was also quite nervous he would do something to inadvertently trigger a temper tantrum that he wouldn't know how to control. Sure, he knew how to deliver a baby into the world, but that didn't mean he knew how to babysit one. Thankfully, Emma was incredibly well behaved and was largely entertained by just lying in her crib and staring up at a goofy Shepard, who had made so many different faces at her, he was sure starting to wonder if it *was* possible to get his face stuck. She was seemingly living for every second of it. By the time she looked like she was growing bored of the faces (thankfully around the time Shepard's face started cramping), he brought out the different toys. She couldn't walk yet, but she could crawl, and she loved crawling for her big, soft teddy bear. He pretended to give it a voice and danced it around her crib, making her laugh to no end. It was the most innocent sound in the world and Shepard felt himself loving her more than he thought he could. It was a type of affection he wasn't necessarily expecting to feel toward Emma. He was sure he wanted a family, but he wasn't sure about the timeline, and kids had previously freaked him out a little. But things were changing faster than Emma could fill up a diaper (and, as Shepard found out earlier, that was *very* fast).

It was like a baptism by fire. All he had to do was spend a good amount of quality time with a baby to realize he knew exactly how to handle them. Beyond that, there was a magic to Emma. He couldn't stop himself from leaning into the crib and giving her a kiss on the top of her head. She smelled like lilac and baby powder. She giggled the second she felt the kiss and then continued crawling to the opposite end of the crib where her teddy bear was sitting, arms open for her. She reached him and grabbed a leg. She fell forward, laughing the entire way as she stuffed her face in the bear's belly. Shepard helped her get back up. She went back at it again and again.

A few hours later and Emma had fallen asleep and Shepard was hanging out in the living room. He was scrolling through Twitter while lying down on the couch when the doorbell rang. Shepard jumped up, not expecting the sudden noise. Emma was a heavy sleeper and seemed to have the ability to sleep through a nuclear attack, so the doorbell didn't wake her. He pocketed his phone and walked toward the door. Maybe Nick had forgotten his house key when he left, or it could have been a package that needed a signature. He looked through the peephole and saw a man staring back, his balding head of thin brown hair lifting slightly in the breeze. He looked down at his watch and went to press the doorbell again. Shepard hurriedly opened the door, not wanting to press his luck with Emma's superpower to sleep through noise.

"Oh, hi," the man said, clearly expecting someone else to open the door. "Is Nick here?"

Shepard frowned and shook his head. "No, sorry, he had an emergency he had to get to at the hospital. Is there a message you wanted to give him? Something you needed to pick up?"

"Sort of," the man said. He was a big guy, with a thinning head of light brown hair. "Is Emma in there?"

Shepard's brows drew together. The man must have sensed his hesitation and realized he was a total stranger to Shepard. "My name is Chris. I'm Emma's uncle."

Shepard nodded then. Now things made a little more sense. "I'm Shepard," he said, reaching a hand out to shake. Chris looked at his hand and back up at his face, smiling weakly in place of a handshake. Shepard took his hand back, figuring he was a germaphobe and maybe preferred to stay away from physical contact. "I'm taking care of Emma until Nick gets back."

"How does he know you?"

"We're, uhm, well, from the hospital. I'm a doctor there." Shepard was stumbling. He wasn't sure if Nick had come out to Chris and he definitely didn't want to out Nick to anyone he hadn't spoken to. Especially since things hadn't gone well with his father, the last thing he wanted was to trigger another family fight.

But it was obvious. So damn obvious. Shepard, as always, had an aversion to lying. His body just couldn't pull it off. He could feel his cheeks getting pink, which only made them turn a shade darker, as if the joke was to see how red he could get. Chris wasn't dumb, either. He could see right through Shepard. Chris already seemed suspicious of him from the second he opened the door, but now it was like he had some sort of confirmation. He crossed his arms against his chest. His posture was straight and stern. His face looked like someone who had just walked past an overflowing trashcan, the scent too offensive to hide the disgust.

"End things with Nick."

"Excuse me?"

"What you two are doing is wrong. You're brazenly raising that poor child in pure sin. Consequences are obvious, don't make them worse for that little girl. Leave. Let me take care of her until Nick gets back. If you stay, things will only get worse."

Shepard was in awe of what he was hearing. A silver cross hung around Chris's neck, catching the white porch light shining down from the corner. "I think you should go now," Shepard said. "You can talk to Nick when he gets back, but I really don't feel comfortable with you threatening me right now." He had to call it out for what it was. Maybe he could get Chris to back off. He didn't want anything escalating, especially not with Emma sleeping a few rooms away.

"Fine," Chris said, chin up in the air. "I came here to make things easier. Anna would have come but she had another migraine."

"Make things easier?" Shepard crossed his arms. "Why would Anna need to be here? Today's Nick's day to have Emma."

Chris looked like he was about to speak but stopped himself at the last second. He brought a hand up to his chest and rubbed the cross. "Have a nice day," Chris said. He turned and walked back to his car, leaving behind a bewildered Shepard.

(End of chapter)

Why does Chris want Shepard to break up w/ Nick?
The story continues...

The first thing Nick did when he got out of the operating room was turn his phone on. He always had a fear of something happening with Emma and him not knowing. He felt good about Shepard taking care of her, though. Usually, whenever he turned his phone back on, the only notifications that popped up were some emails from Banana Republic along with pop-ups reminding him he had pending Candy Crush invitations.

I didn't even know people still played that.

His phone screen lit alive with more notifications than Nick was expecting, and none of the new alerts had anything to do with deeply discounted and well fitting khaki pants. They were all missed calls. He had two from Anna, two from Chris, and one from Shepard. Another three were from his lawyer. Only one of those callers had left a voicemail, and it was his lawyer. His hands immediately clammed up. This couldn't be good.

Nick felt his hands take on a small tremble. He wanted to drop his phone down on the floor. It felt hot in his hands.

Like it was overheating. He knew it was all in his head, but he couldn't shake it. His entire body felt like it was catching fire. He took a deep breath, steadied his nerves, and pulled up Shepard's number. He didn't even think about listening to the voicemail first. He just wanted to talk to make sure Emma was ok.

"Hey, Nick."

"Shepard, is Emma alright?"

"Yeah, of course, she's sleeping. Why? What made you think she wasn't?"

Nick checked his watch. It was eleven-thirty. He had been in the operating room for five hours. What the hell could have happened in those five hours that had everyone calling him?

"I'm not exactly sure," Nick said, gathering his stuff from the lockers next to the OR.

"Something weird did happen. Emma's uncle, Chris, showed up. He didn't really make it clear why he was here, though."

"What does he want?" Nick was sinking deeper into a pit of confusion. "Alright, I'm going to call my lawyer. I'm headed home. Should be there in fifteen."

"See you soon," Shepard said.

Nick was already at his car when he called his lawyer, Sherry Hammer. "Hi, Nick." She sounded upset. It was always obvious whenever Sherry was angry. Her entire demeanor changed. Nick thought that sometimes it was even intimidating. He had liked that passion about her. He thought it would come in handy if they ever had to go into court.

"What's going on, Sherry? I've got Anna and you trying to call me."

"We've got bad news, Nick." He could hear the shuffling of papers in the background, past Sherry's voice. Someone else was speaking. It was probably Ben, Sherry's sharp assistant who was never far from his boss. "Ok, get me the judge, right now." Sherry was talking but it was clear she covered the phone with her palm, her words coming in muted. When she came back, Nick was on edge.

"We got a notice, Nick. It's from the judge. She's denying you any custody and visitation rights, citing proof of your hazardous lifestyle. Effective immediately."

"My *what?*" Nick leaned on his car's open door. "What does she mean *'hazardous lifestyle'*?! I'm a fucking doctor, I've never done any drugs in my life, I'm a responsible adult, what the fuck is she talking about? *Hazardous?*" The heat Nick was feeling earlier started to grow in intensity. He felt like the flames were licking at his chin now.

"That's what I'm trying to find out now, Nick. Something is going on but I'm not exactly sure yet."

"Fuck," Nick said. He was feeling sick. That had to be why Chris showed up at his place. He was probably there to pick Emma up from him. As if they were scared he would run off with her as soon as he found out.

I should. I fucking should. Me, her, and Shepard. We'll run. Far.

Nick knew it was a stupid indulgence, but he let himself think it. He got into his car and couldn't even will himself to press the ignition button.

"You'll need to bring Emma to Anna's right away. I tried everything I could to get them to hold it, but the judge wasn't budging. I've never seen someone so aggressive about it, too. He was insistent that Emma go back to Anna's as soon as you were notified."

Nick felt weak. His limbs didn't really work. He was moving them, but things felt off.

"What can we do?" Nick said. The full weight of it was hitting him. He would be driving home only to say goodbye to his baby girl. Only minutes ago, he was excited to get home so he could see her sleeping face. Now, he would need to wake her up so that he could deliver her back to her monster of a mother. Nick felt his eyes grow wet. He looked in the rearview mirror. Tears already streaked down his cheeks. He hadn't even realized he had been crying.

"I'm doing everything I can, Nick. I've got witness testimony about your character along with all of the documentation you've kept over your care for Emma. I've got pictures upon pictures of you and her, and I've got hope that this won't be permanent. But, for right now, we need to follow the court orders. We can't get into any hot water. Don't worry, Nick. I promise you, you'll have Emma back in your arms soon."

Nick wanted to believe her, but all he could do was sink deeper into the darkness. He could feel inky black tentacles wrapping around his ankles, pulling him down further and further. He wasn't sure how he would make it back up to the surface.

NICK MANAGED to compose himself long enough for the fifteen-minute drive back home. He sat in his driveway, his forehead on the steering wheel, his face contorted as cries lashed through him like whips, coming in waves. He was devastated. He felt helpless. How could this be happening? When everything felt so damn right. When he was feeling more alive than ever. Now, he felt like a husk. He hadn't even said goodbye to her yet and he already felt like a member of the walking dead.

Finally, the cries subsided. He looked at himself in the rearview mirror. His eyes were puffy and red, his lashes dark and heavy with tears. He rubbed his eyes, wiped his cheeks, and steeled himself for the moments to come.

"Nick," Shepard said, jumping up from the couch as soon as the door opened. He ran over to Nick. "What happened?" He must have figured something was up from Nick's slumped shoulders and quivering upper lip. He was trying so hard to hold it all back, but every step made it more real.

"Anna did it," Nick managed to say without breaking down, "She got sole custody."

"No," Shepard said, his hand coming up to cover his mouth. "How? That's impossible. There has to be a mistake."

"Judge cited my hazardous lifestyle."

"Then for sure this is a mistake. Hazardous? What are they thinking?"

Nick shook his head, his hand massaging his forehead. "My lawyer's trying to get more information. The judge wants Emma to go to Anna tonight."

Shepard face cracked. He took a step back, his hand dropping from his mouth but his expression still looking just as shocked. "Nick... no, there has to be something we can do. Someone we can call."

"Nothing. Not for tonight, at least." Nick wanted to put up a fight, but Sherry was right, the last thing he needed was to get in trouble for not following court orders. Now wasn't the time. And it was already the middle of the night. If there was anyone that could help them, they wouldn't be able to contact them anyway, everything was closed. No,

Nick had to give up Emma for now. He needed to keep his record as clean as possible, because he *was* going to fight, and he *was* going to get her back.

For now, though, he let himself fall into Shepard's open arms, his head buried in Shepard's shoulder. He allowed himself a moment of weakness before he had to put up a strong front for his daughter.

Nick just lost custody of Emma (his baby daughter) to Anna (his ex wife!! (insert drama music)...

More intensity is ahead...

(done)

This is my fault. Holy shit. This is my fault.

Shepard didn't want to say anything because he wasn't entirely sure of what was going on, but he couldn't help but think that he was the one to blame for all of this. That must have been what Chris meant when he was giving Shepard the option to leave. Shepard wondered if he was giving him a chance to avoid this entire thing.

But why? And what the hell did he have on them?

Shepard pushed past the guilt. He would deal with that later. What he needed in that moment was answers.

"What's Chris's last name?" Shepard asked, while he pulled his phone from his shorts.

"Santiago."

Shepard opened his text messages and found the ones with his cousin, Zane. "I need you to look into Christopher Santiago. He's Anna's brother, and I think he might be involved in this somehow." He sent the message, knowing his cousin would read it, regardless of the time. Sure enough, a reply was sent a few moments later.

"Already been looking into him. Getting close to putting something together. I'll be in touch with Nick soon."

Shepard read the message out loud. It didn't seem to do much to calm Nick. Shepard sent another message to Zane, explaining that shit was hitting the fan and that the judge was granting sole custody to Anna. He figured there wasn't a lot that could bring Nick out of the hole he was sinking into, but maybe Zane could find something, anything. All Shepard could do for now was be there as a shoulder to lean on. He would help Nick get through this, and then they would figure out a way to get Emma back. They would do it together.

Unless... unless me leaving is the answer to this.

That was what Chris meant. But what did he have to do with the judge's decision?

"What did Chris say?" Nick asked. He was massaging the bridge of his nose, no doubt in an attempt to release all the tension boiling under his skin.

"He said, well he figured out we were together. And he told me to break up with you. He said it would fix things."

Nick brought his hand down from his face. He was looking straight at Shepard. "You don't believe him, right?"

"No, no, of course not." Shepard couldn't lie. His eyes grew moist and his cheeks grew red. Nick noticed the shift.

"You do... *Jesus*, you do. Now you're going to leave me, too." Nick was stepping back and shaking his head.

"Nick, that's not it, at all. I'd *never* leave you. I'm here for you. I'm not going to let you go through this alone."

Shepard's words seemed to have an effect. Nick's shoulders released the tension they were storing and slumped down a bit. He shut his eyes, bringing his hand back up to his face. "I'm sorry, Shep. I'm losing it. I'm scared and angry and fucking helpless."

Seeing Nick like this was tearing Shepard's heart apart. Nick was always a picture of stoic strength, carrying himself with his chest out and chin up. Now, he looked defeated. Slumped and sad. His eyes puffy and his expression tired. Shepard could never find it in himself to leave Nick, no matter what kind of garbage Chris talked. He was going to stick by his man and he was going to get his daughter back, he was sure of it.

"How is he even sure we're together? I never said anything." Nick was trying to put the pieces together.

"I'm not entirely sure. I didn't say anything either."

Nick's phone rang, the sudden sound startling the both of them. Nick looked at the screen and his face paled. "Anna," he answered, venom in his tone. "What the fuck is going on?"

Shepard could hear what she was saying from where he stood. "I'm getting my daughter back, that's what's going on."

"Sole custody, Anna? Because of my lifestyle? What lies did you spit out?"

"I didn't have to lie, Nick. I had all the proof I needed. You're the one lying, Nick. Were you fucking guys when you and I were together, too? Huh? Is that why you divorced me?"

"I divorced you because you're a lying, manipulative cunt."

Shepard felt like that was a line worth applauding, but he stopped himself from clapping.

"I never cheated on you, not with another woman or a man," Nick continued, "And who I love now is none of your business."

"Oh, so you love him? That's rich, considering you could barely say the word to me. I thought you were incapable of it."

"So is that what this is about? Me being with a man?"

"Nick, I'm just calling to remind you that Emma needs to be here in the next thirty-minutes or I'm calling the police." He could hear Chris in the backroom, almost as if he were cheering Anna on.

Nick turned away from Shepard. Shepard reached out and put a hand on Nick's back, thinking it was the smallest gesture he could do, but he didn't want to stand idle either. He wished he had the power to absorb all this negativity, taking it away from Nick. He didn't deserve any of this. He was a great man, an amazing father, an incredible doctor.

"I'll see you in thirty minutes, Nick." And just like that, Anna hung up the phone. Nick's hand dropped to his side, the phone falling out of his grip and landing face down on the floor with a smack. Shepard bent down and picked it up. He set it down on the table and then straightened. He looked into Nick's eyes, seeing the turmoil roaring like a storm in his normally calm gaze. Shepard reached forward and grabbed both of Nick's hands.

"This is so fucked up. Anna somehow found out about us. I read about this happening to another couple online. A gay man's ex-wife cited her morals and values not being consistent with the way her ex-husband was living. The judge, who was a well-known homophobe, sided with the mother. That was in Alabama, I never thought it could happen here."

Shepard felt himself burning inside. He hated how cruel the world could be sometimes. He could occasionally fool himself into thinking things were all fine and dandy, but then prejudice and hate would strike again, reminding

Shepard that there were still people in this world who would rather throw him off a building than allow him a same-sex marriage. It was a terrible thought that took root at the base of his brain.

"I need to say goodbye to Emma." Nick was speaking with his gaze turned down to the floor. He let go of Shepard's hands and walked solemnly toward Emma's bedroom. Shepard waited for him in the living room. He didn't feel right, hovering over Nick's shoulder as he woke up his baby, only to have to say goodbye to her.

A couple of minutes later and Nick was back in the living room, his eyes red, a sleepy and confused Emma held in his arms. Shepard walked toward them, already feeling his eyes well up with tears. He realized this was his time to also have to say goodbye. He wanted to hope against all hope that this would all be fixed, but he couldn't push away that seed of fear and despair that had planted itself. He could barely get the words out. He didn't want to break down in front of Nick. He knew that was the last thing he needed. Shepard had to stay strong for all three of them.

"Hi, baby girl," Shepard said, his throat and chest feeling tight. "This isn't a forever kind of goodbye, ok?"

Nick was sniffling. Shepard didn't want to drag this out any further. Emma was already getting antsy and every second that passed would only made it infinitely more hard for Nick. He had to say goodbye to him, too. But he was certain he'd see Nick again. He wouldn't be going anywhere. He'd be waiting right there for Nick to get home, so they could hold each other as the night grew even darker.

"I'll see you soon, ok?" Shepard reassured Nick, giving him a kiss on the lips. Nick didn't say anything. Shepard knew he was steadying himself for what he had to do. "Want me to go with you guys?"

"No, no, that's ok," Nick assured. "Stay here. Try to get some sleep."

Shepard knew he wasn't going to be sleeping much for the next few days, but he nodded and promised he'd try anyway. Nick turned and left with Emma, locking the door behind him, the sound of the lock blasting through the living room like a bomb sealing Shepard's fate.

With Nick gone, Shepard broke down. He allowed himself to let it all out. He fell onto the couch, his head buried in a pillow. It smelled like Emma. Lilacs and baby powder. Shepard couldn't comprehend what happened. They had spent the entire day together, living it up to the fullest, taking Emma to the park and watching her gawk at the ducks in the water. They laughed when she burped and then cried at the smell. They watched as she met another baby, their gurgles and gagas almost synching up for a moment. Everything had been so damn perfect. Shepard couldn't remember ever having such a great day.

If only he knew the kind of storm that had been heading their way all along.

No. I'm glad I didn't know.

If he had, there would be no way he would have enjoyed his time with Emma.

We'll get her back.

Shepard was putting himself back together again. This all came as a shock, especially delivered in the middle of the night the way it was, and out of nowhere with little to no time to prepare. Clearly the judge had it out for them and wanted Emma out of Nick's life as fast as possible. It made Shepard sick to think about. All Nick did was love the girl.

Shepard got up from the couch. His mouth was dry. A cold glass of water was what he needed. Maybe a cold glass of wine, on second thought. He started toward the kitchen, completely unware of the shadow that had appeared at the window behind him.

Shepard was pouring himself water when he heard the glass shatter.

Who is ^staring Shepard ^at through the window, will he or she harm him?

The story / conclusion is underway...

(finished)

He drove slow, even though the roads were empty. Every mile he put between him and Emma felt like a fresh stab in the chest with the biggest, nastiest butcher knife around. He had the radio playing but had to turn it off. The music was only making things worse. He sat in silence at a red light, wondering how things got to the point where he was losing his rights to see his daughter.

The goodbye was the hardest part. He thought looking into Anna's eyes would be the difficult part, but that didn't matter to him. All he saw when he looked at Anna was a road block. A wall that needed to be demolished so that he could hold his baby girl again. He managed to hold back the tears in front of Anna. His eyes almost hurt with how badly they wanted to stream out. He didn't want to show Anna any sign of weakness. He stiffened his upper lip and kissed Emma on the forehead, promising this wasn't over. Chris had been standing behind Anna the entire time, his arms crossed and his face set as though he were doing a bad impression of a bodyguard. As if Nick was going to start anything with his daughter around. He would never put her at risk like that.

Another reason why this sole custody is bullshit.

Nick had to hold on to that thought. He needed to repeat it like a mantra. He couldn't lose his cool. Logic was going to win. The good people were going to win. He knew the world often gave victories to villains, but not in his story. He was going to make sure of it.

But first, he needed to go home and collapse into Shepard, letting those big arms wrap around him, briefly bringing him back to the good ol' days, when there was barely a problem in the world he couldn't solve. He knew he wouldn't feel completely ok until he had Emma back, but he was confident that Shepard could lift some of the anguish that was coating him like oil from a spill.

He started to tear up, but for another reason now. He was becoming overwhelmed with how thankful he was that he had Shepard in his life. He may not have been dating him for an incredibly long time, but it certainly felt like he'd known Shepard his entire life. And that sense of comfort meant that Nick could truly feel safe around him, even when the world felt like it was crashing and burning all around him. At least, when he was with Shepard, there was a kind of pause button pressed. He could lose himself in the way Shepard smelled, or how he spoke, or the way he smiled. Anything he did had the ability to teleport Nick into a different mindset. It was one of the reasons Nick was sure that Shepard was the one. He couldn't think of anyone else who offered him that same sense of comfort. Or even a fraction of that comfort. Maybe at one point it was his father, who was a solid support against life's tougher times as Nick grew up, but that felt like it was an eternity ago. Things were completely different. And that only made Nick even more grateful he had Shepard in his life. If he didn't, he may very well have been alone. Sure he had a couple of friends at work, and his mother still supported him, but other than that, he wouldn't have anyone to weather this storm with.

He rubbed at his eyes, making sure he could see the road clearly. The last thing he needed was a car crash. He took a few deep breaths and lowered his window, letting the cool night wind blow in as he drove. The street was wide, the palm trees tall, backlit by a full moon that hung unusually low in the sky. Nick could make out the massive craters scarring the surface like huge pimples.

Nick was almost home, still distraught and feeling empty, when he got a call. He was on his street, just about to pull into his driveway. He reached for his phone and saw it was Zane from the detective agency. It was twelve-thirty in the morning, so this had to have been important.

"Zane, what's going on? Please tell me you found something."

"I found quiet a few somethings. I need you to come into my office."

"Now?"

"Right now."

Nick stopped the car and made a U-turn, driving away from his house. He figured Shepard was probably sleeping.

The drive to the agency wasn't a long one, especially since there wasn't any traffic to get through that late at night. Another benefit was an ample amount of street parking. Nick pulled up to the front of Stonewall Investigations. He wasn't sure what he was expecting anymore, but he was trying hard not to get his hopes up. The night was chilly. The trees that sat at the front of the agency rustled in the wind, their dried branches clattering together as if they were praying for a good rainfall soon.

By the time Nick reached the front door, it was already opening. Andrew stood in the doorway. He looked tired, wearing an old pair of gym shorts and an oversized black t-shirt that was probably meant for sleeping only. But Andrew's eyes were bright and alert. He was running on adrenaline, Nick could tell. There were plenty of nights he experienced that rush, knowing exactly what it felt like.

Holy shit, maybe they really did find something that could get Emma back.

"Nick, come in, Zane is in his office." Andrew turned and started leading Nick through the hall. The place took on a different quality at night, when the offices were empty and only the hallway light had been turned on, throwing the rooms past the hallway in shadows that left an eerie feeling in the air. The cozy warmth that Nick had first experienced when he entered Stonewall Investigations was replaced by something colder. The energy was different, and Nick knew it wasn't entirely because of the time of night. This wasn't just because Nick didn't like the dark. There was something else in the air. As if whatever Zane had found was already seeping out into the atmosphere, spreading a miasma of negativity.

"Zane, it's Dr. White." Andrew entered the room with Nick following right behind. Zane's office was a controlled chaos. There were books stacked upon books in a few different piles next to Zane's desk, the glass tabletop covered in organized piles of paper clipped files. Andrew took a seat on an old beige couch that hadn't always been inside Zane's office, by the floor-to-ceiling window, his laptop laying open on the floor, its screen glowing as if it were asking for attention. Next to the couch was a cardboard box, papers and folders sticking out the top. There were papers laying on the couch, too. Andrew's workspace wasn't as organized as Zane's, with no paperclips in sight around the couch.

"Nick, how are you?" Zane got up from behind his desk. Instead of shaking Nick's hand, he opened his arms for a hug. Nick appreciated it. Zane obviously knew what was going on, and although he probably couldn't fully grasp the pain Nick was feeling, his comfort was definitely welcome.

His information was more than welcome, though.

"What did you find?" Nick asked, dodging the question about how he was. He didn't want to get into his feelings.

"Sit," Zane said as he went back to his chair. His voice, still as powerful as when they first met, had taken on a softer tone. The way Zane was acting was beginning to make Nick nervous. What had he found out? He didn't look as bed-ready as Andrew did, but Nick could tell that was only because Zane hadn't left the office in days and was probably wearing the same shirt and slacks he had come in with.

"First let me show you these photos." Zane opened up a blue folder and pulled out a stack of photos. He reached over the desk and handed them to Nick. Immediately, Nick saw the side of Anna's face. She was outside of her apartment building, speaking to someone. A man. He looked vaguely familiar. His face was in full display for the photo, which looked like it had been taken from across the street and zoomed in. The quality was a little grainy, but still clear enough to make out the details.

"Wait... that's Rick. Shepard's ex. What is he doing talking with Anna?"

Nick set that photo down and looked at the next one. This one was taken outside of a church. Nick recognized it, a big chapel near Santa Monica. It had a view of the beach and a beautiful stained glass window set above the entrance. In front of the church stood Chris, speaking to Rick with a hand on his shoulder. They were both wearing church clothes, and other people were coming out of the church, marking the end of a service. Nick looked up from the photo to Zane. Confusion was fully setting in, now.

"I want you to see the photos first so you don't doubt for a second what I'm about to tell you."

The next photo was of Rick, but this one was printed out from a traffic camera. And Rick was behind the wheel of a bright red Ferrari, his hair was a bright blonde and he was wearing a pretty thick beard, but Nick was sure that was him.

"That was shortly after he stole that Ferrari and then dropped off the grid a couple of years ago."

"What's going on?"

"Your suspicions were right," Zane said, "Anna is up to no good. She's addicted to pills and she's getting them from Rick, who was introduced to her by Chris."

Nick's jaw dropped to the floor. "What the fuck?"

Zane leaned in, over the table. "It was when we started tailing Chris a few days ago that everything made sense. He leads a relatively simple life, to people that aren't really paying attention at least. He goes to church, volunteers at the soup kitchen, and works days at a real estate firm as an administrative assistant. Following him painted a different picture, though. One of late nights spent in seedy spots known for cruising for men. I saw him speaking with Rick, who seemed a little out of place leaving the church service one day. Chris was also being very handsie with Rick, something I noticed he didn't do with anyone else. A couple hours later and I followed them to their secret hook-up spot. A Motel Six by the highway."

"But, Chris... but he's, he's gay?"

"Deep in the closet. And resents himself for it, but resents you even more."

"Huh?"

"We found these on his phone." Zane pulled out another set of photos. Nick saw his back in the center of the frame, Shepard next to him, their hands linked together between them. This was from their date in Santa Monica. Nick didn't even ask how Zane got the photos, he just wanted to know why Chris had them.

"These were the photos he sent to the judge presiding over your custody case, who also happens to go to the same church Chris does. Chris and the judge are close friends. Chris knew exactly how to influence him."

"Holy fuck."

"Exactly," Andrew said from the couch. He had been typing away on his laptop and just then chimed in.

"That's what the judge meant by hazardous lifestyle?!" Nick's blood was boiling. This was what had caused his rights to be stripped from him. The fact that he was holding the hand of someone he loved. Oh, the fucking horror.

"And Chris hates himself so much, he's lashing out at you through the judge."

"Is that legal? Can they do that?" Nick remembered the forums he had deep-dived through, but the law was constantly changing.

"The judge is discriminating against your sexuality. Unfortunately, that's still looked past in a few different states. But not here in California. I think this judge was trying to find a loophole, and was probably going to be up all night looking for it. He had until tomorrow to hand everything over to your lawyer. I'm already working on getting another judge to overturn the ruling based on discrimination."

Nick breathed a sigh of relief, but there was still so much to process, he couldn't relax. "And Anna? What drugs? Jesus, I need to get Emma out of there."

He moved to get up from the chair.

"Wait, Nick," Zane said, putting a hand out on the table. "She's ok. I've passed all this on to Child Protective Services. You'll see there's a recording I took of Anna speaking about the drugs to Rick a few hours ago, while she was waiting for you to bring Emma. They were whispering out by the park near her apartment, thinking no one could hear them. I caught it all on tape. It's all the proof they need. They're working with the police to make sure they get Emma out of there safe and sound before the morning. The agent I'm working with is keeping me in the loop with constant updates. They don't want you there in case Anna reacts negatively to you. She's already going to be angry, we don't want to instigate anything. Don't worry, you'll have Emma in your arms again before the sun comes up."

Nick leaned back into the chair. Those were words he didn't think he'd hear, especially not so soon after he had to say goodbye to Emma. This night had been a total roller coaster ride of emotions, and Nick *hated* roller coasters. He wanted to get off the ride and back onto solid ground.

"She's addicted to oxycodone. Chris doesn't know about it. I think he genuinely believes Anna when she says she's feeling sick and locks herself up in her room. He doesn't know Rick is a drug-dealer either. Nor does he know Rick isn't even his real name."

"It's not?"

"His real name is Gabriel Del Valle." Zane pushed a black folder across the glass desk. "This is Rick's criminal history. He's been changing identities for years now, moving from state to state and giving different stories everywhere he went. One of those identities is Hanson Morreno, a man suspected for two murders in Ohio. Apparently he baited two guys off *Grindr*, dated them both without the other knowing, and then killed them both at the same time. I think he joined the church this time around for some deeper cover."

Nick felt like throwing up. "So the guy Shepard dated has an M.O. for murdering guys he's fucked?"

Zane nodded, his lips pursed tight. "But don't worry. The cops already have Del Valle's home surrounded. I called them and filled them in before you got here."

Nick breathed a sigh of relief. He hadn't realized he was holding his breath until then. "So they've got him?"

"From what it sounds like, yeah."

"Holy shit." Nick dropped his head into his hands. He couldn't believe everything he had just learned. Zane was right in showing him the photos first. "Thank you, Zane. Thank you." Nick felt so relieved that everything was all over, and it was because of the incredible detective work Zane and his team had done. He was soon going to be able to hold his daughter and Shepard whenever he damn well wanted, without any time limits or judgment or fear. He was excited for the first time that night. He was allowing himself to feel the hope he had stuffed down to the depths of his soul only hours before. He was seeing the light at the end of the tunnel, after all.

Now, he just wanted to get back to Shepard and wait with him until they could see Emma again.

Life is finally back on track.

End of chapter

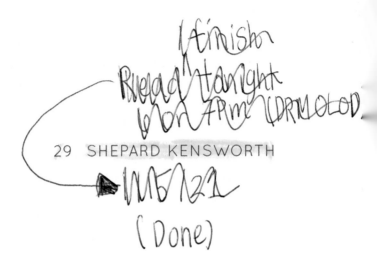

29 SHEPARD KENSWORTH

Shepard dropped the glass of water on the floor, thick glass shards flying in all different directions. Someone was inside the house. The kitchen was an open plan, so it faced out into the living room. Shepard ducked behind the island, as if that would protect him from the intruder. His palms were cold and sweaty. His heart was racing.

"Shepard? I saw you through the window. I know you're in here."

Shepard couldn't believe it. That voice... it was Rick. The man had officially lost it. What the fuck was he thinking? Shepard stood from behind the island, his pocket a little heavier as he got up. He knew there was no use hiding. Rick had seen him. He knew he was inside the house. He was going to confront this and end it once and for all.

When he was standing he saw the gun; its cold, dark barrel raised and aimed squarely at Shepard's chest. He could feel it as though it were pressed up against his bare skin. If he closed his eyes, Shepard was sure he could trace a circle around the spot where the bullet would shred through him. He could see its trajectory as though someone drew it with chalk in the air.

It was a weird feeling, getting a gun pointed at you by a man wearing a sinister smile. Death felt so close, a piece of Shepard was almost welcoming it in like an old friend, one he hadn't seen in years. The other part of Shepard was rocketed into high gear. His blood pressure, his senses, his anxiety. Everything was soaring through the roof. Scents and sights became sharper. Colors more clear. Shepard's thoughts were far from clear, though. It was like someone had pressed play on seven different sound systems. Should he run? Stay frozen? Grab a pan? Beg for his life? Bargain with him?

"What... what, Rick, what are you doing here?" Shepard felt like he had to pull the words out of quick sand.

Rick didn't look disheveled or as drugged out as he looked last time he randomly showed up, but there was still something unsettling about his appearance. Shepard couldn't quite place it. Was it the gun that he held in a steady hand? Or the twisted smile that looked plastered on his face? Maybe it was because he looked more gaunt than usual? His cheekbones were way more prominent than they had been before, giving his face a slightly more hallowed look. "How did you know I was even here?"

"I went to your place, first. I spotted your neighbor. I asked him, very kindly, if he knew where you were. He told me he had no idea. So I pulled my toy out and asked him to think harder. That's when he remembered you mentioning that you've been hanging out with your boyfriend a lot more."

"Jesus, Rick."

"I already knew where your doctor in shining armor lived. I should have just come here in the first place, but eh, we all make mistakes." He took a few steps forward. "Also, about the whole 'Rick thing'. I guess I should probably fill you in. My name isn't Rick. It's Gabriel Del Valle. I had it good, traveling and shedding identities from place to place. Until you had to call the cops on me. You had to get that restraining order. What else did you tell them, huh? Because what it was ended up fucking me over. Is that what you wanted?"

Shepard couldn't speak. Any words that would come to him were completely swallowed by the fear. This man was crazy, and he was blaming Shepard for losing it all.

"You're the reason the police have my apartment building surrounded. If it weren't for you, I'd be fine. But no, you had to go to the cops."

Shepard felt a lump of acidic bile rise to his throat. "No," Shepard squeaked out. "I didn't do anything." He brought his hands up, they were shaking. "I swear."

"You did, though. You could have just opened the door for me when I showed up at your place. I was only going to apologize. Instead, you call the police. You did this. You ruined it all."

Now Rick—no, *Gabriel*— now Gabriel's hand was shaking. His eyes darted from Shepard to the wooden block holding a set of knives on the counter. "This way. Come this way." Gabriel motioned toward the living room with the gun. Shepard wasn't sure if he could get his feet to move. Thankfully, they did. His knees shook as he walked. He could feel the gun pointed at him the entire time.

"You don't want to do this."

"Actually, I do. I haven't done this in a while. I just wish I had more control of the situation. Like I had with my two boys in Ohio." Gabriel licked his lips. His eyes briefly took on a reminiscent gaze, as though he were remembering a birthday or a reunion. Something pleasant. Except Shepard felt like whatever Gabriel was recalling was far from pleasant. "No, no. I've had to give up the control. I'm giving up a lot, tonight. It was either you or that fat guy from church. I thought the church would be a good cover story this time. It was fun, I guess. The guy could fuck, probably because of all that pent up hate and religious guilt. I wasn't sure who I wanted to take with me tonight. But you and I, well, we have more history. You were the first guy I found when I came to LA. And besides, you're part of the reason why I'm in this mess. It's only fair, really."

Shepard started realizing that Gabriel wasn't expecting either of them to walk out of this alive. He was going to kill Shepard and then himself, knowing that the cops were already hot on his tail. He had nowhere to run. A cornered, rabid dog had only one option, seeing as death was already a certainty.

"You don't have to do this," Shepard began pleading. "You can leave and never come back. Take my wallet. My phone. Whatever you need, just take it and go."

"You think I'm that stupid, Shepard? You'll call the cops as soon as I turn my back. No, no, it's over. I had a good run. I fooled enough people. But the end of the road is here."

That's when Shepard thought of Nick. He was going to get home after losing his daughter, only to find a murdered lover. It was enough to steady Shepard's knees. He was filled with a new sense of strength. He could think clearer now. The fear was still there, but he wasn't controlled by it anymore. He had to find a way out of this. Not only for himself, but also for Nick. He loved that man with all his heart, and he knew their story wasn't done. No way. It wasn't going to end like this.

"Like you said, we have a history. We've shared a bed,

memories, laughs." Shepard was trying to appeal to Gabriel's human side, although he doubted if Gabriel even had one. He switched to focusing on Gabriel's innate drive for survival. He was going to need to lie. Something he had trouble doing, and with the pressure of a gun barrel added to the mix, it was nearly impossible. "Maybe there's something I can do to help. I have connections. Maybe I can help get you to Mexico." He was formulating it all in his head as he spoke. "One of my patients, I've overhead him talk about knowing where a tunnel was located. I can reach him. I can talk to him. I saved his daughter's life, I think he'd help me."

Gabriel was skeptical. It wasn't a great lie, but Shepard was selling it as best he could. "Let me call him. You can get out of the country. This doesn't have to be the end. You're twenty-eight, if you didn't lie to me about your age, too. We're young. We've got so much left."

Gabriel's face cracked, the twisted smile faltering for a moment. Something was landing. "You remembered how old I am." Gabriel's eyebrows came together. "No one ever even remembers my birthday."

"October Fourteenth. Libra." Shepard didn't actually care about Gabriel's birthday, he just had a photographic memory, but he wasn't about to tell that to the psycho holding the gun.

"Wow," Gabriel said, sounding impressed. "And it's been so long since we dated... you really cared about me?"

"Yes." Shepard's voice wavered, but he kept his posture strong. He had to sell it. Gabriel had to believe him.

"Really?"

Shepard nodded. "Yes," he said, his voice steadier. "Now, let me help you."

The hand holding the gun wavered for a moment, losing

its laser focus on Shepard's chest. "Where's Nick?" Gabriel asked. "I didn't see his car outside."

"He's at the hospital," Shepard said. He was getting better at spitting lies at a rapid rate. "Working all night. We've got time to do this."

"How do I know you're not lying."

"Come on, let me call the guy." Shepard looked at the gun. "But put the gun down. I won't do anything crazy. Trust me."

Gabriel put the gun down.

Holy shit, it's working.

There was another piece to this place. Shepard had to get Gabriel next to him. He reached a hand into his pocket, being careful to only pull his phone out. "Wait, wait!" Gabriel shouted, putting the gun back up. Shepard immediately dropped his phone. It bounced on a corner and fell flat at Shepard's feet, the cover protecting it from any real damage.

"What?"

"Let me do it," Gabriel said. "I don't want you calling the cops."

Shepard just shook his head, shaken from the outburst but forcing himself to stay cool. What he was about to do next was incredibly risky and crazy dangerous.

"Alright, let me get the phone." Gabriel put the gun down at his side again, not sensing a threat from Shepard. He walked toward the phone, keeping his eyes on Shepard the entire time. Shepard held his hands loosely at his sides, even though he was feeling extremely tense.

Gabriel got to Shepard. He smiled and surprised Shepard with a quick kiss. It was revolting. Shepard wanted to gag on the spot but stopped himself. His breath smelled like rotten eggs and old coffee. Shepard's expression didn't so much as twitch. He had to be strong. "I always knew you were someone special," Gabriel said. "That you'd save me someday."

Gabriel bent down to pick up the phone.

It all happened in a flash. Shepard reached into his pocket and closed his grip around the shard of glass he had picked up from the floor. He didn't even feel it cutting into his palm. He pulled it out and, with all the force in his body, plunged the sharp edge down into Gabriel's exposed neck. The effect was immediate. Shepard knew his anatomy. He knew where to stab. And he did it. The glass sank in and sliced through stretchy tendons and thin veins and one vital artery.

Gabriel didn't know what hit him. Two minutes later, and he would be dead. Slumped faced down into a growing puddle of his own blood.

Shepard was hyperventilating. He stumbled backward and tripped over nothing, his ass falling hard on the floor. He gripped at his shirt, as if it were choking him. He had to get it off. He just killed someone. Self-defense, he kept telling himself. *Self-defense*. He had to do it. There was no other option. He had to stay alive. He had to do it for—

"Holy shit!" Nick yelled. He froze in the open doorway for a moment before bursting into action, running right to Shepard, around the pool of blood. He was already calling the police, telling them they had to be there as fast as they could be.

"Shepard, Shep, baby, are you ok?! What happened? Holy shit, Shep." Nick was holding Shepard, who was shaking like a leaf in the wind.

"He broke in," Shepard said, his throat tight, tears flowing down his cheeks. "He had a gun. Wanted to kill me for calling the police on him."

"Oh, Shepard, you're ok now. I'm here. I'm not going anywhere." Nick's voice was like a lighthouse shining through a typhoon, leading Shepard's ship back to shore. "Can you stand? You're not hurt are you?"

"No, I'm ok," Shepard said. He couldn't feel the deep gash that across the center of his palm, spilling blood onto the floor.

"Shit," Nick said, seeing the wound. He shot up and ran to the linen closet, where he grabbed a clean towel. He ran back and wrapped it around Shepard's hand, applying pressure so that the bleeding would stop. He helped Shepard get up onto his feet. Shepard still wasn't feeling the pain from the cut, but he was thankful he was standing. He wanted to get out of the room that held the dead body.

"Let's go out. Let's get some air." Nick looped an arm around Shepard and walked him out into the backyard, a direction that took them away from the corpse in his living room. Once outside, Shepard felt like he could breath properly again. He took a few deep breaths and let his head fall into Nick's chest. He wrapped an arm around Nick and held him tight, keeping his bleeding hand held out. The pain was starting to appear, but it was nothing compared to the relief he felt of being able to hold onto Nick.

"I love you, Nick. I love you so damn much. I didn't want to die because I thought there was still so much left to do with you. To experience."

"And there is," Nick assured him. He put two fingers under Shepard's chin and lifted his face. Their eyes met, the romantic moonlight drawing a bit of contrast with the amped-up atmosphere. "I love you, too, Shepard. And from this point on, it's you, me and Emma against the world. We're a team, and no one's going to ruin that for us anymore."

"Zane found something?" Shepard said, not knowing what exactly had happened.

Police sirens started to echo through the nearby hills. "I'll fill you in," Nick said. He leaned in and kissed Shepard. It didn't erase everything that just happened, nothing probably ever would, but it immediately calmed Shepard's racing heart. He was with the man he loved, soon to be holding the little girl he loved.

Everything was going to be alright.

End Of Chapter

30 NICHOLAS WHITE

Four months later

NICK JUMPED into the shower and immediately had to jump back out. "Jesus, Shep, are you trying to burn off a layer of skin in there?"

"It's how I exfoliate," Shepard joked, reaching for the knob and turning it toward the cold side. Nick waited a moment before stepping back in. The water was at a much more bearable temperature. Nick had recently upgraded to an overhead shower that simulated rainfall, and wow, did it change the game in term of showers. Not only was it relaxing (when it was warm and not scalding) but it also covered both of them at the same time. No more fighting for the water, and getting cold because half your body was exposed to cool air. It was life changing.

"Emma's asleep?" Shepard asked, passing over the smooth white bottle of soap.

"Yep, knocked out as soon as she finished her bottle."

Nick lathered up. The soapy sweet scent of peppermint filled up the steamy shower. He turned around and offered the loofa to Shepard. Shepard grabbed the loofa and rubbed it over Nick's back. Nick dropped his head, allowing himself a moment to completely relax. He'd had a pretty long day at work and carried a lot of that tension in his shoulders. He felt himself let it go when Shepard brought the rough loofa up to the center of his shoulders. Shepard set the loofa down and started to use his hands to spread the sudsy soap. He gently turned it into a massage, softly pressing into Nick's tight muscles with gentle fingers, increasing the pressure as he continued. Nick rolled his neck and let out a sigh. "That feels so good, Shep."

"You're so tense," Shepard observed.

"I had a close call in the OR today." Nick was happy he could decompress with Shepard. Over the last four months, he had done a lot of that. They leaned on each other, which was what made them such a strong pair. With support coming from both sides, neither would fall. "But it's ok," Nick continued, "Dr. Torres and I pulled off a miracle and brought the man back. He was gone for a good two minutes on the table."

"Wow," Shepard said, his fingers digging a little deeper, working at the large knots.

"How was it here with Emma?" Nick asked, moving backwards so that he could feel Shepard's plump dick against his ass. The water was falling over them in relaxing drops.

"Great," Shepard said. He had the next few days off so they didn't need the babysitter. "We got through the second season of that Pingu cartoon. I swear, someone was on acid when they made that thing."

Nick laughed at that. "The penguin did creep me out a little bit."

"Emma loves it, though. She's already learning how to ask for it."

"What a smart kid."

"Oh, for sure," Shepard replied. Nick turned around. Facing each other meant their dicks were head to head. Both of them were already swollen, and this stance made them start rising into the air. Nick ignored his dick for now. "Something else had me stressed today. My lawyer called."

Shepard's eyes immediately widened.

"Don't worry, everything's ok. She was just calling to say that Anna is being sentenced tomorrow. Officially. She could be sent to jail or rehab."

Shepard shook his head. "Whatever the outcome is, I'm glad we can put most of it behind us."

Nick felt a pang of emotion hit him in the chest. It was only four months ago that he had walked in on his boyfriend down on the floor next to a dead body. It was a shock to both of them. It took a couple of months for things to return back to normal. The first few weeks were spent as if Nick was walking through a dream. Nothing felt real and yet he was grateful for every single little thing. He could count the tiny hairs on Shepard's cheeks and be grateful for each and every one of them. Hell, even the crescent shape scar on Shepard's palm made him grateful. It reminded him of how blessed he was to be able to look into Shepard's eyes and tell him that he loved him.

Shepard had a difficult time sleeping for weeks after the incident. Nick would stay up with him, making sure he knew he wasn't alone. A lot of playtime with Emma helped the both of them. The new judge had overturned the last ruling on grounds of discrimination. Apparently the prior judge was trying to glue together a flimsy case around the photos and the abuse allegations, which was why it had taken a couple of hours for Nick's lawyer to get all the information. Thankfully, the new judge was able to see right through it. He also granted sole custody to Nick, citing Anna's addiction. Nick told Anna that he would consider visitation rights once she got her act cleaned up. Even after all the hurt she had inflicted on him, he still wouldn't be cruel enough to completely take Emma away from her.

Nick reached down and grabbed the shampoo off the gray marble floor. On the way down to get the shampoo, he just so happened to come mouth level to Shepard's stiff cock. He opened his mouth and popped Shepard's dick in, rolling his tongue around the shaft and tasting the water from the shower. He gave Shepard a few good sucks before coming back up with the shampoo in hand. He wiped his mouth with the back of his hand, leaving a naughty smirk.

"So you're gonna tease me like that?" Shepard said, reaching down and grabbing Nick's cock, which was already rock solid. He gave it a few tugs before turning around and rubbing his ass against it. Nick massaged the shampoo into his hair as he pushed his hips forward, his cock sliding up Shepard's wet crack. Nick reached around and grabbed Shepard's dick with a soapy hand. He stroked Shepard, feeling him buck against his touch, leaning his head back on Nick's shoulder so that Nick could bite at Shepard's earlobe.

Shepard reached his hands behind Nick and grabbed his ass cheeks, spreading them open. Nick pushed his dick harder into Shepard's ass, while at the same time enjoying having Shepard open him up the way he just had. Shepard turned around then and their lips immediately connected for a passionate kiss. Their dicks crossed each other like swords ready for a duel.

When Nick parted from the kiss, he turned around. He was feeling like he wanted something else tonight, something that Nick had never had before. He wanted Shepard to take him. To fuck Nick the way Nick fucked him. He wanted to feel what it was like to have Shepard's dick inside him. He had been curious about it for a while, but never felt fully confident about doing it.

Tonight was different. Tonight was the night.

He rubbed his ass back onto Shepard, showing him just how badly he wanted it. Shepard must have gotten the hint because he dropped to his knees and spread Nick's ass open with his hands. Next thing Nick knew, he was gasping and reaching for something to hold on to. He didn't have anything except the glass wall of the shower door. He braced himself as Shepard ate him out.

It was sensational. A fucking earth-shattering experience. And it wasn't even the main course. No, Shepard's tongue was just the appetizer. He had something much meatier for the actual meal.

And even then, Nick was seeing stars. "Oh fuck, Shep, oh fuck. That feels—oh god, oh right there."

Nick was beating himself off as Shepard's tongue swirled in and around his hole. His knees and thighs started to shake from the pleasure. Nick needed more. He wanted it all.

"Come on," he said, "let's move to the bed."

Shepard gave one last lick and got up from his knees. He turned the shower off and both men got out. Nick was rock hard, his fat cock jutting out from him as he ate Shepard up with his eyes. The man was fucking gorgeous. He stood there, his perfect body on display, every muscle dewy with water from the shower. Nick stepped forward, devouring Shepard's lips with his own, their cocks crossing together, throbbing against each other. Steam filled the large bathroom, fogging up the window and mirrors.

"Fuck," Nick said with an exhale. "Come here." He grabbed Shepard and pulled him toward his bedroom. There, he went straight for the night stand and grabbed the already slippery bottle of lube. He managed to pump some out on his palm without dropping it. With his victory in hand, he went back to focusing all his attention on the beautiful man standing in front of him. He spread the lube with his hands, massaging both their cocks before reaching behind Shepard and sliding his fingers between his ass cheeks. He felt Shepard's puckered hole, tender at his touch as he pressed and circled around it. Before Shepard took him, he wanted to play with Shepard, who was already quivering at the touch, his hand finding Nick's cock and pumping it. Shepard leaned in and started sucking on Nick's neck, using his teeth and tongue to create an intense sensation.

Nick pushed a finger in, past the tight ring of muscle and feeling the velvety smoothness of Shepard's channel. Immediately, Shepard bucked his knees and sucked on Nick's neck that much harder. Nick probed with his finger, finding that swollen, spongy spot that he knew would drive Shepard wild. Sure enough, the moment he applied pressure, Shepard's cock jerked in the air and spilled a bead of precome. Nick teased another finger as he continued to press down on Shepard's P-spot.

"Oh my god," Shepard moaned. "That feels so good."

"Yeah?" Nick asked, looking for some more encouragement. He loved hearing Shepard ask for more. He couldn't get enough of it.

"Yeah, put another finger in," Shepard said, his tone pleading, his legs squatting lower so that Nick could have an easier entrance. He pressed his second finger against Shepard's tight hole, feeling him open around him and then shut tight, almost pulling his fingers in deeper. They both released a moan as Nick started to pound his fingers in, rubbing over the spot and slapping his other palm against Shepard's ass. The loud cracks of skin on skin echoed in the bedroom, along with the grunts that started turning more and more animalistic.

Shepard started kissing Nick. His teeth clamped on Nick's lower lip and sucked. Nick only fingered him harder. Both of their cocks were pressed together as they locked lips again.

"That's it," Shepard said through a break for air. "Oh, fuck."

Nick slowed down. He didn't want Shepard to come yet. He had other ideas for how the night was going to play out.

He opened his eyes and double-checked the bed was still behind Shepard. He pushed Shepard back and fell on top of him, their lips coming together in seconds, their cocks rolling over the other, heat coming off them in waves. Nick could feel a streak of wetness on his stomach from where Shepard's cock rubbed against him.

"Shep," Nick said, holding himself over Shepard, his lips twisted in a smirk. "Fuck me. Make love to me. I want all of you inside me."

Shepard's eyes seemed to glitter in the dim bedroom light. All they had on was a large lamp that sat on one of the nightstands, the thick shade covering the bulb and diffusing the light into a warm, soft glow. Nick leaned down for one more kiss before he rolled over so he was on his back.

Shepard got up and grabbed more lube, squirting it on his hand. He climbed back onto the bed and ran his hand over Nick's hard length, sending jolts of pleasure running through him. Nick thought he knew where Shepard's hands were going next, but was surprised when he felt Shepard's tongue against his hole again. It was big and warm and wet and felt like nothing else Nick had ever felt. Shepard had never rimmed him before tonight, and so Nick really had no idea what to expect. Even if he did, he couldn't have been prepared for the intense pleasure he received. It made him squirm, his legs drawing up and his ass lifting into the air. Shepard grabbed onto Nick's thighs and steadied him as his tongue worked circles around his hole. Nick's cock jerked in Shepard's hand. This was intense. Nick pushed his head back into the mattress. He could feel Shepard's firm tongue pressing against his tight hole. He started rolling his hips, moving his ass so that Shepard could eat out every inch of him. Nick felt his ass grow wet with saliva as Shepard licked. Nick's toes curled, his cock pulsed, his body cried out for more. He wanted more than just a tongue. He wanted to feel Shepard entering him, filling him.

"Fuck me," Nick said, practically pleading. Shepard came up from his feast, lining his dick up with Nick's entrance. Shepard was on his knees on the bed with Nick on his back. They had been tested, so condoms were nowhere in sight. Shepard squirted some more lube on his dick and spread it before he pushed his hips forward, teasing Nick's hole with the head of his cock.

It wasn't even in yet and Nick was already seeing stars. He took a breath as Shepard pushed forward, stretching him open.

Shepard was gentle and raw and pure sex swirled with heated passion. Everything about the man was made to unwind Nick. He raked his gaze over Shepard's perfect, naked body. From his sexy legs covered in a light dusting of dark hair, up his strong muscular thighs, that delicious six-pack of his, the hard nipples that screamed to be licked, and that face. Shepard was everything Nick had ever wanted and needed. He lay there, naked on his bed, looking up at the man who stole his heart, feeling so intensely in love. His cock pulsed in the air as Shepard pushed in a little deeper.

"Slow, slow," Nick said, feeling himself trying to accommodate Shepard's size. He was big, which was both a blessing and a curse. Nick felt a sharp, quick sting as Shepard pulled out and pressed back in again. He breathed through it and relaxed even further. Soon, the sting was gone and in its place was a heat Nick had never felt before. He wanted to take all of Shepard, his ass ready for it, his body practically crying out for it. He wanted his man buried balls deep inside him. He wanted to be as close to Shepard as physically possible.

"You're so tight," Shepard said, in a tone that had Nick's body practically go limp (well... not his *entire* body), ready to be used in whatever way Shepard wanted. He had never felt like this. He was always the one giving it, never receiving. He thought he wouldn't like it, the vulnerability of it, but he was quickly finding that he had never been so turned on.

"This feel so good," Nick moaned. "You feel so good inside me."

"Yeah?" Shepard asked, picking up the pace, encouraged by Nick's grunts of pleasure. Nick could take it. He wanted it so badly.

"Here, wait," Nick said, "let me sit on you."

He leaned up, while Shepard was still fucking him, and started sucking on Shepard's hard nipples. This had

Shepard sounding like a wild animal, his breathing coming in harder and his thrusts deeper. Nick pushed up from the bed and sat up so that he was was sitting on Shepard's lap now instead of laying down, all while Shepard still had his cock plunged deep in Nick's ass.

This position allowed Nick more control, and he used that control to bounce down harder on Shepard's cock. Shepard was grunting, pushing his hips upward so that he could meet Nick's downward motions, sinking himself all the way to his balls.

"*Ohhh*, fuck." Nick sat still on Shepard's lap. His ass tightened around Shepard's cock, relishing in the sensation of having him push at his inner walls, filling him up. He rocked back and forth. The motion rubbed Nick's stiff cock against Shepard's belly, adding another layer of pleasure Nick wasn't ready for.

His balls quivered as his entire body was rocked with a pulse. He was getting so close. He rolled his hips backward, slowly, watching as Shepard's eyes rolled back in ecstasy. He rolled them forward. And back. All the while, feeling Shepard inside him.

"You have me so close," Nick moaned. "Come inside me, Shep. I want to feel you fill me up." Shepard started fucking him even harder. He drove his cock upward, fucking Nick deep, pressing that insanely sensitive P-spot like it was a button granting a million fucking dollars. Over and over and—

"Oh, fuck, I'm gonna come," Nick said as his entire body tensed. His cock erupted onto Shepard's chest, shooting warm, sticky come all over.

That had the effect of throwing Shepard over the edge as well. His thrusts became erratic and his face scrunched up as he unloaded his balls deep inside Nick. He could feel Shepard's cock pulse inside him, filling him with his seed.

"Wow," Nick said, breathless, still sitting on Shepard's dick.

"How was that?" Shepard asked, his face saying he knew damn well how it was.

"Mind-blowing," Nick said, laughing. He pushed up, Shepard's dick coming out of him with a pop. He fell back onto the bed. Shepard followed suit, collapsing right next to him, the memory foam mattress absorbing the bounce. "Now I get it."

"You finally discovered the magic us bottoms have been holding out from the rest of the world?" Shepard asked playfully. He rested a hand on Nick's chest and gently played with the small bit of chest hair.

"Oh definitely," Nick said. "The key to happiness is totally in your ass."

"I have to agree," Shepard said. They both melted into laughs and kisses and cuddles.

Love surrounded them both that night and for all the rest of the nights that came after.

EPILOGUE

Nicholas White

Six Years Later

"No, it's my doll!" Emma snatched the Wonder Woman figurine from the little boy's hand.

"But, but, I want it! Mine!" The little boy was struggling to find the right words to express how badly he wanted the doll. Emma was not budging. She got up from the floor and stomped over to her corner of the room. She opened up a white chest that sat at the foot of a twin-sized bed, a light pink princess canopy hanging over the top of it. Emma reached into the chest and rummaged around. The boy was getting closer and closer to crying, his eyes watering at the sight of the doll. He pushed up from the floor and walked to Emma, trying to stomp on the way but not quite understanding how to.

"Mine!" he repeated as he tried to grab the doll back. Emma had the grip of an arm wrestler, though. She snatched Wonder Woman back and pulled something out of the chest all without tumbling over. In her hands, Emma held another Wonder Woman doll. This one was a little older, but still just as cool. "Here, Jude, play with this one."

Jude's eyes lit up. He still looked at the other doll with some suspicion—maybe the one his sister was keeping was more fun after all—but he grabbed the one Emma offered and gave her a hug, too. Their dads always said that the most important part of a gift was the thank you.

Just then, another boy ran into the room wearing an adorable pair of overalls with a green dinosaur T-shirt underneath. "Hey, guys, come on downstairs, we're going to eat soon." It was Billy, Dean and Noah's son. A rambunctious Australian Shepherd came running up behind Billy, nipping at his heels.

"Andy, no! No!" The dog took Billy's protests as a sign to keep going. The dog kept nipping at Billy as he ran out of the room and down the stairs. He took a sharp left and ran right into his father.

"Dad!" he said, "Get Andy off me."

Dean waved the blue-eyed pup away, giving him a stern "no" when Andy wouldn't stop herding. The sharp and sudden "no" seemed to snap Andy out of his doggy urges. Another dog entered the room, drawing Andy's attention. It was Bear, Caleb and Red's spunky little Yorkshire Terrier. The two dogs ran off toward the kitchen, barking and nipping at each other. "Emma and Jude coming?" Dean asked, just as the pair started down the stairs.

"On our way!" Emma shouted excitedly, a Wonder Woman doll in her hand.

Dean squeezed his son's shoulder and walked with him through the living room and out through the sliding glass doors, with Emma and Jude close behind. They were at Nick's house, getting ready for a Thanksgiving meal. It had become a tradition a couple of years back for all the boys to get together with their families and host a big Thanksgiving Day feast. Nick and Dean had grown close working together, and Noah immediately clicked with Nick and Shepard from the second they started their first double date. There had been plenty of others since. They had also bonded from the days Noah would invite Shepard and Nick to come work out at his gym. He would host a private class for the four of them whenever they could get their schedules aligned, and he always kicked their asses, leaving them sweaty messes by the end of it.

"Hey, babe," Dean said, coming up behind Noah. He was having an animated conversation with Caleb. They were standing near a long table set up underneath a couple of tall palm trees. Dean chimed in with, "The food smells great."

"I was so worried I messed the stuffing up," Caleb said. He was looking good, wearing a gray cardigan over a white shirt, sporting a longer hairstyle than usual. "Red was gone all morning filming that new movie he's in, and he forgot to leave me with his 'super secret' recipe. Thankfully, Google is only a phone away. So, it's not the stuffing passed on from Red's great uncle or whatever, but it's still good. Had five-stars out of twenty-four reviews. I also had a great assistant." Caleb looked to his daughter, who was sitting at the table already, playing with an iPad. "Right, Lily? Didn't the stuffing turn out great?"

"I don't know about *all that*," she said, with a comedic inflection reserved for seasoned stand-ups, not six-year-old girls. But she was a sharp one.

Red walked back from the cooler, holding two bottles of ice cold beers. His beard was grown out thick for a role he was playing. He was also asked to put on a little bit more muscle, so he was stretching the sleeves of his polo. He handed one of the open beers to Caleb and stood by his side, cracking a smile. "I think your's actually came out better."

Nick walked out then, holding a large bowl of fruit salad. He had been running around trying to be a good host for most of the day, so he hadn't really taken a moment to appreciate how beautiful the day really was. Especially at that time, when the sun was beginning to set. He looked to all his friends, his family. They were chatting and laughing in his backyard. His kids were already sitting at their table, playing rock paper scissor from the looks of it. Inside, his husband was pouring drinks, getting everything ready for the dinner.

His heart swelled with love. Nick walked the fruit salad over to the table and turned to go back inside so he could help Shepard.

"Need any help in there?" Caleb offered.

"We're ok, thank you" Nick called back, disappearing into his house.

Although house may not have been the proper term. More like mansion. Ever since Shepard graduated medical school and paid off his debts, they were able to save enough between them to upgrade their living situation. It didn't hurt that Nick had gotten a raise at the hospital around the same time as Shepard graduating. Nick went from a comfortable two-bedroom home tucked inside the hills to a seven-bedroom house perched on top of the hills. But that wasn't really what made his life so insanely special.

No, he had three other reasons why he woke up and went to sleep with a smile every day. Two of those reasons were outside right now, fighting over a superhero doll. One of those reasons was inside with him, just across the kitchen, looking dreamy in his light blue button-up shirt and fitted jeans. He had gotten a haircut a few days ago, giving him that crisp clean look that drove Nick wild. He went over and gave Shepard a playfully slap on his butt. He jumped up slightly, almost pouring the champagne onto the counter but managing to keep it in the glass.

"You scared me," Shepard said. Nick stood behind him and wrapped his arms around his man. He kissed Shepard's neck, causing Shepard to tilt his head, exposing more of himself, asking for more kisses without saying a word. They had gotten so good at that, communicating without speaking. Nick could read Shepard's body like one of his favorite books, knowing exactly what each word meant, each movement. Nick leaned into Shepard's body. He smelled good. Like cinnamon and berries. Nick held Shepard a little tighter.

"Everything looking good out there?"

"All we need is the turkey."

"The gobble-gobble machine as Jude likes to call it."

"Ah yes, the gobble-gobble machine." Nick laughed into Shepard's neck. He sucked at the sensitive skin before pulling back. He couldn't get carried away, which was easy to do when he had Shepard's ass pressed against his crotch. The thought alone had Nick's dick twitch in his khakis.

"You guys need any help in here?" said a voice that coincidentally sounded just like Shepard. Nick turned and saw Crow smiling at them from the arched entryway. He had learned the subtle ways to tell him apart from Shepard, who could have filled in for Crow on one of his world tours and no one would have been able to tell the difference.

Well, except that Shepard couldn't sing his way out of a brown paper bag.

But that was only *one* difference between the twins, and that was in skill and not appearance. Nick learned that if he looked closely, he could tell them apart in how they walked and how they spoke. Crow put an emphasis on the ends of sentences, Shepard tended to speak with an emphasis for the beginnings. Their mouths also moved in slightly different ways when they spoke. The biggest tell was a tiny birthmark on the inside of Shepard's ear, which Crow lacked. It was hard to spot, but if there was ever any Parent Trap thing going on for some reason, the birthmark would be the definitive difference.

Other than that, they were identical twins through and through.

Well, there was also another obvious difference: Nick was madly in love with only one of them.

Shepard Kensworth. The man of his dreams and the perfect man to help raise Emma and Jude.

SHEPARD COULDN'T REMEMBER a time when he ever felt happier. Everything in life had clicked right into place. From landing an excellent job as a pediatrician at an incredible practice, to his relationship with Nick, which had been nothing but bliss for years. And then there was Emma, whom he loved as though she were his own daughter from the day she was born. And last, but certainly not least, the newest addition to their family; Jude Kensworth White. He was three now, always reminding Shepard of just how fast time was flying by. He knew that he'd be blinking one moment and the next they'd be headed off to college.

Jude came to them through a surrogate. They had mixed both of their samples together and so they weren't entirely sure which of them was the biological father, but that never mattered anyway. The love he had for both his kids was enough to reach the moon and back.

Ethan popped up behind Crow. He was looking good, sporting a silver-fox look that really worked for him. "Jude is about to flip a table over if he doesn't get a piece of the gobble-gobble machine soon."

Shepard laughed at that. He leaned into Nick, who was standing by his side. "We'll be right out. Tell Jude to be patient. All good gobbles come to those who wait."

"Ah, yes, that famous saying," Crow said. "I think I saw someone with a tramp stamp that said that once, actually."

This had the entire room laughing. Crow and his husband took their leave when the laughing subsided. Shepard turned to Nick, unable to keep his lips off the man when people weren't around. When the kiss was over, he looked deep into his husband's eyes. "I love you, Nick. So, so much."

"I love you, too," Nick said, putting every ounce of meaning he had behind those words. Shepard felt it deep down in his heart. It was a warmth that spread through him, cradling every fiber of his being, and covering him like a plush blanket.

"Let's go out there with the turkey before our kids start a riot."

"I say we're about three minutes out from that happening."

Shepard slapped Nick's butt and got to work, moving the turkey onto a beautiful serving plate he had gotten last Thanksgiving. It had a beautiful hand painted edge around it, showing a motif of different Thanksgiving symbols. Nick grabbed the electric knife and walked out to the backyard next to Shepard, offering a hand in case the heavy turkey suddenly tipped one way or the other. Shepard had a good hold on it. They made it all the way to the table, where everyone had already taken their seats. Well, the adults had.

The children were sitting at a small table just next to them, with adorable tiny chairs and plates and utensils. Jude was looking at the turkey with wide eyes, a string of saliva ready to fall from his open mouth. Emma and Lily showed more restraint, sitting with their hands on the table, waiting for their servings. Billy was already chowing down on a piece of bread. He never cared much for the turkey.

"All right guys, the star is here."

"He does that every year," Noah said to Dean in a stage whisper, "Why does he say that?"

"Because look at her," Shepard said, referring to the turkey, smiling, "She's stunning. She's elegant. She's dripping in class and tasty juices. She's a *star*."

"Great," Noah said, "Now I feel like I'm eating Mariah Carey."

The entire table busted out in laughter. Shepard sat down, catching his breath. Nick took his seat next to him. They were at the head of the table. Across from Shepard, there was a very special guest. Someone new to their Thanksgiving dinner, and someone who Shepard was very glad to see.

"Nick, say a few words and then let's dig in," Shepard said. He remembered he was put on the spot last year and joked about doing it to Nick the next, and so he followed through. Nick looked at him with a smile that said "why I aughta". He got up from his seat and the tables quieted down.

"Alright, so," Nick started. "It's been a great year and I couldn't be more thankful that I get to spend this Thanksgiving surrounded by the people I love so dearly. I'm thankful for this meal all of us helped in putting together. I'm thankful for my incredible husband, Shepard. You're the light of my life and continue to be. And of course, I'm thankful for all those little green beans sitting at that table over there." Nick took a breath. "And someone else is here who I'm very thankful to have back in my life." He looked down, to the seat across from Shepard. Where Nick's father sat. "Dad," he said, "I'm so glad you're back in my life. We have some catching up to do, and I'm thankful Emma and Jude are going to get to know their grandfather."

Shepard felt a cry catch in his throat. He held it back. This was a time for happiness and celebration. Nick's dad had reached out to him a few months back and told him he had made a huge mistake and wanted to reconnect. He said he was still a religious man, but that no religion should be allowed to come between a father and son the way he allowed it to.

Shepard looked around the table. He was surrounded by the people he called family. It was one of the best feelings in the world. He was thankful for that. Thankful that he could experience what true happiness felt like.

When Nick sat back down, Shepard reached over the table and held his husband's hand.

He didn't think he could fall deeper in love, but he found a way.

Every day, he just fell deeper and deeper.

It meant he had found his one. The love of his life. And that was all he could have ever asked for.

The End

THANK YOU!

Thank you for reading *CODE WHITE*. If you enjoyed Nick and Shepard's story, please consider leaving a review. They help immensely in getting these two out to more readers!

My next book is going to be Christmas themed and follow Jude Kensworth White, when he's a twenty-something year old who gets snowed in with his intensely sexy but frustratingly cold boss.

I'll also be starting a new series titled Stonewall Investigations, and it's going to follow the detective agency, starting with Zane.

And be sure to connect with me on Instagram and Twitter @maxwalkerwrites

Max Walker
MaxWalkerAuthor@outlook.com

ACKNOWLEDGMENTS

I have to give a huge thank you to my beta readers! You help make my stories shine. Thank you.

Made in the USA
Coppell, TX
04 November 2020

40768114R00163